Publish and be damned
www.pabd.com

Tales of Mirth and Woe

from the pages of Scaryduck.com

Alistair Coleman

With an introduction by Neil Gaiman

Publish and be damned
www.pabd.com

First published in Canada 2006 by Alistair Coleman
The moral right of Alistair Coleman to be identified as the author of this work has been asserted.

Designed in Toronto, Canada, by Adlibbed Limited.
Printed and bound in the USA or the UK by Lightningsource.

ISBN: 1-897312-14-8

For Vanessa, Hazel and Adam

Preface

So, then, this is the paperback version of your favourite Guardian Award-winning website. The version you can take to the toilet with you without the very real fear of electrocution, with the added advantage of being in a soft, absorbent format should you find yourself distressingly *sans papier*.

Additionally, it is also the version you can read on the way to work, whiling away those hours lost to the commuter crawl with mirth, woe and exciting new uses for your favourite swear-words. I'm also pleased to provide a lovely, soothing picture of a duck on the cover to calm the nerves of your fellow passengers, who, by and large, are probably experiencing a far worse journey than you are. [I have been advised by our legal people to tell you NOT to read this book whilst driving to work. It's neither big nor clever, and I don't think I can live with the blame for the Great M25 Thousand Car Pile-up on my conscience.]

And what are you getting for your money? Number one, you are living with the good karma that you are making me richer - I mean 'happier' - with your kind donation to the Bank of Scary. Weblog-to-book adaptations are notorious cut-and-paste jobs with no extra content, giving the reader nothing they can't already access for free on the internet. Perfectly acceptable for Iraqi war bloggers who've got something important to say to a wider audience, but it just doesn't wash for anonymous fake prostitutes whose prose is about as erotic as a dead salmon, even if there is a small but lucrative market for rotting fish jazz.

So, what you're getting here is a shameless cut-and-paste job from the archives of scaryduck dot com, designed solely to give you a disappointed sense of deja vu, and the urge to send a freshly laid dog egg to the author in the traditional manner, demanding your money back. It is the only language people like me understand.

But no! Each and every tale has been comprehensively rewritten, and I can personally guarantee a 38 per cent increase in both mirth and woe, 17 per cent more nob and arse gags, and similar increases in rampant nudity, gratuitous explosions, and vomit manufactured only from the finest ingredients. There may also be some futile attempt to get these stories into some kind of chronological order, but it's becoming increasingly difficult as I reach my forty-first year to tell where one explosion ends and the next set of bare breasts begins. There is also a gag which I wrote at least seven years ago that is still getting laughs now. Be kind when you see it, it's on the Antiques Roadshow next week.

And because I'm feeling nice/guilty, I've also included some material I have never posted on the internet, and not because it's too crappy to see the light of day. These are short stories, successful and not-so-successful competition entries, and a full range of material ranging from the weird to downright offensive, taking in burst-your-appendix funny. [At this stage, I'd like to pay glowing tribute to my school English teacher, the Eddie Shoestring look-alike Mr Lewis, who taught me never to begin a paragraph with the words "and" or "because". Whoops.]

Try to imagine the whole exercise as your third favourite band releasing a greatest hits collection, cynically marketed with a bunch of remixes and shonky "extra" tracks tacked on to keep even the most sceptical of fans relatively happy. If that fails, I can always sack the drummer over musical differences.

People frequently (never) ask me: "Hey! Scary - are these stories true?", and after feigning offence, I always reply in the affirmative. I can put my hand on my heart and state honestly that each and every tale is a total work of truth. OK, I've had to change names and places for obvious reasons, and one or two stories are - ahem - slightly exaggerated for comic effect, but, yes, it's all real. The Mao tale, in particular, is an amalgamation of about three different stories lumped together for one big, chip shop tale of woe (anyone from my neck of the woods can tell you the Lucky Fish Bar is, in fact, in Twyford), but certain little changes have been made for editorial reasons. And what you don't know won't hurt you. In the words of the late, great Frank Zappa: "This is a true story. Only the facts have been changed."

Naturally, and testament to my generous nature, extending an offer I have generously provided since day one of the website, every tenth copy of this book sold receives all the free, beer, money and sex they can carry [free beer, money and sex offer open only to residents of Brazzaville, Republic of Congo, closes 19th October 1968]. By that reckoning, I already owe the director of the British Library the humping of his life. Such is the price of literary success. That's what sent Archer over the edge. A tragic loss.

Anyhow, here's my book, and I officially declare it this: aces. It is also this: better than gouging your eyes out with a snot-encrusted spoon after watching Garfield: The Movie non-stop for thirty-six hours. If any literary agent or easily-impressed publisher would care to offer me stupid quantities of money to keep me writing this crap (or better still, not to), my bank manager is waiting your call.

There are now 182 official Scaryduck Stories. There are also four in reserve, plus another twenty-five under development. Due to reasons of taste, decency and the fact that I may be forced to resort to fiction, the following tales may never appear on this site:

- The time we pretended to be Catholic Priests to try to pull nuns
- The time nothing got blown up, destroyed or otherwise smashed into a million pieces
- The time we got mixed up in the civil war in Nicaragua
- The time the Virgin Mary appeared to me in a digestive biscuit
- The time I puked in the swimming pool at Disneyland
- The time my dog shagged Sebastian Coe's leg
- The time Sarah, Duchess of York invited me back to see her priceless collection of antique polo mallets
- The time I got kicked out of a job interview for laughing when the boss introduced himself as "Mr Bender"
- The time I accidentally mooned the Lady Mayoress of Nottingham

Actually, one of these really happened, and I'm too embarrassed to say which.

Alistair Coleman
January 2006

Disclaimer: Certain identities have been changed in these stories to protect the guilty and innocent alike. If you think you recognise yourself, you're probably wrong.

An Introduction by Famous Author Neil Gaiman

First of all, I need to make something perfectly clear. I do not know this Scaryduck. Nor have I, to the best of my knowledge, ever encountered anyone named Alistair Coleman. Secondly, I am writing this of my own free will, and neither Mr "Duck" nor "Mr Coleman" are in possession of any photographic evidence of any misdemeanours or sexual peccadilloes on my part. In addition, I would like to go on record as stating that the entire Bulgarian girl "dance troupe" (actually a trade delegation) was over the age of consent, the object I am holding in the photograph is in fact part of a tractor, and the person in the photograph isn't me at all anyway, so all accusations of blackmail are obviously unfounded. I was in Swindon that entire weekend at a meeting of the British Philatelic Association as telephone records clearly demonstrate. Why hound a man over a minor mistake?

There.

The nature of what we have come to know as "Scaryduck" is essentially tied in to the comparatively recent phenomenon of "blogging", a neologism coined by combining the two words "Blow" and "Gging" (an obscure word, possibly of Gaelic origin, indicating that no-one is reading what you're writing except for possibly and unknown to you, the more personal bits and even then it's only your employer, workmates and people with whom you're having sexual relations).

Mr "Duck" achieved notoriety by "blogging". His tales of sexual embarrassment and scatological abandon, mostly written, I believe, under the name pen-name "Belle Du Jour", rapidly made him the talk of the "Blogosphere" (a neologism meaning, I believe, "something that goes round and round") and also made him the easy winner of the Guardian's "Best British Weogbl" Award in 2002. It is, frankly, hard to see how his true (or are they? Surely no man could actually experience such a life) tales of depravity, lust and inadequately restrained faecal matter could find an audience outside of the equally depraved and lust-raddled denizens of the world-wide web – would you wish to read about meeting Kate Winslet while buying pornography? About accidentally smearing dogshit on one's face in the cadets? About puking on trains, how you Can't Get Rid of Porn, or how "Mister" Duck broke his finger in a condom machine? Would you want to read dangerously light-hearted stories of amateur pyromania and explosion, at the concluding moments of which teenage boys usually "cack themselves" in a variety of amusing ways?

You would not. No right-minded person would. These are monstrous tales of humiliation and woe and once read, they cannot be forgotten.

Do not buy this man's books. Do not read his weblog. Do not snigger uncontrollably at his tales of embarrassment and defecation and exploding fish and inadvertent breast-based nudity. Deny him the oxygen of publicity and his moment of glory will be over. There is enough human misery and embarrassment in the world already – this "Scaryduck" merely adds to it and makes it really, really funny. Actually, it's not funny, "Mister Scary", it's not clever, and nobody's the slightest bit impressed. Er. Well, I suppose it's funny, obviously. And thousands of gullible people have been impressed. But for heaven's sake, it's things like this, along with mucky seaside postcards, the Carry On films, and the Fiesta Reader's Wives Specials that have brought the country to the state it's in today. And I haven't even mentioned the Piss stories.

Wake up, world! Stamp out this evil in your midst! This filth must be eradicated!

Also, I am assured it will make an excellent birthday and/or Christmas present.

I thank you.

Neil Gaiman, Famous Author.

Part One: Days of Youth

"In which a small boy wantonly destroys property, sets fire to things and drives without due care and attention; thereby narrowly avoiding painful death, humiliation and the wrath of his parents."

Drunk

And so it begins.

Many people have a happy first memory from childhood. Playing in the garden with friends, a day at the beach, or a particularly happy time with mother or father. Not me. My earliest memory is of getting as pissed as a little beetle.

Early days in West London: I remember sitting in a huge pram with my brother and sister in the pouring rain outside The Greyhound Pub on the Fulham Palace Road as mum talked to a friend from work at Charing Cross Hospital; going into the outside toilet to find it inexplicably full of lawnmowers; the ghost that lived on the upstairs landing that kept me howling in my bedroom for days. But the memory that sticks in my mind, against all odds, as it turns out, is seeing my dad off from the living room window. It explains an awful lot about my life. Start, they say, as you mean to go on.

My father was an officer in the Territorial Army. He's a doctor, and he got a Major's rank and a job as an army surgeon. It had its privileges, the cheap bar at Chelsea Barracks being one of them. He'd have to spend every other weekend at the mercy of the armed forces, and every year there was a two-week exercise, usually somewhere glamorous, up to their necks in mud in Aldershot.

As a recently self-aware three year old, dad disappearing for two weeks was a Big Thing. The lads turned up on the day in a great big Army ambulance, and half a dozen or so came in for "farewell drinkies", before going out in the garden to talk loudly and postpone the inevitable moment of departure as long as possible.

Forgotten by the big people, I was left alone in the front room. The drinks cabinet, that great locked mystery, had been left open revealing a fascinating array of multicoloured bottles. If it was good enough for the grown ups, it was good enough for me. So I got stuck in.

Unsurprisingly, there were a number of failures. A big green bottle turned out to be Gordon's Gin. It tasted like rat's piss, an opinion that is still valid three decades later. Similarly, the great big bottle of Tonic Water had my tongue stuck to the roof of my mouth and left me barely able to spit the rest out into a pot plant.

Third time lucky. Martini. A sweet bottle of yummy stuff that was oh-so-easy to drink. Before I knew it, I was as pissed as the proverbial little beetle, rolling around on the floor giggling, clutching the bottle to my chest. Given half the chance I'd have called everyone "You're me best mate hic", but I was alone with my bevvy, and dad was just getting set to leave.

I staggered up to the living room window, hoisted myself up onto the sill via the sofa and waved frantically to him as he got into the big green army ambulance with the big red cross on the side. He waved back as he started off up the street, and I opened the window and shouted "Bye-bye Daddy!" as he went. The further up the road he went, the further I had to lean to see him, and drunkenly waving with one hand, it made my position all the more precarious.

Headfirst I went, landing on my three-year-old booze-addled noggin right in the middle of the flowerbed. I don't know how long I lay there amid the roses, but by the time I came to it had started to rain and I was covered in a mass of mud and scratches. I had not been missed.

I staggered to my feet, and yowling, banged on the front door until mum opened up to see me, wet, bleeding, muddy and crying.

"Oh!" she said with surprise "I thought you were upstairs."

I puked neat Martini all over her foot. The truth was out.

Start as you mean to go on, baby.

The Scaryduck guide to smuggling penguins onto airliners

It's always the same. You go on holiday, have a few drinks, and before you know it, you're faced with the problem of getting that ill-advised purchase onto the plane home. Don't sweat - you'll get Mr Flippers back home with minimal jail time if you follow our foolproof guide.

- Wear dark glasses and claim he is your guide penguin. Any attempt to harass you is discrimination against the disabled.
- Superglue a handle to his back and insist that he is the latest line of designer handbag: "Gaultier's got one"
- "Airport security - we understand there is an illicit shipment of fish on this aircraft. Go fetch, boy!"
- "Are you stupid? Can't you see my son supports Newcastle United?"
- Hide it inside the llama you are also smuggling on board
- Buy him a first class ticket, and continually refer to him as "Maestro"
- Pretend to be a BBC film crew from TV's Jim'll Fix It, and produce a letter saying "Dear Jim, please could you fix it for my small flightless bird to go up in a plane."
- Put him inside a condom, swallow him and carry him through customs inside your stomach. Back at home, just wait for nature to do its course, et voila! (Only works for very, very, very small penguins)

And the best of British luck to you all. Please be aware that the penalties for penguin smuggling are severe and vary from country to country.

Mushy Peas

Mushy peas made my life hell. Words cannot describe my hatred for mushy peas, but by God, I'm going to give it a try.

They're not natural, obviously the result of some sort of evil scientific experiment involving nuclear waste carried out at Porton Down during the Cold War, and there seems to be an endless supply.

Mrs Duck loves mushy peas, and she accuses me of being strange. She might have a point there, come to think of it. Dissolve to 1972....

I still remember my dinner hall nemesis today. Blue-rinsed perm, horn-rimmed glasses, scowling face, monstrous sheepskin coat. Mrs Green the dinner lady, a million hateful school-yard clichés rolled into one. The harridan of Melcombe Infants School on the Fulham Palace Road. I was six, she was evil, the battle was lost before it even started.

Let's clear up one misconception. The six-year-old Scary was by no means naughty. Slightly adventurous, maybe, but not bad. He just wanted to be A Good Boy and stay out of trouble. And by and large, I succeeded, it was Mrs Green who brought me down.

I actually liked school dinners. Those were the pre-Thatcher days when you actually got free milk and a decent sized, balanced meal, usually with a rather yummy pudding to finish the whole thing off. Naturally, Thatch came along in 1979 and murdered school meals - my kids' school doesn't even have a kitchen. The cow.

The only problem was Thursdays. Thursdays promised the best evening TV (Blue Peter, Tomorrow's World and Top of the Pops), but first you had to negotiate school and mushy peas at school dinners. Torture.

In order to get your hands on your pudding and your route out to the playground, you had to finish your dinner, show your plate to the dinner lady, who would then allow you to join the queue of duff. Four days a week, I had no problems with this. Thursdays, though, meant mushy peas and the wrath of the evil one. It was no good. I couldn't even force a single mouthful down and my attempts to get to the slops bucket without her seeing me always ended with failure.

And when you were caught, you weren't sent back to your table. Oh no - you were sent to the Naughty Table, where you had to stand and finish your meal in front of the entire school. And because it was right next to the playground window, your humiliation was completed by older kids coming up and pulling faces from the other side of the glass.

Entire Thursday lunch-breaks - a whole hour and a half could be spent at this table while Mrs Green glowered at me and my fellow mushy pea dissenters. Brought up in wartime London where to waste food was a crime, not finishing your dinner was handing victory to Hitler and his cronies. He'd only been dead for twenty-six years. He could come back any day, all thanks to the green crap on my plate.

"Waste not, want not" she told us. Too bloody right - it was nuclear waste.

Revenge was not long in coming. It was a particularly rainy Thursday in the London Borough of Hammersmith, and mushy peas were on the menu again. True to form, as all my friends tucked into a rather lovely looking sponge pudding with pink custard, yours truly was at the naughty table again, trying to outstare a pile of green stuff, and losing.

It came to my attention that there was something under the table that I hadn't noticed before - a pair of Dunlop's finest Wellington boots. Mrs Green's Wellington boots, which she had worn to work, and changed into a pair of carpet slippers once she got there. Dear reader, I simply don't know what came over me...

An experimental forkful of peas found their way under the table and into a boot. Then another, and another. No evidence, just forkful after forkful of those cursed peas surreptitiously disappearing off my plate, and as far as everybody else was concerned, into me. My plate empty, I was able to strut to the front of the school hall in triumph and present my plate - completely wiped clean - to a jubilant Mrs Green who gave me a smile, the like of which I never want to see in my life again. She was so pleased with me, I was allowed extra pink custard.

I shall spare you the sordid details, but I was called to the headmistress's office later that afternoon to confront a grimacing Mrs Green and my mother who had been called out of work to "discuss my unacceptable behaviour". Mrs Green, I noticed, was wearing one boot and one carpet slipper.

Rumbled.

Head bowed, I apologised to her, the head, Mrs Green and anyone who happened to be in earshot, and dammit she would make me like mushy peas in future. She didn't fight a war for children like me to waste perfectly good food, you know.

But a plan had formed in my head. Every Thursday, I would slip a greaseproof paper bag - lifted from the kitchen drawer at home - into the pocket of my shorts, and with Mrs Green's attention elsewhere, I'd load the bag up, stuff it back in my pocket and furnish an empty plate to the old bag, convincing her that I was a reformed character. However, this presented me with the same problem with the tunnellers from The Great Escape - what to do with a pocket of crap once I'd left the confines of the prison hut.

Flushing it down the bog didn't seem to work. For starters the toilets just didn't seem to have the power to take a bag of shite round the U-bend, and secondly, you had to run a gauntlet of juveniles chanting "Who's in the bog, then?" as soon as you entered the cubicle. And most tellingly, living in a third-world inner city, these were outside toilets, and my classmates were masters at the art of "highest mark on the wall", or in this case "over the door."

I was soaked in piss and still had the evidence, sopping wet in my pocket.

There was only one other place I could think of, and here I must blame my father for regaling me with stories of how they used to ping their rock-hard peas at the school trophy cabinet at his school in Greys. The trophy cabinet with its sole trophy was just round the corner from the boys' cloakrooms - where I spent many a morning hiding from the none-more-scary "Boy from Space" on schools' television.

I waited for a quiet moment, opened the cabinet and slipped my package into the house cup, and pushed down the lid until it stuck. And there it remained, forgotten, festering, until the last day of term prize-giving.

I shall spare you the sordid details... all I am saying is give peas a chance.

PiSS
Dedicated to Rik and Chris, sledgehammer-wielding number one duck-fans

Growing up can be painful, even for a small boy at the heart of a middle-class family. With everything on a plate, the failure to learn from experience is a fact of life.

We weren't poor, we weren't rich either, just a family with three kids getting away from London and settling in the relative comfort of the suburbs. Just the middle kid of three going through school in a quiet Berkshire village. Where's the harm in that?

Just about everywhere it turns out. At eight years old, I shared a bedroom with my younger brother. My bed was a huge wooden thing, with a headboard carved out of an entire tree by prisoners during the Boer War. Nonetheless, it was the biggest thing in a small boy's life. And it spelt my doom.

It was under this bed that I kept my most secret secrets. All my top toys. A Great Universal catalogue in which I was showing an unhealthy interest in pages 220-245. Approximately 200 spent matches. It was a wonder I'd made it this far.

In my own defence, I claim that I was far too easily led. So I blame the BBC entirely for showing a TV programme about the work of engravers and the intricate work they do in the medium of wood. Inspired, I felt I should copy their work. So I did, with the only large piece of tree I had to hand.

I found the first relatively sharp instrument I could lay my hands on - a metal cogwheel from my Meccano set, and set myself to work in my first attempt at the art of wood engraving. With unshaking hand, and knowing not exactly what I was letting myself in for, I neatly engraved the word "PiSS" onto the headboard of my bed in eighteen inch high letters. I sat back and admired my handiwork. Lovely job.

It was about ten seconds after this particular point-of-no-return that I realised something was not quite right. I had written the foulest word known to my eight-year-old mind on the wooden headboard of my bed. And nail me to the ceiling and call me Tracy, it wouldn't come off.

PiSS.

It had to go.

I rubbed it. I soaked it in a mixture of water, soap and spit. It came off. Joy.

Ten minutes later, it had dried, and there was the word PiSS, back again, taunting me. Woe.

I was mortified, and I could hear mum was coming upstairs. Double woe. Time to think quickly. I draped the curtains over my headboard and announced as she entered the room, "From now on, I want to sleep like this".

"You'll get a draught down your neck" was her reply, steeped in years of accumulated parental wisdom.

"I don't mind, I get hot in bed."

She was right. For three dread-filled months, I slept with a stiff neck, with the curtains covering the word PiSS on my headboard. I did anything I could to cover it up, diligently making my bed each morning so mum wouldn't have to. Slapping stickers over the PiSS, but having to peel them off as they might "spoil the wood". I cut out pictures of airplanes, pets and family photos and stuck them over the dreaded PiSS, only for them to fall off in the night, exposing my Nemesis for the world to see.

Every night was a struggle against discovery. PiSS was taking over my world. I was tired, stiff in the neck, and my school work was suffering. I was pilloried by Mrs Jones at school for absent-mindedly doodling "PiSS" on the cover of a school book and sent to stand outside the headmaster's office. It was getting too much. I was turning into a pre-teen crack-up.

PiSS.

PiSS. PiSS. PiSS.

PiSS. PiSS. PiSS. PiSS. PiSS.

All I could see was a lifetime of PiSS, stretching away into the far future. Even as I die, the word PiSS would be engraved on the lid of my coffin.

Then - the glorious day.

I came home from school one afternoon, and ran upstairs for the daily ritual of guarding the PiSS against discovery. Instead of the two beds side by side - my brother's World War II relic and the PiSS bed - was my saviour, a lovely brand spanking new bunkbed in glorious white-painted wood. I danced with joy.

It gleamed. It sparkled. And best of all, the PiSS bed was already on its way to the dump. Gleefully, as older brother, I bagsied the top bunk and revelled in my new found freedom, getting a good night's sleep for the first time in months.

It was not long after that I noticed that brother Nigel was becoming a little particular about covering up the end of his lower bunk. He developed the habit of hanging spare clothes, pyjamas and his dressing gown over it in a frankly suspicious manner.

I took a peek.

"ArSE".

I was saved. For now.

Lost in Cornwall

Who the buggering hell planned the roads in Cornwall - Helen Keller?

The ideal Cornish "road" is a single track of dirt with grass growing up the middle, surrounded by twelve-foot high hedges. It should lead precisely nowhere, and have as many blind ninety degree bends as possible; which will deliver you directly into the middle of a herd of cows accompanied to the milking parlour by an old fella with trousers held up by string, face agog at one of these new-fangled horseless carriages bearing down on him at 90mph.

A short-cut, then, from the local shop back to Dad's house - a distance of four hundred yards - took an entire morning of careering around this maze of primitive tracks, hopelessly searching for familiar landmarks, or at the very least, a signpost. A tiny, unnamed village rose out of the morning like a Brigadoon, and seconds later it was gone, never to been seen again for another century.

The emergency rations consumed, we were marooned, starving in a hostile land

Navigating by the sun, we eventually hit the A30 at Redruth - a town so drab, grey and lifeless, the building of a Tesco superstore had the locals out on the streets with rakes and flaming torches and a burning effigy of Jacques Delors as the infernal, satanic bulldozers went about their task - and we arrived home just as a search party was being organised.

"You were a bloody long time. Where the hell have you been?"

"I. Don't. Know."

PiSS II - Son of PiSS

When I was eight-years-old, I carved the word "PiSS" on the headboard of my bed, and suffered months of angst and bloodcurdling fear as I tried to cover up my piece of wanton vandalism from my parents. Did I learn my lesson? What do you think?

Less than a year after the PiSS bed ended up as so much landfill somewhere in rural Berkshire, I found myself in the boys' toilets during lunch break at school, piece of soap in my hand. I looked in the mirror, the devil stared back. I had a flashback of evil work done in the privacy of my own bedroom. I was tempted. My hand moved to the mirror. And wrote.

21

P. I. S. S.
"PiSS."

I stood back to admire my work, and in my horror, I realised I'd only gone and done it again. Damn you Demons of PiSS! I went to grab a hand-towel to wipe it off, but too late, I'd been spotted by one of the more vindictive kids in my year.

"Oooooh, I'm telling on you."

And he did, despite my offers to "Be your best friend" or "I'll give you any money", the urge to be a stoolpigeon was far too great for Benny.

If only I'd drawn an ejaculating nob, like all the other boys did, even if, at that age, I didn't know what it meant. Good grief, our current favourite game was running round the playground in a frenzy shouting "Wankwankwankwank!" at the top of our voices, wondering why the dinner ladies were having kittens at us.

I spent the next hour hiding behind class eleven pretending to play war and hardly shouting "Wankwankwankwank!" at all, but it was no good. Mr George's excellent network of spies found me, and I was trooped off for an audience with the head.

Those weren't the wishy-washy days we live in today when teachers can't even give kids a good talking to without written permission from parents, police and judge, for fear of denying their human rights and damaging their self esteem! Oh no! None of that bollocks at all - I got six of the best with twelve inches of finest wood - Mr George's dreaded ruler across the back of the legs before being torn off a strip about vandalising school property. All thoroughly deserved too. It was even left to me, in my shame, to tell my parents. I chickened out, naturally, but with half the school trooping past the Head's office, they found out eventually.

After my ordeal by wood, he made me stand outside his office for the next hour while every teacher in the school made snide comments as they walked past. It wasn't the pain, it was the fact that even my favourite teacher, Mrs Jones, said "Who's been a naughty boy, then?" as she came out of the staff room. That was the last time I had pre-pubescent fantasies about her. Even at the age of nine, it was the blondes.

Meanwhile, skulking in the shadows was the dark figure of Benny. He'd been given what for from the Head as well. And his crime - being a tell-tale for the thirtieth time that year, making full use of his season ticket for the space by the tuck shop supplies. There came the crunch of Golden Wonders and the tell-tale whoosh of a bottle of fizzy pop opening, the sly little weasel.

Justice works in mysterious ways. I reflected on this for the next hour or so, as I doodled the word "PiSS" in the dust.

I'll never learn.

Christmas at Grandad's

Isn't Christmas lovely? It's that time of year when families get together, united in love and understanding, to get outrageously drunk and blow each other up. Sounds perfectly reasonable to me.

We always used to go to my Grandad's for Christmas. He lived in Basildon, a horrible concrete mess on the other side of London where Cockneys go when they've had enough of the East End. My dad's brother and his family also lived there, so you could always guarantee a full house and a pretty lively celebration. A knees-up, even.

Grandad was a pretty practical chap, and like anyone who lived through Second World War hardships was adept at growing-their-own, digging-for-victory and all that guff. He had a garden to die for, and won horticultural awards all over the place. He also made his own wine, and his spare bedroom was always filled with huge demijohns (look it up) bubbling away with his latest brew. The pea-pod wine was his speciality, and had a variety of uses as paint-stripper, patent cure-all and weapon of mass destruction.

Scene: Grandad, Gran, five of us in our family, four of Uncle Dave's mob, one over-excited dog, all in a kitchen-diner the size of a postage stamp. If one of us wanted to get up, at least four others had to move. If the dog wanted to get up, we all had to go out into the garden. So Grandad opened the front parlour, a room that hadn't seen human life since 1963 apart from the comings and goings of his gardening trophies and enormous stock of homemade booze.

Ah, but it was Christmas! Gifts were exchanged. My cousin Andy gave his dad a marvellously fat Cuban cigar. Quite where an eight-year-old kid got it from is another matter, but in those days you could send your bairns off to the corner shop for twenty Bensons and a bottle of vodka without the shopkeep even batting an eyelid, but there you go.

What Uncle Dave didn't know was that Andy had also been to a joke shop on the seafront at Southend, and his cheroot was positively brimming with exploding cigarette ends. Before the day was out, there would be hell to pay.

A quick aside - Andy is the most accident-prone person I have ever met. He was always falling down stairs, off ladders, out of trees or over the handle-bars of his Raleigh Chopper. He had a season ticket for the local Casualty department, who'd always wave him off home with a shout of "See you next week". He once caught his Johnson in his zip on the beach at Southend and spent the rest of the day having it frozen by hospital staff who could barely stifle their laughs. When he got married, the car broke down on the way to the church, so he arrived on the back of a tractor, with the heap of junk towed behind. He is, of course, a most excellent individual.

The Christmas dinner came and went, Gran catering for the assembled masses like she'd done it for her entire life. Grandad let us kids have one thimble-sized glass of his homemade paint-stripper, and we all toasted the Queen, family, friends and the downfall of the Bay City Rollers. And that was enough for most.

But not me. As the rest of the family snoozed in a post-dinner stupor, I sneaked into the front parlour and helped myself to another glass. And another. And another. Before long, my ten-year-old head was spinning round like a spinny-round-and-round thing, and I was feeling more than a little queasy. It was then that my body decided it wished to part company with Christmas dinner.

Page 374 of The Thoughts of Chairman Mao says "You can't hold back puke", and how right he was. In a drunken panic, I darted around looking for somewhere to spew. The room was filled with Grandad's best furniture and an impressive looking carpet which was his war-loot from North Africa. If I chundered on that I would be dead meat. Only one thing for it. The Laindon and District Horticultural Society Challenge Trophy. It brimmed. And by God, I felt better.

Holding the cup above my head like a drunken seventies footballer, I staggered up the stairs and flushed the diced carrots down the bog. I would have got away with it too, if, in my drunken state, I had remembered clean the thing out.

I arrived back downstairs just as Uncle Dave lit up his Christmas cigar. Laying back in his easy chair, he inhaled deeply, drawing in the sweet aroma of the Cuban tobacco, puffing out smoke rings to the general amusement of the massed throng of the Scary family. In the minutes before the Queen's Speech and the afternoon's Bond movie, it was a most tranquil moment. As a matter of fact, even Andy had forgotten about the time-bomb waiting to go off.

BANG!

There was a flash, and Dave was thrown halfway up the wall behind his easy chair with shock as an entire packet of explosive cigarette ends went nuclear.

Gran screamed "It's the blitz!", realised the Anderson shelter had been dug up thirty years previously, and hid under the kitchen table with the dog. Grandad dashed off for his war-loot gas mask and German bayonet. The rest of us collapsed in fits of laughter at poor old Dave.

The cigar looked like he'd just walked into a door as part of some Groucho Marx film stunt. A pathetic smoke ring curled up from the end, a wisp of tobacco clung to his nose. He was livid.

"Right, who's been playing silly buggers?" he scowled, scanning juvenile faces for guilt.

There was only one thing for it. We shopped Andy to him. It was a fair cop, and Uncle Dave eventually managed to see the funny side as a second non-exploding cheroot was produced.

After all the excitement Grandad decided that we deserved some more home-made wine to calm the nerves. I politely refused, finding a nice warm corner to curl up and die.

Two days later, with my hangover still raging, they found the dried up huey in the gardening trophy. Whoops.

Let Uncle Dave be the bringer of the moral to this tale: "Oh yes, it's all fun and games until somebody loses an eye."

Unfortunately for me, I still had both my eyes, it's just that they refused to look in the same direction for weeks. Kids! Just say "No" to paint-stripper!

Terrible One-Liners Department: On Gayness

For those of you thinking of joining the gayers at some time in the near future, the World Federation of Homosexualists offers a bargain membership plan designed to attract new recruits to their ranks. It's called "Bi now, gay later."

Oakdale

Our junior school of the 1970s was incredibly forward thinking. We had our own school minibus while other schools still had a man walking in front of a horse and cart with a red flag. We had a swimming pool while our nearest rivals were still jumping in puddles. We also had our own Outdoor Activity Centre, halfway up a mountain on the Welsh Borders years before they became fashionable.

Granted, the minibus was an old ambulance with a couple of benches screwed to the floor, but hardly any pupils ever got killed, and the sliding about as the bus went round corners was all part of the fun. Even for the kid at the back who had the job of making sure the doors stayed shut.

All of this was down to the head teacher, the God-like David George, who loved his school, the kids and the village.

As far as I can remember, Mr George had bought Oakdale - a clapped out old farm house on the Welsh borders - for the school around 1970 at some ridiculously low price, which may have included the bartering of some sheep, a handful of magic beans and a pile of scrap metal. He'd done the place up, quite possibly out of his own pocket, in his own time and produced a homely little centre which could comfortably accommodate fourteen kids and a couple of teachers to do the kind of stuff you can't get insurance for these days.

On any given Monday morning, a bunch of kids aged between eight and eleven accompanied by a couple of teachers would pile themselves and their luggage into a converted death-trap of an ambulance and cart themselves off up the M4 to the Wye Valley.

Our parents tearfully waved us off at the school gate, before running off home for a "Thank fuck they've gone" party. The minibus had wooden bench seats, no seatbelts, and we all piled in on top of the bags, cases and junk. One lucky kid - judged the most likely to puke up - was allowed to sit up front, belt-less, with the teachers. It would be enough to give any modern solicitor a heart attack.

Mr Morgan - our Welsh wizard of a form teacher - slapped the school's only music tape into the slot, and we would be treated to a "Now That's What I Call Fucking Awful" musical compilation for the first of fifty-eight times that week. To this day, I still have nightmares about The Wurzels singing "I've got a Brand New Combine Harvester"; and don't get me started on J.J. Barrie 'singing' "No Charge", the kind of saccharine-sweet bollocks that can only drive you to commit murder, and by God, we came close that week.

By Monday teatime, following an afternoon's diversion to the SS Great Britain and Bristol Zoo we descended on the house. Seven to a room, we bagsied beds and settled in. Giggling could be heard and an eye appeared just above floor level.

The dreaded enemy! Girls! They'd found a hole in the wall of the boys' dorm in the stairwell and were spying on us in the time-honoured fashion. And did we do anything to block it up? Of course we didn't. Instead, Andy squatted down onto his haunches and let rip the most terrifying fart into the hole that only a cow-herding farm-boy like himself could manage. It lasted for a good ten seconds and sounded like a motorbike going down the road outside.

There was a scream.

"Miss! Miss! The boys are being dirty!"

Yeah, it was OK for them. They'd only been rumbled spying on the boys' dorm, a stunt they repeated on a regular basis for the entire week. We had to live with the consequences of Andy's pickled arse. All week. Day or night. And the windows were stuck closed with gloss paint. They say that pet owners soon come to resemble their pets. Andy's farm had 200 cows, and he had somehow inherited their digestive system.

In the end, he and his mate Simon were "allowed" to sleep in Mr George's caravan out the back, much to our relief.

We spent a week of doing the most dangerous stuff that we could get away with, as our teachers *in loco parentis* treated us with such a laid-back attitude, they may as well not have been there at all. Up mountains, through forests, down caves, over rivers, eating Miss Hill's cooking. Back in the World, she lived in a hippie commune. By Friday, I had grown to love cardboard..

We lived on the edge, and by and large, we escaped uninjured. Whatever the teachers were getting paid for their week of juvenile hell, it was nowhere near enough. We were wild, we were out of control, we were lucky to be alive. So, what did they do to keep us entertained of an evening? Our spartan accommodation didn't have a television. In fact, the whole valley seemed to be blissfully unaware of such modern comforts as electricity and running water. They took us down the pub. Corporate lawyer has heart attack...

With our teachers either cooking for the bunch of gannets nominally under their control, or having a nervous breakdown somewhere private, we were allowed to wander the countryside around the house virtually unsupervised. That was, it turned out, a Bad Thing. The sheep were worried, and so were the locals. They knew about us from previous visits, and we were frequently threatened with "I'll make sure Mr George hears about this!" Did that stop us? Surely you should know the answer to that by now.

Geoff led an assault on the top of the valley to "see what's on the other side". Like pint-sized adventurers, we followed him up and up through the bracken, heather and gorse, thrashing the undergrowth aside with sticks. Before long we reached the summit and took in the view. There was a telephone pole. And lots of trees.

"You git!" I complained. "We followed you all the way up here for *this*? It's like... like... trees!"

He had to die.

It wasn't Geoff's fault that some thoughtless bastard had planted trees as far as the eye could see, but he got a hail of "crow pecks" on his noggin for his pains. Steve, Steve and Simes had already started back to the house to see if there was anything worth smashing up down there. It was then that we found The Tyre.

It wasn't huge, just something off the front wheel of a tractor. Not quite big enough for the old "stuff Geoff in the middle and roll him down the hill for knackering us out for nothing", but it had possibilities. We were on top of a big, steep hill. It was round. We were young and open to temptation, and farm-boy Andy was the first to get his hands on it.

With his shock of blond hair blowing in the wind, he hurled the thing down the valley. The first thing that happened was that it bowled Steve, Steve and Simes over like skittles, much to the amusement of those still at the top of the hill.

It picked up speed, ricocheting off rocks, trees and stumps, changing direction almost at will. Changing direction until it rocketed straight towards a farm house where a large, middle-aged woman in an apron stood in the garden taking in the day's washing, surrounded by a brood of chickens foraging for food round her feet.

"Oooh noooo....."

Helpless, we knew what was going to happen. Fat Old Dear was going to wake up in some hospital in Chepstow with a tyre-print running up her front and down her back, and there was nothing we could do about it. Apart from laugh, obviously.

Vaguely aware of her impending doom, she looked up just in time to see black nemesis approaching with increasing speed. Her mouth took a vague "O" shape as if to scream, yet words failed her. The chickens, knowing that an appointment with the oven and a packet of sage and onion stuffing could be only seconds away, scattered. Like... err... chickens.

At the last moment, just as her doom - not to mention ours - looked sealed, the tyre hit a rock and bounced into the air. It sailed over the astonished Welsh housewife, tore the TV ariel off the roof and bounded on its merry way, before landing with a resounding splash in the brook at the bottom of the valley.

Caught like escaping airmen from Stalag Luft 17, we froze in the icy glare of Mrs Farmer. An old man, aged about 150, tottered out of the house on a walking stick.

"The damned TV's broke", he said, voice almost lost in the distance.

The lady said nothing. She just pointed up the hill. We scattered.

"I'll tell Mr George about you, you see if I don't" she bellowed with a voice that could flatten trees.

She did, too, and the following Monday we were summoned to the great man's office.

Faced with damning evidence, and with a lack of "bigger boys" to blame, we confessed all, and put it down to a moment of collective madness.

A twinkle appeared in the old fella's eye, and we knew we were off the hook.

"Such honesty cannot go unrewarded. Get out of my office before I change my mind."

He even fixed the ariel out of his own pocket, too. You don't find men like him every day.

Slide of Doom

For an eight year old boy in 1974, the world was more-or-less the shellfish of your choice. You had the freedom to go anywhere, try anything, and more often than not you'd arrive home relatively unscathed.

A quick wriggle through the hedge at the bottom of the garden, a dash across the school field to the shouts of the caretaker, and we were in the park. At one end was the playground, a death-trap of cast-iron play equipment with jagged edges and unexpected hinges just right for severing fingers, ears and stray bodily appendages. A little mutilation's good for kids, so that's where I went with Nigel.

He climbed to the top of the slide, a fifty foot tall monstrosity that appeared to have been left over from the construction of HMS Belfast. Such was the pressure difference from top to bottom, your ears would pop and you'd get a nosebleed on the way down. You were also travelling at something approaching the speed of sound, with nothing to stop you at the end except your backside against solid concrete. And there we considered ourselves lucky. Woe betide should you arrive home covered in mud.

Nigel at the top. So it's only natural that I should stand on the slide at the bottom. If I was retarded. "Get out of the way!" he shouted. "I'm coming down!"

"No!" I replied. "When you slide down, I'll jump over you. It'll be a great stunt."

Great stunts were the be-all and end-all of our lives, and for this I blame television. Everything had to be done with style, panache, and above all, looking good for any passing girls. Movie stuntmen plan their gags down to the last possible detail, measuring the risks and ensuring that

30

nothing remotely painful ever happened to them. I, on the other hand, was standing in a forest of steel and concrete without a single cardboard box to fall onto. Worse still, there were no female witnesses for the Great Stunt that was about to occur.

Nigel slid.

He came down like a lightly-greased Exocet missile. Concentrating totally on the upcoming glory of my Great Stunt, I forgot to jump, and my life was rudely interrupted by Newton's Laws.

His feet caught me square in the shins, causing me to catapult up into the air. By all accounts, my one-and-a-half somersault with pike would have graced any diving competition as I flew through the air, gravity waiting in the wings to slam me back to earth.

In beautiful slow motion, the slide came up to meet me, followed by the blinding white light of pain. I landed face first and teeth and blood went everywhere. I looked like I'd gone ten rounds with Ali, and the Russian judge docked me points for the shonky landing.

Luckily, Nigel had the presence of mind to pick up the severed molars and shove them back in from where they came. I spent the next two hours in the dentist's chair having sharp edges painfully filed off and loose teeth fixed back in. Thirty years later, they're still there, thanks to the wonders of superglue.

The following week, we tried it again. I remembered to jump. I was right. It was a most excellent stunt.

Slide of Doom II

Playgrounds are dangerous places. I should know, having lost teeth plying silly buggers on the slide at Twyford Rec. The whole place was a death trap. These days, it's all safe play, loads of wood chipping and rubber matting to fall into, and not a single sharp edge or masses of exposed mechanics to rip off innocent fingers. More's the pity. Kids need to be exposed to bone-crushing danger, I say. It made me the social misfit I am today. Back then, if you were going to fall off the twenty foot monstrosity of a climbing frame of tubular steel and exposed bolts, you would land on concrete or tarmac and like it.

Hideous accidents were legion at our park. In fact, there was an ambulance bay by the main gate and a permanent supply of bags of frozen peas to keep severed fingers fresh. The swings were made out of the hardest substances known to man, and could decapitate anyone foolhardy enough to walk past (in fact, it's how One-Bollocked Rick lost his bollock). The concrete tunnels housed wild creatures and broken glass, while you got exactly what you deserved riding a piece of torture equipment called the Witches Hat, while the whole thing was surrounded by a hawthorn hedge. If the swings didn't get you, the thorns would rip you to shreds.

Parents didn't give a monkey's either. If you didn't come home from the park, they knew to drive to Casualty where they'd pick you up after having your bits sewn back on. The human body can take a lot of punishment. You could do yourself a lot of damage yet still walk away, often with crucial parts in a shopping bag. My father - the doctor - once showed us how bendy it was, on a rather unnerving visit to his lab. It toughened you up.

Today's toughening up exercise will be brought to you by Stupid Scary and his friends.

We'd done plenty of stupid stuff before, usually ending with pain, explosions, or pain and explosions. Today, having seen some crap-fest on television, we were - as usual - The World's Greatest Stuntmen, and we were going to do The World's Greatest Stunts. At the park. On our bikes. And a skateboard.

Doomed, then, before we even started.

We started off with the easy stuff. We set up a small ramp with a bit of wood which had once hidden rather important and life-threatening rotating machinery on some of the more fiendish equipment. We jumped over on the skateboard. We jumped over one of the bikes. Then we jumped over Russell, taking great care not to cause him any physical harm. Well, as little as we could get away with, because we secretly wanted to know what his insides looked like.

But we wanted speed, we wanted thrills. We wanted stolen cigarettes and hardcore pornography. But at the age of thirteen neither was forthcoming. So we settled for mind-bending death-defying skills instead, which basically involved jumping over hawthorn hedges on your mum's Raleigh Shopper.

Try as we might, there was just no way we could get up enough speed for the jump. John had already chickened out at the last moment and come within an ace of severe mutilation. We needed speed. And there was only one way we were going to get it.

It was my idea, I am forced to admit. Carry your bike to the top of the slide - a thirty foot high behemoth of cast iron and a sheer drop that rivalled Beachy Head as one of the country's most notorious black-spots for gravity-induced death - and zip down as fast as you dare.

I lugged the bike to the very top, and in fear of my life, mounted up. I was scared shitless, I don't mind saying, the only thing I could see below being cold, hard tarmac. Following parental advice, I was wearing fresh underwear "just in case you have an accident", but alas, my pants were on inside out and lightly soiled. I chickened out. I let the bike go, and it careered down the slide on its own, catching Russell squarely up the arse with one of the handlebars.

I followed it down at a more sedate pace to the jeers of my mates. Fate! Why do you mock me at every turn?

"Out the way you great poof" said Matty, "I'll show you how it's done."

He grabbed his bright green skateboard and hoofed it to the top of the slide, while we readied the ramp for his do-or-die stunt attempt.

He was as scared as I was, but was determined not to chicken out. With a whimper, he jumped onto the board, and shot off down the slide like Eddie the Eagle's less talented and rather more mental brother.

With a thwooosh! he shot off the end of the slide and landed, with Tony Hawk-like agility, on the board and careered his way towards the ramp and certain glory.

"Go for it Matty!", "Ride that board!" we yelled after him as his moment of triumph approached. Only cruel, cruel fate could let him down now. Or, forgetting the crucial detail that the ramp was made of wood an inch thick, obviously.

TOCK!

Matty hit the ramp.

The skateboard stopped.

Matty didn't. He flew.

It was majestic. It was beautiful. It was sweary.

"OHSHITOHFUCKOHSHITI'MDEAD!"

And oh! He nearly made it.

The hedge claimed him. Wood, leaves, branches and thorns, thorns, thorns swallowed his thrashing body.

There were screams of pain. There was blood. There was a fear-wracked teen in his death-throes, clutching his groin which had come into contact with something solid. There was only one thing for it.

"Leg it!"

Half an hour later, a blood-drenched wraith dressed in rags appeared at my front door on all fours.

"You... you... you.... GIT!"

"Err... you alright mate?"

"Me fookin' skateboard's bust!"

Ah.

He held up his skateboard. A piece of green plastic and a couple of wheels.

"And me bollocks are killing me."

"Pffft..."

"Take a look at them, will ya?"

"Oh no, I don't do other fellas' testicles. I'm no bumgay, y'know. Lie to your dad. Say it was bigger kids."

The catch-all excuse of 'bigger kids did it'. He told his dad. Dad didn't believe him.

Glider

Call me a dweeb, a geek and a nerd, but I went through a pubescent phase where I liked nothing better than sitting down with a big pile of balsa wood, some needlessly complicated plans and a frighteningly sharp craft knife; building enormously detailed scale model gliders.

Sad, isn't it? While my contemporaries were poring over magazines full of naked women, the only models I had an interest in involved several weeks of construction. The glider would be covered in tissue paper. Everybody else was going through BOXES of the stuff. The end result of my innocent labours would be about four feet long with a wing-span of six feet, and with a following wind could do some serious damage if you accidentally took one straight in a soft, vulnerable part of your body.

Of course, we went to enormous measures to ensure that this sort of thing could never happen.

With the right radio control gear, and a large, windy open space, your fragile creation of balsa wood and tissue paper became a fearful weapon for frightening grannies, dive-bombing dogs and getting hideous and bloody revenge on the snotty little creep of a kid who just wouldn't leave you alone.

I had spent months building my craft, and even managed to finish it despite overcoming the obstacles of watching the dog eat it, for which he was greatly chastised; and having to go to my best friend's house to ask for my glue back, which he was busy sniffing out of a plastic bag. Up the park Graham (who, I should point out for legal reasons, was not the glue fiend) and I went, he to launch the thing, and myself to twiddle the knobs on the radio control unit and pretend I knew what I was doing.

"Can I have a go?"

Oh crud. Greebo.

Greebo was one of those snotty little bastards who followed you around everywhere like a lost puppy, and then run home to his dad when you told him to fuck off, or, on one memorable occasion, broke his nose.

"Fuck off Greebo."

"I'm telling my dad on you."

So he did. His dad told my dad, and my dad told me to "let the little shit have a go and perhaps he'll fuck off."

We let him have a go. Dads, eh? What do they know?

Up, up, up into the air my beautiful, beautiful glider went. Soaring away into the blue, blue sky, climbing and diving, turning and err... soaring a bit more. You get the idea. I handed the remote to Greebo with a shrug.

His inexperienced fingers played over the controls, and my wonderful contraption lurched this way and that, narrowly missing a line of trees, and almost disappearing into the wilds of the London Road and certain destruction. Suddenly it hove back into view, coming straight at us, diving madly like a German Stuka on a bombing run.

Funny, both Graham and I - friends since the age of five - seemed to have a telepathic connection. We always seemed to do or say the same thing at once. And so in this case:

"MWAAAAAAAAAAAAAAARGH!"

Graham and I fled for our lives, but Greebo stood there, transfixed, the monster getting closer and closer, his fingers frozen on the remote control as it whistled towards him.

Wwwwwwheeeeeeeeeeeeeeeeeeee-OOOMPH!

Right in the love spuds.

"Haaaaaaaaaaaaaaaaaaaaaaaaaaaaaaaaaarrrrr!" said Greebo as the air burst out of his body. He keeled over, and remained in a foetal position for several moments, whimpering softly to himself.

My beautiful, beautiful glider was no more - the impact had sheered the wings off and the fuselage was now about eight inches long, the rudder flapping forlornly like the tail on a naughty puppy.

It had been most excellent, made even more gratifying to find that Greebo had fallen directly into the kind of turd that could only be left by a Great Dane.

A week later, Greebo was back, still limping.

"I've made me own glider," he proudly announced, his voice an octave higher than usual.

Grudgingly, we agreed to meet him over the park to witness its maiden flight. And what a glider it was. He had eschewed the usual lightweight designed favoured by most model-makers, and gone for an old broomstick, with wings of scrap wood covered in newspaper. It took two of us to lift it, left alone get it airborne.

But fly it did, for five wonderful, glorious seconds. Graham and I took a wing each, and bowling along down the slope we got up enough speed and launched the lumbering thing into the void.

Up, up, up it went as Greebo operated the useless controls. Over, over, over, it flew in a great loop with a mind of its own. Down, down, down it screamed, picking up speed as terrified onlookers fled for the safety of their homes.

Wwwwwwheeeeeeeeeeeeeeeeeeee-OOOMPH!

Dear reader, let us count Greebo's blessings for him, and they are but one: he was facing the other way.

Straight up the arse.

He keeled over forward, the leviathan still stuck there, and unerringly allowed a Great Dane shit break his fall.

There were only two things Graham and I, trained first-aiders, could do in the circumstances, and we did both. We laughed ourselves shitty, and we left him for dead.

The next one I built had a spike on the front. Just in case I got lucky a third time.

Octopus

We rode the Octopus.

These days it would be seen as a fairground ride for wimps, but back then it a test of hardness to the youth of Twyford as the funfair made its twice yearly visit to the village.

The big question was "How long could you stay on?"

It was a trial by g-force that lasted as long as your money did, until you were thrown off or you could take it no more. Stories were told of those who managed five, six, ten rides in a row and hardly needing hospital treatment at all.

Melanie (known as Melon-y for two reasons I cannot even begin to express here) looked well set for a mammoth ride. With a wink to the ride operator, she was allowed to stay on for as long as she wanted, and every time the ride finished, she dipped into what seemed a bottomless purse for another fare and another ride on the swirling behemoth.

Quite a crowd built up underneath. Not simply because the entire fair consisted of a whole four rides and every bugger and their dog had had enough of the merry-go-round, the dodgems and the other whirly-round thing whose name escapes me, and wanted a go on the Octopus - word of Mel's impending triumph was getting around. She had been in flight for the best part of 45 minutes, and records were being set.

It was rumoured that one year, car eight hadn't been bolted on properly and it had flown off at the top of its arc, killing some friend-of-a-friend's aunt as it plunged into a nearby back garden. Mel - Cthulhu save her - was in car eight. Surely history wouldn't repeat?

We watched in awe as the ride started up again. Somebody was keeping count, and great cheers went up every time our heroine hove into view.

Round and round went the bloody great wheel, up and down went the cars, spinning the occupants this way and that in a dizzying dance to thumping rock music and flashing lights.

"Hey Mel! What's the weather like up there?"

"YAAAAAAAAAAAAAAAAAAAAAAAAAARCH!!!!!"

Raining.

She could have least waited until she was round the back, or on the bottom of a swing. But no, car eight was at its highest point, right above our heads as Mel's stomach decided enough was enough and the words "projectile vomiting" entered my vocabulary for the first time in my young life.

Half digested hotdog, candy floss and cheap cider flew in a graceful arc and rained down on the attendant crowds to shrieks of great woe and gnashing of teeth. This, unfortunately, unleashed a domino effect of vomiting, as those who had also been overdoing it on the supermarket own-brand cider, junk food sourced from at least one named animal and consecutive rides on the Octopus decided to join in with the chorus of Rolf and Huey.

I've been on some rough Irish Sea ferry crossings, but the devastation below the Octopus that night made them look like a ride on the boating lake at Regent's Park. Days of chunder, indeed.

As the ride came to a halt, Mel wiped her mouth with the back of her hand, and with a nod to the ride operator said "Again, please."

The next day, the fair left and the seagulls came.

Bottle of Fire

The Summer of '76 was a scorcher. It didn't rain for months, and water was rationed as reservoirs ran dry. Instead of a beautiful lush green, England was brown, withered and fit to burst into flames.

Which is probably a very bad thing if you're a ten-year-old pyromaniac.

I just couldn't help it. I had a thing for fire. My parents didn't help much by putting me in the cub scouts, which was rubbing sticks together and camp fires all the way. My grandfather had a bonfire almost every weekend, we'd pile anything flammable on top and watch the flames scorch the feathers off birds in a hundred yard radius.

I had a perfectly natural urge to burn things, and that is how I found myself on the wasteland behind Twyford Youth Club with a packet of Swan Vestas rattling in my pocket, looking for flammable materials. I didn't have to look far. That summer, everything from little old ladies to white dog turds was flammable.

A hedge ran along one side the youth club from the park, and that's where I found the empty glass coke bottle.

It was no good. I had one of those inevitable light-bulb-over-your-head moments.

"Wouldn't it be great", I thought to myself, "if I could light a fire in this coke bottle and carry it around with me?"

To a ten year old son of the television, this genie in a bottle stuff was pretty sound logic, but on reflection, nigh on impossible. I stuffed the bottle with scraps of paper and tinder-dry sticks, of which there were a plentiful supply. I struck my first match and put it in. Nothing. As soon as it passed the lip of the bottle it went out. I tried it again and again with less paper and sticks in the bottle. Clearly this was one bright idea that wasn't going to work.

My second light-bulb moment.

"What if I lit the fire outside the bottle, and put it in?"

Genius. I set about building a small fire out of the materials to hand. One match, and up it went like Mount Vesuvius. Within approximately five seconds, my small fire had become a raging inferno. There was no way on God's Earth I was going to pick it up and shove it in a bottle.

In fact, the fire was spreading at such an alarming rate over the sun-darkened grass and into the bushes that all thoughts of fire-in-a-bottle were forgotten and replaced by an overwhelming urge to run away from the conflagration I had started as fast as I could and hide under my bed.

So I did.

I only lived a few hundred yards away, and my feet barely touched the ground. A glance over my shoulder confirmed the worst - the entire hedgerow was aflame in biblical proportions. I bet Moses shat **his** pants in the same circumstances. At least he had a convincing cover story. I ran upstairs and dived under the bunkbed.

By the light of a blazing match, I could see that I was barely singed and clearly hadn't been followed by the forces of law and order.

After a decent interval, I went downstairs. My mother was standing at the kitchen window watching a column of thick black smoke rising into the sky, punctuated by the odd lick of flame. The sound of sirens could be heard.

"Ooh. I wonder what happened there then?"

I wouldn't know, mother, I wouldn't know. I just hoped my eyebrows would grow back before she noticed. I vowed there and then never to play with fire again. For at least three weeks, anyway.

Hair Woe

A small, telling vignette that neatly illustrates my life:
She: "Where have you been?"
Me: "Washing my hair."
"I hope you weren't using my shampoo."
"As if I would. I used that new stuff on the window sill."
"Which one?"
"Primrose oil. The one with a picture of a golden retriever on the label and ...oh..."
"You do realise that's dog shampoo, don't you?"
"Woof."
Call me Cujo.

Ski Jump: White Christmas Woe

White Christmases have always been a bit of a rarity in my lifetime. Apart from the short period when I lived at the foot of the Rockies in Canada, they have been, sad to say, few and far between.

The only one I can remember in the UK was at the back end of the seventies, a cold, snowy winter that followed a summer of endless sunshine. For a ten-year-old kid, that's exactly the perfect kind of weather we should always be getting. Cooked to a cinder one day, up to your eyeballs in the white stuff the next.

So, Christmas Day, where the snow lay, if not particularly deep, certainly crisp and even. After the present-opening ritual, we ran out into the street to discuss the day's swag with friends, and to get down with the serious business of our favourite hobby: chaos.

I've mentioned in other stories that our road in Twyford was on the side of a hill, and certain houses had driveways which resembled the north face of the Eiger.

One of these houses remained empty for years (the speculation was that it was haunted following the mysterious death of the owner), and had the perfect drive for racing go-karts, bikes and skateboards. And with several inches of untouched snow, it was now the perfect ski slope.

Except there were just a few minor problems with this concept:

1. Nobody had any skis.

2. Nobody knew how to ski.

3. There was the small matter of Matty's house and several cars parked in the road opposite.

As if that was going to put any of us off.

Rummaging around in freezing cold sheds and garages provided we merry few with planks of wood and endless supplies of gaffer tape, which would serve as bindings for our makeshift skis.

They were, I am afraid to say, an utter disaster. You couldn't walk in them, you couldn't even stand up straight in them, and worst of all, their usefulness as ski-ing implements was zero.

Using a couple of bean-poles as sticks, you'd push yourself off at the top of the hill, slide about two feet before the tips snagged on something, and you'd be left face down in the white stuff. Complete waste of time, and as we were called inside one-by-one for our Christmas dinners, it was agreed that we should try another tack later on if any fun was to be had out of the day.

A couple of hours later, we emerged into the dusk, fuller, wobbling slightly from too much turkey and the misguided parental application of "Oh let him have a glass of wine, it's Christmas after all".

John was carrying a large tea tray "A souvenir from Brighton" which he had swiped from under his mum's nose. Tea trays, as we all know are ten times better than any sledge or toboggan you can buy in the shops, and have the added advantage of being useful as giant, deadly frisbees when the snow melts.

41

To the top of the drive we struggled, and with the shove to end all shoves, John careered down the slope at speed, between two parked cars and clattered into Matty's front step opposite. Magic, so we all had a go. In fact, we all had several goes, and the ski run got faster and faster as the compacted snow turned to ice.

But there was something missing.

"What we need," I mused, having seen the world's greatest athletes on Ski Sunday, "is a ski jump."

Yes. We needed a ski jump. So we built one, right there on the pavement at the bottom of number 32's drive.

It was a monster, carefully crafted with every piece of snow from miles around, curving upwards from a gentle slope to a frightening forty-five degree angle, four feet off the ground. Evel Knievel would have had second thoughts about taking it on. And like Evel Knievel, we thought "Danger? What's a few broken bones amongst friends?" and got on with it. Because of the dangers involved, we thought it best to ask for volunteers to try out the great ski jump. There were none, so we hit Squaggie until he gingerly sat on the tray and cast off.

Down and down he went, picking up speed, before he hit the ramp with a blood-curdling scream, rose gracefully into the air and executed a perfect landing on Matty's lawn.

What a disappointment.

"That hurt my arse," he said, so an old cushion was rescued from our garage and put to good use.

All of a sudden there was a clammering to have a go on the Great Ramp before grown-ups rumbled what we were up to and put and end to our fun. Just as long as they were glued to the Morecambe and Wise Christmas Special, we were fine.

John next, and defying the law of averages, he too executed a fine jump-and-landing that would probably have won a medal in the Winter Olympics, if tea-tray surfing ever made it past the demonstration event stage. Matty, however, his "wee glass of wine" and grandmother-administered sherry getting the better of him, decided he just HAD to be different. "I'm going down standing up," he declared.

"That's crazy talk!"

"You're mad!"

"You're gonna die! Can I have your presents?"

There was no talking him out of it. He stood on the tray, and pushed himself down the slope. As a fresh flurry of snow fell, the world fell silent in dread expectation.

Fffffffffffffffffffffffsssssssssssssssssshit! went the tray.

Flapflapflapflap went Matty's flares.

"Meeeeeeeeeee-aaaaaaaaaaaaargh!!!!" went Matty.

It was close, so very, very close. The tray struck the ramp at a slight angle, and instead of hitting the gap between the two parked cars, Matty executed a perfect back somersault before spread-eagling himself across the bonnet of his grandad's pride and joy - his immaculate Mark I Ford Cortina.

We slipped and slid down the driveway to rescue our fallen comrade. He had landed straddling the front wing mirror, missing his meat and two veg by mere inches. He lay groaning in what could only be described as a boy-shaped depression on the bonnet.

"I don't feel too good."

He was right, too.

"Yaaaaaaaaaaaaaaaaaaaaaarch!"

Rich, brown, steaming vomit filled with turkey, roast potatoes and all the trimmings, sweets, fizzy pop and some foul substance that we later realised was marshmallow.

All over the front of the car it went, running down into a little brown pool round his stomach. It would take them forever and a day to get the last of it out of the windscreen jets.

"Yaaaaaaaaaaaaaaaaaaaaaarch!" he said again.

There was only one thing to do under these circumstances of extreme vehicular and vomit woe: flee for our lives and let Matty take the rap. It was only fair, and after all, his sacrifice would be appreciated for many Christmases to come. It turned out, however, that he too had fled the scene of the crime, limping back to his house, with his family none the wiser.

During the night, the vomit froze.

The following morning Matty's grandad left the house for the long, slow drive back to Southsea.

"What's that on my car?" he asked.

John's tea tray was never seen again.

Commercial Break

"Become a Ninja Master with these free deadly throwing stars with Practical Ninjitsu Magazine! Learn how to kill, maim and inflict bodily pain on your friends and relations with everyday household implements, just like that Jackie Chan fella. We'll show you how to dress in black and remain stylish without being mistaken for Marilyn Manson. Find out about shuriken etiquette and the correct way to order pizza without maiming the wife.

"I was a pathetic weakling until I read Practical Ninjitsu Magazine, and now I'm the world's first Ninja Daytime TV Presenter!" - Dale Winton.

"Building up in weekly parts, you'll find yourself a master of the ancient Japanese code of honour in no time. Free binder with issue three! All at the stunning price of 1.99 (normal price 3.99, and we'll be hiking that up to 5.99 at issue 108, just when you're within sight of completing your collection, you mug – and just think, you could have bought the book for a tenner at Smiths)."

I have already started on the road to becoming a Ninja. Yesterday, I painted the garage door a rather fetching shade of blue. Master Splinter says it needs another coat, or he'll tear my gizzards out.

Bicycle/Gravity woe

I'd like to brag at this part of the proceedings and say that I've got A-Levels in Applied Mathematics and Physics (Grades E and D). I know all kinds of stuff about forces, angular motion and Newton's Laws. Like for example, what would happen to a bicycle being towed down a steep hill by a frayed piece of rope, and round a sharp bend at the bottom. You know, useless stuff that never happens in the real world.

Our cul-de-sac in rural Twyford was perched on the side of a hill. Don't look for it now - it's still there and they'd probably chase you like Gary

Glitter from a branch of Top Shop. Being a dead-end, there was hardly any traffic, and we were pretty much free to bike, rollerskate and stakeboard to our hearts' content without the fear of ending up under the wheels of the maniac from number thirty-eight, which only ever happened to me once.

The fashionable thing to do was to meet up at the top of the road on our bikes, and race down as fast as we could, leaning into a huge left-handed bend and braking at the last second just in front of John's house. No-one wore helmets. This was the 1970s, and only bike racers had helmets. It wasn't as if we were going to fall off or anything.

Webby, who lived at number one, had a rich dad who had bought him a speedometer for his bike. We would take turns trying to break "the record" for fastest run to the bottom, even if many of us couldn't actually reach the ground perched on his monster of a machine. We all lied through our teeth, with people claiming to have recorded speeds in excess of sixty miles-per-hour. With my legs pumping furiously, I got up to thirty-six. Or fifty-six, as I triumphantly declared when I got back to the top of the hill.

No matter how fast we went, we had to have more. We had to rack up the danger. The envelope, as they say, had to be pushed. This was when Matty produced a battered old bike from his garage. It had been ravaged for spare parts, and had no mud guards, pedals, chain or brakes. Apart from that, it was sound.

So how to make it go? Easy. Matty also produced a rope. He'd tow the little blue death-trap behind him down the hill. It would, he declared, be the thrill of a lifetime. A very short lifetime, it would prove.

The bikes were prepared. Matty mounted his steed, and with the rope tied firmly to the handlebars of the death-trap, I jumped on behind him. Matt pedalled like fury, and as the rope went taut, the other lads gave me a hearty shove, chasing us down the hill whooping and shouting.

"Go for it, Scary!"

"Take it to the moon!" and

"I'll visit you in hospital."

And this is where those lessons in maths and physics might have come in handy. With the ninety degree bend in the road fast approaching, I suddenly realised I had absolutely no control over the bike. I couldn't slow down, and with Matty already disappearing round the corner a good thirty feet in front of me, I couldn't steer the thing either. I was a projectile, under all kinds of forces outside my control. Up in heaven, Sir Isaac Newton was rubbing his hands with glee.

Matty shot round the corner, doing a good seventy-five miles per hour by his own reckoning. My bike proscribed a huge arc, rapidly approaching the speed of sound, fully obeying all sorts of laws of angular motion and Quantum Theory into the bargain.

That didn't last for long. I let out a blood-curdling scream as the bike swung round and smashed into the low wall in front of number fifteen.

Angular motion gave way to projectile flight. I was airborne, making a perfect arc through the air, sailing over flowerbeds filled with prize-winning roses.

I landed face first on the lawn, creating three yard-long furrows in the grass with my chin and knees. I was carted home with concussion, where I spent the rest of the day being sick.

The old guy from number fifteen was in apoplexy. He'd spent the last hundred and seventy years cultivating that lawn, just for me to turn it into a landing strip for retards. I was lucky to be alive. He was planning on using me as fertilizer.

The next day, I took my bruised body to Matty's house, where he showed me what was left of the bike I'd been riding. You could have carried it home in your pocket, and used what was left over as iron filings.

There was, naturally, a lesson to be learned from this whole affair. It was: Don't play silly buggers. And did we learn?

Go-Kart Woe

In America they're called Soapbox Racers. They have organised leagues, TV rights and world-famous professionals. In the real world, they're called Go-Karts, and the only autographs you get are the ones on your plaster cast after you've broken both arms and legs.

John's old man - officially the coolest dad in the world - had been to America and had brought back the latest craze - skateboards, which we roared down the hill with our lives in our hands with not a hint of a helmet or kneepad to protect us. It was ace, but we wanted more.

"More" came in school assembly one morning. To celebrate the Queen's twenty-five years on the throne, there would be a Go-Kart Grand Prix, and an Easter Bonnet competition for the girls. By Royal Appointment. Matt, John, Nige and I were up for it, and set out building our karts for the big event. It was, after all, our patriotic duty. Hedging our bets we built two, and in a solemn ceremony, they were given names by Matt's five-year-old sister. In the absence of champagne, the karts were christened with stolen Babycham.

The Bee-Buggy-Bum was nothing but the bottom half of a 1930s style pram with a plank of wood screwed on for a seat. The wheels were huge, and superbly put together in a lost age of workmanship with quality bearings that would run and run. There was a hefty hand-brake which could stop you on a sixpence, and we found that by pulling on the front suspension rods you could warp the frame enough to turn in a decent circle. It didn't need fancy decoration, go faster stripes or anything, it was everything a decent go-kart needed - wheels and a seat. Nothing more, nothing less. It rocked.

The Bum-Tiddly-Um, on the other hand, was small, slow and made of some old wheels we found on a scrap-heap, with the entire contraption held together with six-inch nails. It sucked.

Our main rival was "Tiger", owned by Luke and Jonesy, two lads from the next street. It was a beautiful, beautiful go-kart, built in Luke's garage by his far-too-enthusiastic over-competitive father. It had a proper steering wheel, a sleek, streamlined body with the wheels hidden underneath so it looked like it was flying along; and a magnificent tiger-skin paint job. It was the clear favourite to win by looks alone. The flashy sods were even seen practicing in matching overalls and racing helmets.

The die was cast. It was us against them. David against Goliath. Good against Evil. Enid Blyton against Aleister Crowley, sort of.

The day before the big race, we went out for one final practice session. We pulled the carts to the top of the road and shoved off, gliding downhill, the Bee-Buggy-Bum leaving the Bum-Tiddly-Um in its wake. That was all fine and dandy on a nice, gentle slope, but we were pre-teen speed demons, and as usual, we wanted bone-crunching danger. This was, after all, the final practice session. We had to see what our karts were made of.

This time, we found "more" at number thirty-two, the house opposite Matt's. Number thirty-two had lain empty for over a year, and its unlocked garage acted as our unofficial gang headquarters for dirty deeds and general hiding from parents. It was also right on the steepest part of the hill and had a driveway that was like the north face of the Eiger.

This was it. The big test. If our carts were good enough for the Big Hill, they were good enough for anything. We set up. Nige on the Bum-Tiddly-Um with John pushing, Matty on Bee-Buggy-Bum with me ready to shove.

"Three! Two! One! Go!"

John and I gave a huge run-up and shoved the carts into the abyss. With a scream the lads disappeared over the edge and down the driveway, Bee-Buggy-Bum leading the way, closely followed by its sonic boom.

Down the drive they roared and out into the road, John and I bounding after them with giant steps to see the action. Nige hadn't been able to turn the Bum-Tiddly-Um fast enough and had instead pulled on the brake, slamming both feet down on the road, burning through his best school shoes, while Matt was still hammering on down the road, picking up speed as he went.

Now here comes the tricky bit. After turning out of the driveway, he had to pull another turn to avoid running out of road and slamming straight into his house. Not particularly difficult in the super souped-up Bee-Buggy-Bum, but even to our untrained eyes, he was leaving it remarkably late.

The three of us watched in awe as Matt yanked on the brake handle. There was a cry of "Muuuum!" as it snapped off, cartoon-style, in his hand. The front wheels smacked against the kerb, showering broken spokes and pieces of wheel rim in all directions, and Matt and the Bee-Buggy-Bum took off.

It was a short flight, the width of the pavement plus about six inches, as Matt and the kart hit the fence about halfway up with a sickening, bone-crunching thud. The entire fence panel, a lovely piece of delicately woven lattice that probably cost a bomb, shattered all over the place, revealing the touching domestic scene of Matt's mum and dad pulling weeds in the garden and his little sister playing dolly with a friend. All of them with astonished looks on their faces. It was beautiful.

We fully expected Matt's dad to go ballistic, but instead he was on his knees crying with laughter. Matt, like any other idiot who brushed with death, was completely unscathed, and staggered from the shattered wreck of the Bee-Buggy-Bum, still clutching the severed brake handle. The kart was completely mangled, a complete non-starter for the following day's big race. We were down to one kart. The rubbish one. We were doomed.

We turned up the next day with the Bum-Tiddly-Um. It was awful. We had to sit through the unending hell of the Easter bonnet parade before we could even think about the humiliation of coming last. Everybody came to gloat at our pathetic little machine, especially Jonesy, Luke and Over-Competitive Dad. And our worst fears were confirmed in the Big Race. Everybody roared past us as we huffed and puffed to get even the slightest semblance of speed. Even the kid with only one foot disappeared into the distance.

All except Tiger. They'd been found out. It turned out that Over-Competitive Dad had gone for glamorous good looks over speed and had based the thing on supermarket trolley coasters. No one had bothered to tell him that the race was over grass on the school field, and he watched in horror from the sidelines as his pride and joy sunk into the mud and stuck there like a dog turd to the bottom of your shoe.

So, who won? I had absolutely no idea then and still don't know to this day. Luke and Jonesy didn't show their faces round our street for weeks, and Tiger was never seen again. As far as I know, it sunk into the mire of the school field, and is still there twenty-five years later, an interesting divot on the outfield of the cricket pitch for future archaeologists to find.

And worse. I still remember that dark, dark day if it were yesterday. At least three boys had Easter bonnets, and one picked up second prize. For shame, for shame.

Armageddon Days

I grew up in the shadow of The Bomb. My parents were married around the Cuban Missile Crisis of 1963, not knowing if there would be a world left to bring kids into. Those Roman Toga Party days at medical school must have seemed so long ago. We lived in fear of the four minute warning, and had a copy of Protect and Survive to guide us through the worst Reagan and Brezhnev had to throw at us.

It was a world of Mutually Assured Destruction. If anyone was damn fool enough to start a war, it was more or less acknowledged that civilisation as we knew it was doomed to fry in its own fat. Hence, a nuclear war was, by this logic, well nigh impossible. Try telling that to a fifteen year old kid having nightmares of firey nuclear destruction on a regular basis, his school exercise books filled with doodles of mushroom clouds. Two nuclear establishments within a few miles of Twyford, and NATO Command just up the road in High Wycombe, meant the Soviets knew exactly where to target their biggest, shiniest warheads.

I could just about live with this, if it weren't for the fact that I saw a TV programme about witches. One of the stories featured an old hag who lived in a cave in the North of England several hundred years ago. She made several uncannily accurate predictions, the last of which before they threw her on a great big bonfire was that the world would end in 1981. You know what that meant: I was going to die a virgin.

My brother's best mate Giles had seen this programme too, and claimed to have read in Mad Old Bastard's Almanack that Armageddon was due on 12th September. Just to make matters worse, this would be a Saturday. The world didn't even have the decency to end on a school day. Giles was so confident in his boast, that he bet us 50p that he was right. We happily shook on it, and it took him several minutes to realise it was a wager he just couldn't win. Not only that, his Almanack still had entries for October, November and December, confidently predicting second favourites to do well in National Hunt races.

As the End of the World approached, was I worried? Was I terrified at the thought of facing destruction on Biblical proportions with my cherry still intact? Too bloody right I was. For starters, my attempts to leave this mortal coil without my virginity were foiled by two simple factors:

a) none of the girls I approached on this matter believed a word I said, leaving me with a post-armageddon reputation of lacking marbles; and

b) I was a teenage geek of huge never-gonna-lose-that-cherry proportions.

I was blissfully unaware of point b.

Come the big day, I was a bag of nerves. Ironically, it was actually Battle of Britain weekend, commemorating the one time in the twentieth century where we managed to save the known world without American assistance, and we went on a day trip up to RAF Abingdon for the airshow.

The cream of NATO's airborne fighting forces screamed overhead in close formation, when they really should have been preparing to face the Red Menace that was pouring over the German border as we spoke. Giles was still confident, yet the forces personnel present looked decidedly unruffled about the forthcoming call to arms.

I watched planes.

I took loads of photos (can't think why - it would have been hell finding a chemists in the radioactive rubble of British civilisation).

I went home.

I went to bed.

I woke up on Sunday 13th September 1981.

I was still alive. The world had not ended. Presidents Reagan and Brezhnev, senile pair of lunatics that they were, had both stubbornly kept their fingers off the button. It was, I remember, a rather pleasant sunny day, and I took the dog for a walk down by the River Thames. It felt good to be alive.

On the other hand I felt bloody cheated. All those years of worry utterly wasted. I hadn't bothered doing my school homework either, on the grounds that there wouldn't be a school to go to on Monday. I spent a whole Sunday afternoon, nose to the page, writing a compare-and-contrast essay about My Family and Other Animals. Somebody was going to pay.

And the next day, at school, it was Giles. To be honest, he paid up his bet with remarkably good grace for someone who'd been nailed in his first lesson for not doing his homework. He was rather proud of the fact that Mr Wallace (son of the inventor of the bouncing bomb, celebrity spotters!) had told him "That's the worst excuse I've ever heard, boy". As for the end of the world: "Give it a couple a days. These things take time."

I'm still waiting.

Some twenty-four years later, when doing a bit of background research on this book, I found out that Mother Shipton, the mad old witch mentioned in this story, had predicted the end of the world for the year 1881. I had, it turned out, misheard her prediction on BBC Nationwide and had subjected myself to years of unnecessary terror. I just hope that when the baying hate mob came for the crone, they toasted her good and proper.

On religion

I went to church yesterday. Getting churched-up isn't part of my regular routine, I'll be the first to admit, but it was a lovely sunny morning, and Scaryduck Jr was on church parade with his scout group. It was, all told, a rather pleasant experience, with songs (apparently they're called "Hymns", and they've got a WHOLE book of them), near-the-knuckle jokes from the bloke at the front who dresses like Eddie Izzard, and a nice lady at the back who does tea and biscuits.

Enthused by the spirit of the occasion, I bowed my head, thanked Him upstairs for my family and in return promised not to swear quite so much.

Now, I'm not a total ignoramus with churchy things. The whole idea of spirituality is the result of a complex set of belief systems deriving from folk superstitions, evolving into a vast organised religion with disparate value systems which pervade the lives of many, whether they realise it or not.

Take the act of Communion, for example.

Communion is representative of Christ's Last Supper with his disciples, which was closely followed by The Last Argument Over The Bill. "I thought Judas was paying - he's come into some money." The bread is representative of Christ's body, and the wine is his blood. We protestant types know this is purely symbolic. The bread is bread, the wine is a quid a gallon from Threshers. Catholics, on the other hand, take this as gospel. As soon as the sacrament touches the lips, it truly becomes the body and blood of Our Lord and Saviour.

Now here's the nub. What happens if you're a veggie? It's OK telling yourself it's just a biscuit and a sip of free booze, but then you're denying that you've got your gnashers round a big chunk of Our Lord and Saviour. And then, it's terribly non-specific. Which bit are you getting? For all you know, you might be munching on a bit of His Arse, or something far, far worse. Have the health inspectors been informed? There should be clear food preparation guidelines to this, ones that don't involve a nice tablecloth and two chunky candles.

So everybody queued up, got their bread and wine - which I politely refused as I was scared of making an arse of myself - and returned to their pews. With all-comers perfectly happy with their lot, one slight detail became all-too-clear to the vicar. He'd blessed-up far too much bread and wine, and the altar was swimming in the stuff like a kitchen table after a barbecue.

It turned out to be no real problem for the vic. He scooped up a huge handful of wafers and forced them into his mouth, cheeks bulging like a chipmunk, and followed it down with a quaff of wine, hoping nobody had noticed. I was mortified. One tiny wafer - fine. You could easily get away with that. But a whole pile of the things? That's just greedy. It is, in fact, rather a large part of Our Lord which He might have wanted to use later. And let's not forget all that wine as well. In the words of the great prophet Tony Hancock: "A pint? That's very nearly an armful!"

I decided to take issue over this unashamed gluttony with the vicar after the service, as I'm well aware that it is one of the seven deadly sins. Not just run-of-the-mill sins. Deadly ones. As the faithful streamed out, blinking, into the sunlight, I caught him in a half-nelson and forced a confession from his quivering lips.

"Sirrah!" I raged, aiming a punch at his kidneys, "You are nothing but a gluttonous, hypocritical murderer and the lizard-spawn representation of the Illuminati that crushes the human spirit underfoot in a global conspiracy to control our minds and bodies! What say you to that, eh?"

Or I could have just shaken his hand meekly and say "See you again soon." After all, I'm overdrawn at the Bank of Eternal Damnation as it is.

And did I say he was a vicar? As a matter of fact, I found out he's a canon. Tell him he's fired.

I was a Teenage Bomber

History: This was the first Tale of Mirth and Woe I ever wrote. That pie-eating double act of wireless wackiness Danny Kelly and Danny Baker had appealed for stories on the theme of "Dangerous Things You've Done", and of course, having lived a life of brazen stupidity, I was happy to oblige. It's been rewritten and revised several times since its first airing on Radio Five, and I promise this is the absolute final never-going-to-be-rewritten-ever-again version. Honest.

The whole affair started so innocently with long, lazy afternoons hidden under my bed ignoring my parents' warnings about the dangers of playing with matches. It was dark in my secret den, and with my torch batteries deader than Marc Bolan, I needed matches so I could see.

From those illuminating beginnings, my fascination moved on to "genie-ing" entire boxes of Swan Vestas and chucking them out of the window. Within weeks, with myself as self-appointed ringleader, there was a whole gang of us diligently scraping the heads off matches and watching with abject terror and no little joy as they all went up in about a quarter of a second, usually depriving at least one of our number of their eyebrows.

It would have stayed at this innocent level had my best mate Graham not got involved. Graham was a total whizz at science, and he filled our heads with ideas of rockets, bombs, and certain combinations of garden chemicals and innocent kitchen ingredients which I won't go into right now because I'd be experiencing the inside of Guantanamo Bay at first hand if I did. He would turn up after school with something he'd knocked up in his shed-cum-mad scientist's laboratory, which we'd pack full of "substances", light the fuse and dive for cover.

At the peak of our art we had rockets that could travel a good quarter of a mile, and what the bomb disposal people would call "viable devices" that would leave a sizable crater. We would change our match-buying rota on a regular basis, as we were sure the authorities would notice such large purchases by a group of youths covered in burns, twitching in a strange manner.

Refused service in the local garden centre, a sweet old lady who lived near us took pity and vouched for "such sweet, young lads taking an interest in gardening", as we humped a catering-sized sack of weed killer home. If only she knew.

It was gratifying to see that some of the innovations we brought about subsequently turned up in the Iraqi Supergun a few years ago, and Osama bin Laden cites the Twyford Nuttyboys as one of his major influences. This success, inevitably, was to be our downfall.

Being 14 year-old kids, we didn't have a firing range to test on like the army did. So we used the school field. One evening, after one particularly excitable device had veered off course and set fire to a hedge, we were chased home by a baying hate mob of equally excitable teenage vigilantes who had witnessed the whole affair from the adjacent youth club. In our confusion, we ran through the wrong hole in the fence into a neighbour's garden, and it was quite a relief that the little squirt took the rap for the whole affair and not us.

But had we learnt our lesson? Up the local chalk pits we went the following weekend with a satchel of the things determined to make a noise. Wedging our devices between rocks and using a Graham-designed detonation device powered by a car battery, the results were spectacular and a tribute to our scientific *nous*, patience and blind stupidity in bringing bright orange fireballs and ear-splitting roars to a residential area on an otherwise quiet Saturday morning.

In retrospect, dressing in combat gear probably didn't help our cause much: there was a blue flashing light as the might of the law eventually rumbled our little game of world domination. The village Plod informed us that someone had panicked, dialled 999 and used the key letters "I" "R" and "A", and if he didn't get on his radio pretty sharpish, half the army would be here within minutes. Luckily, he found - as he had suspected - that there were no terrorists, just idiots.

Being the cowards that we were, we laid the blame squarely on Stuart who had got cold feet and had run off home to watch Saturday Superstore on TV. No charges were pressed, and he didn't even bother getting out his notebook which would have spelled doom for all of us. Most importantly of all, he didn't even tell our parents. Bombs, prison, the might of the British Army I could live with. A parental bollocking - no bloody way.

Graham is now a research scientist. At least one of our gang has used the experience gained in this little episode to forge a career in Her Majesty's Armed Forces, while another is using his position to invest money in the possibilities of Star Trek-style matter transporters. I, for my sins, still have the scar tissue on my right hand, and most importantly, survived to tell the tale.

On religion, again

Theological argument says that God is omnipresent - He is in all places all the time.

Following that logic, this means that He's got front row tickets at the Raymond Revue Bar for every single performance and knows the dark, dark secrets of Dolly Parton's chest.

On the downside, He also gets to see Tottenham Hotspur play every Saturday. No wonder the world's in such a mess.

My Illustrious Football Career

Spurred by the success of "I was a Teenage Bomber", I wrote this - the second Scary Story. Again, it was for the Baker and Kelly show on Radio Five in response to their plea for stories proving "My team is worse than Guam because...". Guam - officially the world's worst international football side - had shipped nineteen goals in a World Cup qualifier against Iran, and the Dannies were on the lookout for someone who'd give them a run for their money.

When I was a mere lad of nine years old or so, I used to go to cubs in the tiny village where I lived. Hurst, Berkshire, population wavering between nine and eleven, depending which day they had a funeral.

We had a football team. A very small one of laid-back village kids, kicked out of the house on a Saturday morning by parents with better things to do. As you can imagine, with such a small pool of players to choose from we weren't exactly endowed with the best of talent, and if we managed to keep the opposition to less than 10 goals it was seen as a moral victory. In other words, we were shit.

In fact, there was myself, my brother and nine others who would all have been the last players picked by any sane manager. One lad was told by his dad not to run around after the ball "because of his weak chest", and Peter wore callipers on his legs, but he gave his all nonetheless. Our goalie was as deaf as a post, and tended not to hear our shouts to remind him the ball was coming until it was far too late. I am certain we had a player with only one foot at some stage, and he was still more mobile than some of the other lads.

At least five members of our team never actually got a touch of the ball in all the time I played for them, and one kid was so frightened of getting hurt, he'd run away as the action came towards him. Our nine-across-the-back rearguard was frequently seen cowering in terror, arms down the fronts of their shirts for warmth in the traditional manner, egged on by our coach Mr Hoskins, who would frequently bring his goat to graze by the side of the pitch.

We played on the school playing field, a postage stamp patch of land which gave us a pitch that was wider than it was long. We frequently conceded goals which were, frankly, hopeful punts from the opposing penalty area, which would roll limply into the goal as the defence fled in terror at the round white thing in their midst.

The problem was that being near to a big town, we'd usually come up against teams with a less laid back attitude to football than ours. We'd turn up on a Saturday morning, jog around a bit and possibly even get the odd touch of the ball (usually kicking-off after the other team had scored), while the well-drilled opposition colossi with a shouty coach on the sidelines would pummel us into submission.

"Memorable" games included 14-0, 17-0 and 21-0 hammerings in consecutive weeks, yet still we turned up for more. In one match, I played in goal and up front simultaneously as our keeper "had to go home" and we only lost 6-2, the most goals we ever scored in one match, and our narrowest ever defeat. As a matter of fact, the delirium I experienced on scoring our second was so frightening, I vowed never to score again. I still have nightmares about being mobbed by midgets.

It all came to a head when we attended the District Camp. We fled into the woods after non-stop taunts of "1st Hurst are the worst" for the whole weekend, and never played again. Strangely, we won the local five-a-side tournament that year (mainly because we didn't have to make up the numbers with the hard-of-breathing), but only after my dog ran on the pitch and sniffed the opposing forward's arse as he was winding up for a shot. Shame does terrible things to a small boy.

I still have the newsletter from that season, and it makes for painful reading:

Played 16
Won 0
Drawn 0
Lost 16
Goals For 4
Goals Against 177
Points 0

Player of the season: Mr Hoskins' Goat.

Scouting for Boys

In 1908, a war hero by the name of Robert Baden-Powell, impressed by the work of young scouts in the Siege of Mafeking, decided to try the idea out back home in Britain. He grabbed a bunch of street urchins and dragged them off to Brownsea Island, a large wooded area in Poole Harbour, from which you could barely hear the screams. He promised them tents, whittling, ging-gang-goolie and their own woggle.

It went down a storm and the worldwide Scouting movement was born. And seventy years later, my parents decided it was my turn.

I was dragged, along with my younger brother, down to 1st Hurst for a spell in the cubs before I was allowed into the Scouts proper. We tied knots. We played daft team games that you only played in the Scouts and we helped little old ladies cross the road, whether they wanted to or not. I got a woggle and a sheet of paper with the words to "Ging Gang Goolie" which I was told to guard with my life.

We also had to engage in "fundraising". The Scouts aren't exactly rich.

We had a shack made almost entirely out of asbestos that had previously been used as a bakery, and before that for manufacturing chemical weapons in the War. We also had a van which looked like it had been used to ferry casualties around Beirut. We held jumble sales. We collected old newspapers for recycling. But 1st Hurst, being a rural troop, had a secret weapon.

We sold shit.

Not just any old shit, either. We had a deal going with the local stud farm. We'd turn up in the Beirut Bus armed with shovels and plastic sacks, and we'd shovel prime quality racehorse shit into the bags and sell it to people to put on their gardens. It was a big money deal - we could make as much as twenty or thirty quid in a day, the equivalent of over 1,500,000 clicks on an Ask Jeeves banner in this chic modern world of the interwebs.

Sadly, the shit, once our saviour, was to be our downfall. Shit got everywhere. In our clothes, in our hair, but most importantly it got into the workings of the Beirut Bus, and eventually it was led off to the glue factory, but not before we managed to beat the crap out of it first.

And soon, summer came, and we had to go camping. This was the big one - the District Camping Competition. Six of us against the *creme de la creme* of the Thames Valley. Reputations would be won and lost here. Pride was at stake. This was important, dammit!

In reality, it was a mob of schoolboys living in a field for a weekend loaned out by a gullible local farmer, presumably in return for a cut of the valuable shit-digging rights. The best part of all was that everybody knew each other - apart from the Woodley boys (who went to Waingels Copse, aka "Wanker's Cock"), we all went to the same school, and most of us actually hung out in the same gang. We were Hurst, the poor country cousins; there was Wargrave, cool as hell and had enough money not to have to go digging shit; and there was Twyford who were, and let's be generous here, as thick as two short planks.

And so it came to pass that while my parents were arranging a "Thank Fuck they've gone" party, we leapt out of the back of the Beirut Bus, reeking of horse shit and choking on exhaust fumes. Myself, brother Nigel, Cooky, Greebo, Smithy and Clive, the latter two foolishly being left in charge.

Getting there early got us the prime camping ground, right in the middle of the apple orchard, giving us an ample supply of ammo in case things got nasty. Our gear was cutting edge - huge six-man patrol tents that had probably seen action in Baden-Powell's original 1908 Brownsea camp. And no bugger was going to come near them either, oh no! Not with the reek of horse shit still hanging about us like a ...err... bad smell.

The rest of the district turned up in dribs and drabs, almost entirely in the back of daddy's Volvo. And with the parents out of the way, this bunch of teenage boys broke out the "gear".

This had been a meticulously planned operation. Cooky and Clive had been slowly weedling away their parents' supply of cigarettes for several weeks now, and they had as many as fifteen. Nigel and I, on the other hand, had got our supply in one fell swoop, raiding Dad's box of top-quality Cuban cigars, where we'd got a big fat stoogie for everyone on the team. Bloody luxury, and we were feted like heroes.

And that was right up to the minute until we saw what Cool Wargrave had brought with them. There were huge clouds of smoke rising from their camp, and they hadn't even started a camp fire yet. We went and paid a "courtesy visit", to find them sitting on crates of cigarettes, sweets, beer and pornography. They were so cool it hurt. Bastards.

Payback was sweet though. Within six hours, they'd puffed their way through over 200 smokes and drunk all their ale, and Sean had spent the entire afternoon spewing his guts up on a cocktail of chocolate and Shandy Bass. Julian and Ernie came over as part of a delegation.

"Got any smokes?" they asked. "Ours have all gone"

"I am authorised by our leadership to tell you to piss off"

"We've got money"

CH-CHING!

The motto of the Scout movement is "Be Prepared". We sold them a box of 250 PG Tips teabags at a substantial mark-up, which they rolled up and smoked over the entire weekend. I've got to say that our parents were pretty bloody impressed by that. To this day, they still think we drunk over forty cups of tea each in two days.

"We like tea", we lied, and another catering box was put on order.

Back on the ground and dossing about with school mates, it was easy to forget we were in a competition. We had to carry out a number of tasks and projects, take part in daft scout games and set fire to things whilst singing "Ging Gang Goolie" in the traditional manner.

We had to build a weather station.

We had to cross a river, and the steady stream of soaking wet idiots passing our camp proved we were WELL in the lead on that one.

We had to Cook For A Leader that evening.

And we had to do A Special Project.

First came The Meal. We built a fire, specially like, as we were going to cook proper backwoods style for The Chief that was coming to dinner. Chicken, potatoes in their jackets, corn, the works. The fire was huge, with flames twenty feet in the air and a heat haze you could feel fifty feet away. One of us donned the fire-proof gauntlets and lead-lined suit and stuck the tucker onto the conflagration. It was burned to a crisp within thirty seconds. Whoops.

The Chief was due in twenty minutes and his dinner was a pile of ashes somewhere beneath the Towering Inferno. "Bollocks", we said in the ensuing crisis meeting, "we'll cook him pancakes, the rest of us can live off chocolate for the weekend". So we did.

There was a horrible crunching noise which turned out to be The Chief's dentures cracking in two.

"What in the name of blue blazes was that?" he said, spitting bits of dental plate and lumpy pancake out.

"Err.... chewy nuts"

"Cheeeeewy Nutssssss?!?!?!"

We got top marks for improvisation.

Ours wasn't the only disaster that night. As the rain came down, idiot Twyford troop had decided to take their cooking indoors, and lit a fire INSIDE their tent. I can still see Stuart sitting there, where his tent had once been, surrounded by ashes and the remains of his gear wondering what had happened. As with all idiots, he was completely unscathed.

The next day, our Special Project, our grand design, was to be an aerial runway. One of those things you see the SAS or Royal Marines sliding down on a rope from tall buildings. They're fast, they're flash, they're super cool. And what we didn't realise, they're bastard difficult to build.

Smithy sent us off into the woods to find wood. Really big wood. We found two fallen trees, tied ropes round them and dragged them back to the camp. We lashed them into an A-Frame and using a bastard long bit of rope and as many easily impressed passers-by as we could muster, we hauled it into an upright position.

There are actually official Scout HQ-approved guidelines on building these things, mainly to stop idiots like us trying to knock something together with a couple of tree trunks and zero safety gear, and ending up killed to death.

Now, I'd seen aerial runways before. And they usually had rather more bits of wood than this particularly poor example, and they tended to be held up by rather more than tent pegs. "And, hey lads, isn't the rope rather slack?" My warnings went unnoticed as the thirty foot tall Slide of Doom was readied for its first - and last - passenger.

It was to be Greebo, as he was the smallest and most obnoxious member of the team, and frankly it wouldn't matter too much if he was killed in the line of duty because I don't think even his parents wouldn't have missed him that much either.

The previous night, he had refused point-blank to do the washing up "because that's my mum's job" and threw a rather embarrassing hissy fit in front of The Chief. Smithy had punched him on the nose, causing blood to spurt everywhere and Greebo stormed off home, about five minutes sulking time up the road. About ten minutes later his dad dragged him back by the ear with the fatherly advice "Do the fooking washing up you lazy little bastard and don't come back until tomorrow".

Greebo, then, was marked for death.

With thinly veiled threats of physical violence still ringing in his ears, Greebo shinned up the A-frame, which wobbled ominously even under his pathetic weight. By now, there was a growing crowd of onlookers as the entire campsite sensed something unusual was about to happen. I backed away to a safe distance, and joined Cool Ernie from Cool Wargrave for a puff on a teabag. Greebo sat on the slide's makeshift seat, and with a blood-curdling cry of fear, launched himself into the void.

The sliding rope was so slack, he dropped like a stone, ending up flat on his back in one of the cow pats we'd spent the entire weekend trying to avoid. There was a ripple of applause and a small cheer from the gallery. This was followed by a hollow "thwack" as the tent pegs holding up the A-frame gave up the ghost and pinged out of the ground, covering the prostrate and shit-covered Greebo with a shower of rope. This was followed by a brief moment of equilibrium as the entire construction decided which way it was going to fall.

It went backwards.

There was an ironic cry of "Timber!", and I'm sure I heard a drum roll as the two bastard great tree trunks toppled in slow motion straight onto the Beirut Bus. It beared up rather well, considering. The windscreen exploded outwards, and the back doors burst open, revealing the entire contents of our booze, smokes and porn collection. The roof was stoved in with a huge comedy dent. The crowd went wild.

"Lads", said Smithy. "Get your shovels out. We've got to things to dig. Shit, and our own graves."

As it turned out, the Beirut Bus had been condemned to the scrap heap the week before, and this trip was to be its last before the final journey to the dump, but no-one had bothered to tell us. Our lives were only made a misery for about ten minutes when Skip turned up to drive us home; and to our relief, the death of the bus also meant our shit-digging days were over.

As for the camping competition - we won. Naturally.

PiSS III

Scouts! I joined up and found, to my disappointment, that they no longer dybbed or dobbed, nor did they teach the young recruits secret martial arts skills that could kill a brownies at ten yards. But look on the bright side, they sent us on a week's camp in some terrible corner of the Kent Countryside (or, as Sir Trevor McDonald once said on the News at Ten "Cunt Kentryside".

With our minibus sadly deceased - rotted from the inside by the acid effects of the horse shit we sold to raise funds - we piled into a hired bus and headed off to a camp, heaving at the gills with the cream of scouting from up and down the country. It had everything - climbing wall, rifle ranges, go-karts, football and a huge assault course.

In retrospect, it seemed to be run by a bunch of dodgy types in uniform, as camp rules dictated that "all boys should wear shorts - no long trousers", and there were regular nude swimming events in the camp swimming pool, from which visiting girl guides were strictly excluded. Bunch of no-good killjoys. These days, the police and social services would be hammering at the gates, while a baying hate mob stormed the place with burning torches. Such was youthful innocence, however....

So, it was a week of far-too-cheerful organised events, including a remarkable egg-throwing competition in an attempt to break the world record which stood at something over three hundred feet. Cue a day of food wastage and teenage boys shouting "IgotitIgotitIgotit!" before covering themselves from head to short trousers with smashed egg. The world record remained safe.

The rest of the time, we were more or less let off the leash to do as we pleased. This included most of the day on a trip to Calais, where not only were we mostly unsupervised, but we were unsupervised in a foreign country where the drinking age is only fourteen, and there's a sex shop on the road between the ferry terminal and the main town.

Apart from drunkenness, an ill-advised wanking club (of which, you may be surprised, I was not a member) and scooting round at high speed in petrol-driven go-karts, this freedom mostly involved trying to get ourselves killed. From the materials available around us, we built weapons. Most of these were incredibly workmanlike catapults and bows-and-arrows, showing that all those cold evenings in the scout hut practicing knots and whittling technique were going to good use. Baden-Powell would have been proud (apart from the bit about the wanking).

We split into teams and prowled the woods on a man-hunt. How nobody ended up in hospital is beyond me. Only one person was knocked unconscious (by a large flying log, a device employed by Arnold Schwarzenegger in "Predator"), and he was revived by a good slap round the face and threats of a nude swimming gala with the creepy camp commandant.

Litzermann, our American recruit had honed his archery skills to a fine art with a rather spiffy crossbow. Just a shame that no-one told him not to try climbing a tree with the thing loaded. There was a "twang!", a scream, followed by a pause and the sound of a body hitting the ground. We ran to his aid, fearing the worst. He lay there, and arrow protruding from the front of his shorts, where it had gone off, missing his tackle by millimetres to come out the other side. Litzermann was the only one of our number who had ever "seen a lady naked", and was rather relieved to have survived to repeat the experience.

He only had one comment for us, words that will live with me till my dying day: "I've pissed me pants!"

That wasn't the end of the drama. There was a troop on the site from Liverpool - 2nd Toxteth, or something. And let's be charitable and say that they were a bit wilder than most. Oh bollocks to that, they were a bunch of thieving scousers that confirmed everything you'd ever heard about the City of Liverpool. Some of them even insisted on long trousers, the bastards. Everybody knew they were out on the rob, and some bragging overheard in the camp shop indicated that we were next.

Plans were laid to defend ourselves for that night's raid. We all slept with our boots on, and a sign saying "Stores Tent" was hung on a tent filled with the biggest bruisers in the troop. As darkness fell that summer evening, a none-too-subtle rustling was seen in the trees and bushes at the edge of our camp site.

Scousers! Dozens of thieving scousers, all working for their thieving proficiency badge!

There was a tense stand-off. They knew we were watching them, waiting for the raid; but they still had to go through with it as a matter of pride. We knew they were there, and it was just a matter of not backing down and seeing them off. Hours passed.

A day of heavily stewed scout tea (25p for 600 teabags) was resting heavily in my bladder. Something had to be done, and I did it.

I staggered out of tent to the hissed warnings from my paranoid comrades, who seemed certain that I was going, like Captain Oates, to my certain death. Instead, I went for a piss into the first bush I came across.

"Oh 'ey!" screamed a young Liverpudlian voice from the bush which I was watering with no little relief. "Youse pissin' on me 'ead!"

"Was I? Oh, I am so terribly sorry young man. Now why don't you and all your pissy little mates BUGGER OFF AND LEAVE US ALONE?!"

There was no battle, there were no running charges through the night, just a bunch of thieving idiots breaking their cover and sloping back to their tents. Which we'd thoughtfully let down for them while they were away.

You don't need a tough attitude or the biggest guns. Just a weak bladder.

Yay for PiSS!

Part II: Teenage pricks

"In which a teenage boy destroys his school, college and most of a small rural town, and leaves everything around him a charred ruin. Still, you've gotta laugh"

Filthy Dave

Filthy Dave – where do you start with Filthy Dave?

You could only describe Filthy Dave one way: filthy. Filthy of mind and filthy of body. His school jumper was full of holes, and his ears dripped with enough wax to keep the Catholic Church in candles until the Second Coming. And his mind - we prided ourselves on being a pretty cosmopolitan, depraved bunch, but Filthy Dave was a breed apart.

When somebody suggested what a laugh it would be to spy on the girls' changing room during PE, Filthy Dave was the one who marched in and had a good look round while high-pitched screams shattered the windows. The only words we got out of him for the next two weeks were "Tracey... Tracey..." and a glazed, faraway look which could only be erased by a well-aimed punch to the scrotum.

When Miss Shagwell was sensitively discussing the subject of female genitals during a sex education class, Filthy Dave was the one who asked for a hands-on demonstration. And knowing Miss Shagwell's reputation, he probably got one too.

Filthy Dave's idea of a good laugh was to open a box of fishing maggots in the dining hall during lunch - and eat a handful; while one of the ingredients he brought in for a home economics class was an unidentifiable road-kill picked up and stuffed into a Sainsbury's carrier bag on the way to school.

Filthy Dave started the school craze for crapping through letterboxes, and leaving a well-placed turd exactly where you least expected to find one. For example, on the rear pew of the local church during the school carol concert. Filthy Dave was a filthy, filthy boy, and gained a cult following not just for his filth, but for the fact that as far as I know, he never, ever got into trouble for anything he ever did.

Filthy Dave once shaved his head during Maths. "It's the lice, miss," he explained, and not a word was spoken on the subject.

One day, Filthy Dave found that by drinking enough blue ink (either from ink cartridges or straight from the bottle, the filthy Quink addict), he could do a blue poo. Laying a log on a piece of yellow paper nicked from the art class, he discovered, with a bit of prodding, that he could make a passable example of the school badge in faeces. The school motto was an entirely different matter, but it's amazing what you can achieve with ear wax, snot and Lord knows what else extracted from bodily orifices.

So, over a period of several weeks (I could be wrong with this detail - subsequent police reconstructions suggest that it may have taken him "ten, maybe fifteen" minutes), while the rest of the class were out playing football and fighting over pornographic literature, Filthy Dave beavered away at home over his *meisterwerk*, crouching over a piece of paper, pants round his ankles, eyes bulging with the strain, in a way which I can only leave to the darkest pits of your imagination. He sculpted it, varnished it, and submitted the result as part of a project in "three dimensional texture modelling" for his CSE in Art.

Mr Law - the mad bastard's mad bastard - was so impressed he showed it to the Head, who, in turn, was so impressed that he had it hung in the school entrance hall, where I gather it remains to this day.

I still see Filthy Dave every now and then. He is no longer filthy, just plain Dave. It's sad how age mellows people. But God, you should see his kids.

School Trip

In these litigious days, you cannot send your children on a school trip without a taking out a full risk assessment, life cover insurance, third party insurance, legal insurance and let's-sue-the-teacher-anyway-if-the-kid-comes-back-with-so-much-as-a-dented-lunchbox insurance. Not that they go anywhere exciting anyhow. Exciting means dangerous, and dangerous means legal action. About the most exciting you get these days is a trip to the cotton wool factory across the road from the school.

Mr Wilkes ran the Outdoor Activities Club, and anywhere that Wilkie went, hero that he was, we followed. When he announced a trip to the frighteningly-named Devil's Punchbowl somewhere in the south of England for a weekend of youth hostelling, walking and general larking about, we signed up in a shot. One minibus, two teachers, a dozen kids as the biggest stash of sweets in the known universe. We had planned this one for weeks, and the quantities of chocolate-flavoured trash were frightening indeed. We'd even brought some real food, to bring us down from the sugar rush.

All the usual suspects had signed up - Cookie, Ernie, Rob, Downsey, Enders, plus a few more who I've forgotten through the years of brain damage and selective amnesia. Basically, we left the soft boys at home. What am I talking about? I **was** one of the soft boys. And I was trapped in the middle of nowhere with a bunch of teenage maniacs.

The Devil's Punchbowl is a funny old place. Just off the main London to Brighton road, you have to leave your transport up at the gates and walk a mile down a wooded track to the Youth Hostel. It's hidden somewhere in a wooded glade, about halfway down the bowl, and at one stage it was the home of some child-eating witch. It's old, it's got a huge log-burning fire, and most important of all, there's a hole in the wall where you can see into the girls' dorm. They found out after about three seconds.

And so the weekend began. Stuff your face with sweets. Cook breakfast. More Chocolate. Hike through the local army range with chocolate snacks. More sweets. Lunch. Sweets and a furtive smoke. It was late afternoon and getting dark by the time we got back to the hostel.

"If you guys want a log fire", announced Wilkie, "You'd better get some wood together.", and he went off to do whatever teachers do when they've had enough of us.

At this point, our esteemed teacher has left a small group of fifteen-year-old kids buzzing about on a saccharin high, only rivalled recently by the introduction of Sunny Delight, alone in the woods with a bow saw, two large axes and a two wheeled trolley-cum-wheelbarrow to get the logs back up the hill.

We were responsible in our duties. For about five minutes. We diligently found fallen trees and branches, cut them into logs and wheeled them up the hill in the barrow to the hostel. That lasted for about one trip, while Wilkie sat with his feet up, shouting words of encouragement out of the door and smoking roll-ups. It wasn't long before the slacking-off qualities of the barrow became apparent.

"Bollocksed if I've walking all the way back down there" said Ernie, "I'm getting in the cart".

So he got in. And it was the Devil's own job getting the extra weight back down the hill without letting go, while Ernie sat like a king in his sedan chair, waving to his passing subjects. But teenage minds were already working towards greater things...

And so, as we dumped another load at the top of the hill Downsey looked fear in the face and jumped in. God alone knows what I was thinking, but I jumped in behind him and yelled "Ride 'em cowboy!" as the cart slowly trundled down the ever-steepening path. The trouble was, nobody else was holding onto the barrow as they were far too busy with the logs. It was just me, Downsey and Newton's Laws.

It took us about 1.2 seconds to realise that something was wrong.

We were staring over the abyss and gaining speed rapidly as we rattled down the track. I distinctly remember lovely, lovely Trudy pointing at us and saying "Aren't you supposed to be..." before saving her own neck and diving out of the way. Nothing was going to stop us now. The wind was in our hair as we accelerated at 9.81 metres per second squared towards escape velocity. All those months of sitting in Wilkie's classroom learning physics weren't going to be wasted, I could tell you for nothing.

About halfway down, we hit a root, and for a couple of seconds we were flying. Really flying. It was also at that point that Downsey and I grasped the notion that we might not actually survive the trip, and frantic thoughts spun through my head like "Will this hurt?", "I'm going to die a virgin" and "What are my parents going to think when they discover all my porn?" We clung on for dear life as we roared towards the bottom of the hill, axe-wielding schoolmates scattering before us.

Newton's Laws of Motion finally caught up with us as we neared the bottom of the valley. Luckily, we only caught the tree a glancing blow. Someone, who turned out to be me, yelled out a bloodcurdling cry of "Fookenhell!" and Downsey and I were airborne once again, this time leaving the twisted wreckage of the cart behind us. I landed in a holly bush, scratching my face to buggery but otherwise saving my life. Downsey, being at the front, flew a bit further and touched down with a spectacular belly-flop into the stream at the bottom of the hill.

We both stood up, dazed. My face was a network of scratches and dirt. Downsey was a black spectre of water and mud. I puked my guts up as a sackful of chocolate came back to haunt me, and I slowly came round to the noise of my classmates actually cheering and applauding us. We were stupid. We nearly died. We were heroes.

"Shit man", said Downsey, "As soon as we get that trolley fixed up, I'm going again." So we did. And we had to wait bloody ages for our turn.

We did so many trips with that barrow up and down the hill, we virtually stripped the entire Punchbowl of trees; and the ensuing log fire nearly burned the hostel to the ground. Our teachers, as far as I know, never found out, or if they did, they turned a blind eye as hardly anyone got killed or badly hurt. Well, not until the raw egg eating competition the next day. Ernie, mate, you weren't supposed to eat the shell.

School Fight Club

Our little school in the suburbs of London was nothing special. We had our fair share of triumphs and tragedies. We had people of a certain genius who would go on to great things; and we had our fair share of stupids.

If there was one thing our school WAS good at, it was fighting. You see, far from being middle-class suburbia defined, someone, somewhere had decided in the early 1970s to move "problem" families out of dark, deprived inner-city London and out in the country, where the open spaces would, presumably turn them into better people, skipping through fields and being nice to fluffy animals.

What a load of bollocks.

We ended up with a village full of psychopaths, crooks and close relations of the Kray Twins who'd cut your knackers off and rob you blind as soon as look at you. OK, I'll concede that some of them were lovely people, and I'm not just saying that because of the coffee table nailed to my head, either. And their psychotic kids went to my school.

No-one remembers how it started. There was probably a playground argument at some stage, or at the very least a whole host of bragging followed by someone fetching somebody else a damn good kicking. The upshot of it was that it was decided that all the fourth form boys would be "compelled" to fight for the honour of being The School's Hardest Fourth Year. Someone even had the idea of taking our school champ and facing him off against the champs of other local schools, but subsequent events meant we never quite got to that stage.

A secret For-God's-sake-don't-let-the-teachers-find-out committee was set up and rules laid out. Fight until the other boy surrendered. No weapons except fist, boots and head. Non-triers would be ridiculed. Every boys' name (and one girl as well - Linda was a savage animal who cared not a jot if you were a boy or girl. She'd kill you anyway) was put in the hat and a draw was made for the first round. With an elaborate system of seedings based on whether you were deemed "hard as nails" or "a poof", the first round parings were made and the tourney started.

The secret committee were masters of their work. They scoured the playground at break-times and made sure the fights happened. Some boys were willing, some were not. The protagonists were taken (some kicking and screaming) to the Hallowed Place between the sports hall and the science block, where no school law held sway and teachers never went. Most of the time it was fighters, seconds and referee, specially selected to ensure foul play. It was like a duel, only with Bovver Boots.

The early rounds went off relatively quickly, with the wimps tending to run away and hide when it was announced they would be fighting someone called "Bozzer". Like myself, for example. I eventually gave in to official "persuasion", came out of the toilet and took on third seeded Turnip in a one-sided contest, which saw my limp body peeled up and posted back to my parents within thirty seconds of the start.

The competition itself lasted for a couple of weeks, a tribute to the skills of the Secret Committee as they managed to get fifty kids to beat crap out of each other over several rounds. The veneer of secrecy was wearing a little thin though, as teachers soon got to hear the classroom gossip as the event reached a climax.

The first rule of School Fight Club was not to talk about School Fight Club. But we all did. All the time. The whole thing wasn't helped when Sean opened a book on the final outcome, and large quantities of lunch money began to change hands, mostly backing Psycho Tommy, one of the London refugees who'd been to Borstal for clocking some kid twice his size over the head with an iron bar. Tommy was ace: it was rumoured that he'd even had sex with a lady once, without having to pay. He once made me shit my pants, and for that I was thankful.

As we reached the last four, bravado got the better of the competitors. The Law of the Hallowed Place was soon forgotten, with the American Paul versus Psycho Tommy rumble going off right in the middle of the playground in front of an audience of hundreds.

This was our undoing.

Paul dived in with a haymaker of a punch, missed, and ended up on the floor.

Tommy kicked Paul in the head.

Tommy kicked Paul in the head again.

And again. And again. And again. And again. And again.

For several minutes.

There was blood everywhere, the Headmaster stormed down from his office along with the entire school staff, whistles and cattle prods. The police were called. The entire school was kept indoors for a week.

There was no winner, but no-one was going to argue over Psycho Tommy's victory by default. No-one had been so consistently maniacal throughout the entire tournament or spilt more blood as he single-handedly destroyed the flower of Britain's youth. I'm pretty sure that the other two semi-finalists were secretly relieved that neither had to fight him, as by the law of averages one of them would probably have ended up on a slab in the local hospital, or worse still, in trouble with their mum. Sean the official bookie, called all bets off and kept our money, wisely giving a generous cut to Tommy to ensure his survival.

The event's passing was marked by a school assembly in which the local vicar was called in to lecture us on his shock that we were brawling like "seafront Rods and Mockers", while several of us sniggered at the back, comparing bruises and the contents of a recently discovered stash of pornographic magazines. It was during this assembly that the Headmaster made his infamous "If this is the law of the jungle, then I'm King Kong" speech for the first time.

The bloody liar, he wouldn't have got past the first round.

"You just can't get rid of porn"

There are some unshakable truths in the world which just cannot be changed. You can't vote, because the Government will get in. Policemen are younger than they used to be. And no matter how hard you try, you just can't get rid of pornography.

Disposal of porn is like trying to get rid of chemical weapons or nuclear waste. No matter what you do with it, you're running the risk of discovery, humiliation, and worse still, contamination of an innocent population. Take a look at Saddam Hussein. Huge piles of nerve gas and weapons grade uranium hidden in a hole in his garden, but it's the sack of porn under his bed that George Bush nailed him with.

"If we cannot liberate... errr... destroy Saddam's evil arsenal of Hustler, Asian Babes and Naughty Over Forty slag mags, then the terrorists have already won."

"Ah-ha! Mr Scary", you are saying already. "You're going to tell us about the time you had a shed-load of pornography that you couldn't get rid of, in the pithy yet humorous style we have become accustomed to."

Damn right I am. And there's a moral too. Flashback...

It was early 1981. Thatcher had been in power for two years, unemployment was rampant, and Britain was rocking to the sound of Joe Dolce's "Shaddap You Face". In short, society was already doomed. Not that this bunch of fifteen-year-old school-kids cared, kicking a soccer ball round Stanlake Meadows that evening. It was when a misdirected punt ended up in the bushes that our lives would change forever. Well, for a month, tops.

Rob had waded past the knee-length grass and into the bushes. There were shouts of excitement that had us all crowding round. There was Rob. There was the ball. And there was an old sports bag stuffed to the gills with pornographic magazines. Paydirt.

The football game was long forgotten as the filth was passed round for "sampling". It wasn't particularly strong stuff by today's depraved standards, but for a bunch of pimply fifteen year-olds from a village west of London, even page three of The Sun was seen as the acme of jazz smut.

With time getting on, the decision had to be made. What to do with it?

Disposal, at this stage, was not an option. Someone had to look after it. Step forward Mickey.

Mickey was a bit special. We was rich for starters, and he got time off school because he was an actor, and once had a small speaking part in a BBC costume drama. Because of this, he was a little bohemian in his tastes to say the least. He claimed to have once "seen a lady naked", and already had a burgeoning collection of smut hidden in his bedroom. That was enough for us. Mickey had experience where it mattered most, and he promised on his dog's life to bring the spoils to school the next day.

Come the morning, there was Mickey at the school gates. The sports bag was now a sleek attaché case, and he dialled the combination (696969, the perve) as we all crowded round like that scene from Pulp Fiction. The goods were there, glowing slightly, and one or two hands made a grab for the top copies. The lid snapped shut amid cries of pain.

"There'll be no touching until break time," explained Mickey. "As you can see, I've taken the liberty of cataloguing the mags, and I've added one or two from my own collection". He produced a small school exercise book, where each mag had been meticulously catalogued with name, date and contents. There was also a column marked "Who".

"Who?"

"That's for who it's loaned to. Nobody's going to take stuff from **MY** jazz library without my knowing it".

Yeah, right.

And thus was born the Mickey Porn Library. The bastard stole our stash, and would only let the rest of us take the filth home one at a time on a system of tickets and record-keeping that would have brought a tear to the eye of our school librarian. It was when he started charging kids outside our gang to see our scud that we decided enough was enough. There could only be one punishment. The Tree.

It's simple. Lure the victim onto the school field. Get him on his back, grab his body, arms and legs, then run at the tree. One leg to the left, the other to the right. End of punishment. Mickey still persisted in his role of School Porn Baron, only now on a rather more democratic basis. It's amazing what crushing your gonads against a tree will do to your attitude.

The collection was mind-boggling in its variety, but most highly prized was a recent edition of Fiesta magazine, the Rolls Royce of British top shelf smut. There, across the centre pages was a shapely young lady called "Julia". You could see her flanges and everything. We all knew Julia as "Miss Shagwell" (name changed to protect the innocent, but believe me, I didn't have to change it much), our biology teacher. She had taught us all about human reproduction, while sitting on the corner of her desk wearing a very tight, white dress that finished just above the knee. We hung on to every last word.

Getting hold of the Shagwell Edition was a nightmare. There was a waiting list as long as your arm to get hold of it, and a black market in crude photocopies which just weren't the same as the real thing. If you were lucky, you might get a glimpse in the playground for half a second, but that was all. There were major arguments, and bribery to get up the waiting list was not out of the question. When Julian finally got his turn he kept it at home for a week, only bringing it back after repeated use of The Tree.

Alas, the arguments over possession of the Shagwell Edition would not go away, and would often spill over from the playground to the classroom, and this was to be Mickey's downfall. Mickey had kept possession of it for rather longer than was absolutely healthy and Ernie really, really wanted his go on her. A whispered conversation in maths got louder and louder until it developed into a vicious tug-o-war over the attaché case.

"What the hell is going on back there?" thundered "Shagger" Willis as the fight turned into an out-and-out brawl. Ernie let go, just as Mickey gave one final, resounding tug. The case flew from his hands, soaring over the classroom in a low arc - narrowly missing your narrator - to score a direct hit on Willis's desk. Pens, pencils and exercise books were crushed under the assault. The case burst open and slag mags exploded everywhere in a shower of tits, flange, arse and filth. And as if ordained by fate, the Shagwell Edition flopped open at Willis's feet, exposing our favourite teacher in all her glory for her colleague to see.

"There had better be a damn good excuse for this" whispered Willis, looking frighteningly like a volcano about to explode.

"Yes sir," said Mickey in that annoying sing-song voice of this that you knew was going to get him a visit to the Headmaster, "It's our porn collection."

So it's **OUR** porn collection now, is it? Cheers, mate.

Mickey was marched off to see the Head, and Willis had the entire class working through break-times for a week.

Because of his special status as school TV star, Mickey got off lightly. The porn was confiscated, and proving that You Just Can't Get Rid Of Porn, was fished out of the school bins and sold back to him within two days. However, the Shagwell Edition was missing. And so was Miss Shagwell. The school had known about her out-of-hours "photographic work" and had decided to brazen it out. As it had become common knowledge amongst pupils, she was transferred to another school many miles away, who, I found out later, were very happy to have her. On a regular basis.

But that was not the end of it, by any stretch. Mickey had decided his library needed a headquarters, somewhere he could work under the cover of legitimacy like Capone's speakeasies in prohibition Chicago. And that headquarters was to be the school darkroom. Ironically, he had hidden the entire stash in the roof space above the staff toilets. By pretending to be an ardent photographer, he could run his little business empire with impunity.

This was all well and good, but it soon got on the nerves of the genuine photographers, myself included, who found the constant comings and goings a bit of a nightmare when you're trying to get your exposure right. So we swiped the lot and decided that The Porn Had To Go.

And thus, Cookie and I found we weren't the first, and certainly not the last to discover that You Just Can't Get Rid of Porn.

God, we **TRIED**.

The fear of discovery mortified us. Bins - at home or elsewhere - were out, somebody might find it, and the thought of my mum finding a pile of jazz mags was just too much to bear.

We considered dumping it in the hedge where we had first found it, but on our reckoning it had only been there about ten minutes before we discovered it, so that was out of the question too. Burning, illogical as it sounds, was "a waste of good porn" and would just draw attention and, knowing our luck, the Fire Brigade. So we buried it.

Two figures could be seen behind the allotments on the Hurst Road digging a bloody great hole and dropping in a bin-liner full of naked tarts.

Within a week, drawn by the sound of Jumanji drums (not to mention a particularly tasty bribe which I never saw a penny of), a group of perverts from the year below us had dug the lot up, and there was a new Porn Baron in town.

And the moral of this tale? Greed is a terrible thing, and You Just Can't Get Rid of Porn.

Postscript: Being in the school camera club had its advantages. One evening, going through the tangled mess that was the negative drawer, we found an entire roll of film shot by a sixth former the previous year showing the voluptuous Miss Shagwell in various states of undress. We made a fortune.

On wanton acts of vandalism

I did A Very Bad Thing on the train to work. Busting for a piss, I broke the habit of a lifetime and used the on-board toilet (instead of the usual paper cup). It was a primitive thing, just one step removed from a hole in the ground, and appeared to have been previously occupied by an IRA "dirty protest."

In the process of straining my onions (no mean feat on a train, I can tell you) I noticed a sign which read "Do not flush the toilet while the train is in station", a sign just crying out for a slight amendment. Taking the pen out of the notebook I routinely carry around for the benefit of you lucky people, and making sure there were no hidden cameras or highly-paid midgets spying on me, I added two words.

"Except Basingstoke."

This is the town that gave the world Liz Hurley. I thought it was time the world gave something back. If you're reading this, Mr South-West Trains, I'm really sorry*.

* not sorry at all.

Kingy

The Law of the Playground is quite specific: "Games shall be as brutal as possible, and there shall be no snitching to the teachers if you get hurt." Are we absolutely clear? Good. It was tough out there.

Take the gentle game of "One Touch" for example. You've got to kick a ball against a wall. You've only got one touch of the ball to do it (hence the name, stupid) and if you fail, you're out. Last person left is the winner. Simple enough.

At our school this pursuit mutated into "One Touch Dobbings". Nobody dared to miss the wall because not only were you out, but you had to make it to the edge of the pitch without receiving a kicking from the other players. The later into the game, the worse the "dobbing" as frustrated "out" players dealt out harsher and harsher punishments. A particularly good game of One Touch would actually attract non-participating spectators whose sole purpose in life was to "dob" the vanquished. The more the better, and one or two of the lads would resort to wearing protective clothing.

Woe betide you, however, if you played One Touch Dobbings with Jonah. His idea of a good dobbing was a steel-capped boot to the testicles. You only played One Touch Dobbings with Jonah once, usually minutes before you crawled into a quiet corner to die.

One Touch? Pah! Why play that wusses' game when you had Kingy. In America they've got Dodgeball. It's played with a huge great ball and nobody gets hurt. Hell, there's even an International Dodgeball Federation for crud's sake. And leagues. And twenty foot high trophies that you can only get in American minority sports. I bet there's even an ironic movie, too. Ah.

Hell no. That won't do. We took the "game" of Dodgeball and turned it into Kingy. We didn't have no truck those great big soft balls. We wanted action. We wanted power. We wanted pain. Being the maniacs that we were, we had tennis balls injected with water. In skilled hands, they were deadly weapons, and some people actually preferred the risk of playing One Touch with Jonah over the painfest that was Kingy.

The rules were simple: One person is Kingy and has the ball. He has to chase the other players round the playing area chucking the ball at them.

If he scores a hit, the two then team up against the rest until everyone is hit. The last guy left is the winner and is Kingy for the next game.

Early on in the game, you're more likely to get a fluky hit that won't hurt so much. The longer you last, the greater the odds against you and the bigger the chance of receiving a close-range whupping. And that, I'm afraid is the price you pay for being so bloody good at it.

And boy, could you get some power with half a pound of water-filled tennis ball. A good hit would leave a bruise that would stay for weeks. I saw with my own eyes James taking a hit from close range right between the arse cheeks courtesy of a member of the school cricket team. The ball was travelling with such force that it wedged in there and James silently keeled over forwards, the ball still up his arse. As far as I know, it's still there.

But playing this wide-ranging game of chase and pain on the school field was not enough. We wanted more! One damp day, with the field closed off, we decided to play Kingy in the enclosed space between the maths block and the sports hall. Holy Mother of Donkey Poop. There was nowhere to hide. It was brutal.

A whole game, which would normally last twenty minutes out in the field would last maybe two or three. Bodies would lie scattered across the playground nursing wounds or crawling to safety. If you were hit and went down, they'd hit you again "just to make sure", or resort to the time-honoured tradition of "Dobbings" in a horrific playground crossover that took the genre just a little too far. Break-time, once a fun refuge from the rigours of the classroom soon became something to dread; and wary of breaking the Rule of the Playground and wimping out, we grimly got stuck into our brutal task.

However, the line had been crossed and there was no going back. And like drug addicts, we wanted more. And Mad Jonah of the bollock-crushing boots provided it.

"Screw the tennis ball", he said, "Look at what I've got".

It was a golf ball. One ounce of white plastic malevolence. Not only did it hurt, it had the ability to draw blood. And in the enclosed maths block/sports hall space, the thing would ricochet around to catch you unawares, leaving you in a groaning heap on the deck, just ripe for a dobbing prior to your trip to the emergency dentist.

One break-time of that was more than enough. People were about to crack. To hell with the Playground Law, teachers would have to be told. Luckily, honour would be preserved. One break-time of Golfball Kingy was all we got.

The trouble with golf balls on a hard surface is that they bounce. A lot. And once it's going, no bugger on Earth is going to try to stop it. So come lunch time, out came the Ball of Fear and off we went with another game. Jonah was Kingy and let fly with the Mother and Father of all misdirected throws. We watched with astonishment as our nemesis bounced once, twice, three times, right across the playground, younger kids diving out of the way, scattering in abject fear.

There was a sickening crash of glass as Jonah's Exocet missile scored a bulls-eye on the dining hall. Witnesses on the inside speak of an explosion of glass, panic, outrage and a free meal to anyone who claimed they had glass in their food. And there, at the very epicentre, was Mrs Taylor, the fearsome dinner lady, who had taken the full force of a supersonic golf ball right in the left tit.

Shit. Fan.

Mrs Taylor's tit had to be avenged, and the head stormed out of his office like a big fat, sweaty angel of death to collar the culprits. There are times when you have to say bollocks to the Playground Law of landing your mates in the shit, and this was it. Month upon month of Jonah's steel-capped boots in the nuts was enough for all of us, and his time had come. One day we might want to have children, or at the very least, See A Lady Naked. He was handed to the authorities on a plate, and our ordeal of Death Kingy was over. And thank God for that, we could get back to regular brutality.

If there's a moral to all this, it's that sometimes we have to bend the rules. Playground Honour is one thing. A boot in the nads is another.

On profanity

Swearing on television is neither big nor clever, and I fear I may have blown my chance for TV stardom again. For there I was, doing a bit of window shopping in town, when I was brutally accosted by a camera crew filming a TV commercial for Walkers Crisps.

"Eat some of the crisps", said the rather too happy girl with a microphone resembling a small, fluffy dog, "and tell the camera what you think. Be honest."

So I did. A great big cheek-bulging mouthful, trying, but failing to stop myself from spitting half-chewed lumps of deep-fried potato at the lens, I spoke my brains.

"They're fookin' ace."

Obviously, I'm not going to get on the prime-time advertising slot with a potty-mouth like that. Not unless they do a Tourette's Syndrome special. I've been on TV before. It's grossly over-rated.

Rugby

A history lesson: In the year 1823, during a school game of Association Football, the young William Webb Ellis picked up the ball and ran with it in his hands. Not only was the cheating git immediately hauled up in front of his fuming games master and thrashed soundly, he also invented the sport of Rugby and inflicted decades of insufferable pain and wanton violence on the generations of schoolboys which followed him. The bastard.

I remember a time when I was actually quite enjoyed the oval ball game. At the age of twelve, I was Mr Quinn's secret weapon in the school team, a nippy little scrum-half who could throw a mean dummy followed by a blind-side run to the try-line that suckered the opposition every time. A scrum to the Blues invariably meant four points; and on one occasion, the joy of being carried from the pitch on the shoulders of my team-mates.

If only they had let me down before they reached the dressing room door. I've still got the scar above my left eye.

I picked up another scar weeks later, just above the bridge of my nose. This time, courtesy of American Paul, who having just settled in England, was still ignorant of the rules of the game. Any game, in fact, and he leathered me in the face with his great size nine boots. And like a fool, with blood streaming down my front, I played on.

Despite this, my love affair with the egg-chasing continued. Dad had me doing all the physical jobs round the garden to "build me up like JPR Williams", but I couldn't help thinking this might have had something to do with the fact that he couldn't be arsed to rake the leaves himself.

I hero-worshipped the All Blacks, those rugby geniuses from New Zealand, and JPR Williams, the flying Welsh fullback with the pork-chop sideburns. I got a real leather rugby ball for Christmas and slept with it in my bed for three months (and we'll have no smutty comments at the back, thank you very much).

All of a sudden though, I wasn't twelve years old any more. By the time me and my schoolmates reached the age of fifteen, late developer Scary stayed more-or-less the same size. The rest of the rugby squad had grown to the size of brick shit-houses. Quinny didn't have the heart to drop me from the team, and moved me further and further back, away from the bone-crunching action.

The last straw came in a practice match. Turnip burst out of the pack, ball resting in the crook of his arm, sweeping all before him. Turnip was a farmer's boy, used to hauling bales of straw around and didn't take any shit, not least from the skinny little full back cowering between him and the try-line.

To be fair, I *did* try to get a tackle in. I dived at Turnip's thrashing legs, there was a sickening crunch, and that was the last thing I remembered that particular day. Just like a Tom and Jerry cartoon, they peeled me up from the mud, leaving a student-shaped impression on the pitch and carried on with the game as if nothing had happened.

Quinny didn't even have to drop me from the team. I begged him to drop me down to the bottom group full of fat kids, asthmatics and One-Legged Mike who only had one leg. I could blend in with the crowd there, dodging the half-hearted tackles of full-backs shivering in the mud with their hands up their jerseys, never once worrying about where the next boot in the head was coming from. Bliss.

And that was the end of Rugby Union for me. It was far too dangerous. Sport was for watching.

Cake

I never wanted to do home economics. The trouble was, I already had an ashtray in my bedroom, and I didn't fancy wrapping myself around a lathe making another. On the other hand, the kitchens were virtually empty, with Miss Horton teaching to a small knot of girls made to do cookery class by their parents.

We were given a choice. Hot sweaty metalwork with the sadistic Mr Callaghan, or the easy life cooking cakes with Miss Horton.

Mr Callaghan was the king of the cruel and unusual punishment, normally involving particularly inventive ways of inflicting pain on his hapless pupils. We put this down to the fact that he had lost a foot in a bizarre and unspecified classroom accident, and as such, it was his life's mission to wreak his awful revenge on the poor kids that came through his workshop. He was known as The Penguin.

On the other hand, Miss Horton was a lesbian, something she told us every five minutes, but as far as we knew, the girls she taught weren't. It was no contest for me and Tim, who really wanted to be a museum curator. This was about as close as the curriculum got to curating, so we signed up in a flash.

Tuesday mornings became ace. We came in and cooked stuff. Cake. Pie. And once, a whole three course meal, which we then ate, bursting at the seams. Pretty soon, the message got about that Scary and Tim were having a great time stuffing their faces while Mr Callaghan was crushing their bollocks in a vice, and within weeks there were further defections from the metalwork class.

One day, the fragrant Miss Horton came to us with an idea. Mr Bull, the school head teacher was about to celebrate his 60th birthday. Wouldn't it be nice if we were to make him a cake? Too bloody right it would, that man made our lives hell with petty rules, meaningless punishments and a habit of lecturing us all to sleep in morning assemblies.

At the time, there was a strict one-way system operating in the school corridors, punishable by instant death. This was one of Bull's big ideas to, and I quote "prepare us for our entry into a structured and ordered society". You had to walk halfway round the school just to get to the class next door, and transgressors were taken away to the "special" classroom, never to be seen again. He had to pay. We would make the cake. Oh yes. The cake.

It was a beautiful cake. We spent a wonderful Tuesday morning all doing our bit to give Bull the happiest of birthdays. Sugar. Magarine. Flour. Eggs. Vim. Icing Sugar. Some mouldy cheese somebody found at the bottom of the fridge. It all went in, and more. Despite our giggling protests that he was taking it too far, Seany dropped a huge green, pulsating loogie right into the mix. Seany had been on the end of Bull's wrath far too often, and today it was payback.

We did, however, physically restrain him from running his finger round the toilet bowl and rubbing the result into the mixture so that "he really would be full of shit". We didn't want to poison the old goat. Not much, anyway.

The *coup de grace* was "Happy 60th Birthday Mr Bull" piped out expertly in green icing by Tim, a skill he is undoubtedly putting to use now in his chosen career as a museum curator. We didn't have any green food colouring. So we used washing up liquid.

At the end of the lesson, as we all packed up for lunch, the door to the forbidden zone opened, and in walked our leader, Mr Bull, for a royal visit. Miss Horton grovelled and fawned round him, and it was all we could do to stop her from spreading rose petals on the very ground he walked upon. Eventually, she led him over to where we stood with The Cake of Doom.

There was a brief, sycophantic ceremony. He complimented us on our cooking skills, expressed his deep joy that his students had thought of him on his most special of days. We sang "Happy Birthday", and he blew out the one oversized candle planted in the middle of our masterpiece.

"See that candle?" Seany whispered to me as Old Man Bull blew it out, "It's been up my arse."

Then, as I stifled my giggles, we heard the words we dreaded most: "Won't you boys join me in a slice?"

Not on your bloody life, mate, we know what's in it.

He took a knife, and cut himself the biggest piece you could imagine, the great guts. He wasn't known as "King Kong" for nothing. He tucked in. We held our collective breath, waiting for the eruption.

It never came. He demolished the slice in about two mouthfuls, swallowed, and said, "This is actually rather good. You won't mind if I take the rest home for Mrs Bull?"

Of course we didn't mind. As a matter of fact, we were all for making him another one, just to finish off the job good and proper. Fair play to him, he showed up for work the next day showing no ill effects. Hardly surprising - the amount of washing up liquid we used to get the icing the right shade of green probably left him with the cleanest insides in the known universe.

A victory for the kids, for the first time ever. And like that episode of South Park where Kenny didn't die, I felt strangely dissatisfied. It just wasn't right, and I'm still waiting to be collared for this one now, over twenty years later. You'll be pleased to hear that Mr Bull is still alive and meting out bizarre punishments from the comfort of his centrally-heated bench in the High Courts. I'm still out here, running free and as guilty as hell. The cycle of crime and punishment is yet to be fulfilled.

Cross Country

Don't get me wrong, we loved school sports. In the autumn we got rugby, followed by a spring of football and a summer of athletics. Even the most lethargic of kids would take part, a testament to the enthusiasm of Mr Quinn and Mr Curtis.

If everything was so great, then why did the sadistic bastards keep sending us on cross-country runs? Right in the middle of bastard winter, too, when there were ice-cold howling gales in your face no matter which way you were facing.

Our school was drawn from three country villages, and was built between them right in the middle of farmland. Running behind the school was the railway line to Henley-on-Thames, with sweeping views of the local sewage works and the River Thames.

And right in the middle of that was Quinny's tried-and-test cross-country course. For decades, the man has sent the cream of the Thames Valley out into those fields, some as punishment, some in competition, and most perversely, some because they loved it; to run the three miles down to the river and back.

It was called "The Sewers", because that's what it was. A run round the sewage works, with the smell of shit forcing itself up your nostrils as you struggled for breath. The girls weren't even spared this hell - they had "The Short Sewers", an abbreviated version of the course, no less shitty and if anything, even muddier than the boys' course.

The first mile or so was relatively easy - a jog across the school field, up the main road to the farm track. Tarmac all the way and fine if you liked that sort of thing. The farm track wasn't too bad either. There's the odd pothole filled with water, and with a leap and a bound you jumped over it and headed on towards the sewage works.

That's when it hit you. The fetid smell of shit, piss and God knows what else, with the knowledge that it is also YOUR crap that was in there. Crap that is then pumped back into the Thames for the people of London to drink.

And that's when it got horrible. You were no longer running on a track, you were now in the Somme. With every step, your foot sunk into the goo up to the ankle. Mud built up on your feet like giant dinner-plates, making running nigh on impossible. But run we did.

I was ten yards behind little Stevie. He was waning, energy being sapped out of him yard by yard. I wasn't doing terribly well either. Suddenly Stevie was gone. He'd run into a puddle, thinking that like the rest, it would only be ankle deep. This one was a trench going down about two feet, and he'd fallen in head-first and was swimming for his life.

I had to stop and fish him out with the help of another couple of runners. He was covered head to toe in mud, his face a look of steely determination with the thousand-yard-stare of a shell-shocked soldier. As we pulled him free of the quagmire, his legs still going, so we faced him in the right direction and off he went with the rest of us following.

At the front of the course was Jimmy. Jim, so it turned out, was a county-class runner who actually enjoyed this kind of thing. He had just moved to the school, and desperately wanted to make a good impression of himself for Mr Quinn. He was miles out in front.

Before the race, Quinny told him the route so he wouldn't get lost. "Down to the river, follow the path along until you get to the railway. Then follow the railway line back to school." Couldn't be simpler than that, could it?

Unfortunately, Quinny didn't realise that Jimmy wasn't playing with a full deck. I think the correct diagnosis is "thick as pig shit". He could run like the wind, but you needed to tell him when to start and stop and someone to tell him which way to face, otherwise he could end up anywhere. You can just imagine where this is heading...

"...Follow the railway line back to school..."

So he did. He vaulted the thin wire fence and ran along the railway line. What the hell, the rest of the boys, struggling for breath, freezing cold and soaking wet all followed. It was like that scene from the Railway Children, only without Jenny Agutter to save our lives and take us home to rub us down with baby oil.

"...Follow the railway line back to school..."

Jim reached the school, and finding that the fence was now twenty feet high with no way through, kept on going.

At that point, if the station-master at Wargrave hadn't called the police, we'd have been halfway to London before we realised something was up.

Police cars and vans screeched to a halt on the bridge. Boys were physically dragged up the embankment, where, not knowing what to do with us, let us run back to the school. Stevie, still covered head to toe in shit, refused all help, giving the evil eye to the coppers as they tried to reach for him. Sensibly they let him go, and one-by-one we arrived back at the sports hall.

Quinny went ballistic. He was lost for words, waving his hands over his head as his mouth opened and closed noiselessly. Eventually, he managed to speak:

"You... you... you... twats! Are you trying to lose me my job?"

"But, sir, you told us...." said Jim.

"Never mind what I said! Haven't you got a brain in your head?"

Apparently not.

The next week he made us all do it again. The previous seven days had seen rain only previously witnessed by people saying "Hey, Noah! Stop working on that stupid ark of yours and come join us worshipping this false idol." Jim, streaking away at the front and deaf to our cries of "Come back you stupid tart!", turned the wrong way out of the school and ended up in Henley, and was rescued hours later by Mr Curtis in his car. The rest of us stuck grimly to the course, which was even muddier than the week before, arriving back in the playground, exhausted, each and every one of us fully qualified for our long distance swimming certificates.

Little Stevie is still missing.

Rocket

It was a science project about soil.

Easy, just dig some out of your garden, bring it in, and pour chemicals over it, and if you're lucky you might get some pretty brown bubbles. But, no, that wasn't good enough for Greebo, Hackett and Mickey. They thought they could earn extra marks by comparing our top quality soil in Reading with that in Bristol, where Mickey's Gran lived.

Mr Wilkes thought it was a good idea too, and looked forward to her posting a small envelope of the stuff to the school, an act that would spark a full-scale security alert these days, and earn the poor old dear several years without trial in Belmarsh Prison.

But Greebo and company were, let's put it tactfully, mentalists. Instead of just asking her for the dirt, they decided to build a rocket that would fly eighty miles to Bristol, where Mickey's Gran would fill it up with soil, and fire it back with the kind of accuracy that Werner von Braun could only have dreamed about when he designed the V-2.

After a huge class-room bust-up in which Mickey screamed and shouted at his "rank amateur" co-conspirators, there was an official divorce and Mickey went off to work on his own top secret project. This was almost certainly nothing to do with Greebo and Hackett's initial design. It was a used Coke can with a cardboard nose-cone filled with gas from the science lab. With the top-level technology afforded to these geniuses, the gas was held in the can by a blob of plasticine. NASA had nothing on this lot. It flew thirty feet on its maiden flight - as far as Hackett could throw it. And he threw like a girl.

While the rest of the class worked on their presentations with huge quantities of local muck, the mad duo were forced to explain, in front of the entire class, what, exactly, was the point of all this messing about with empty Coke cans, and why they had produced exactly nothing. After open ridicule of the cardboard nose cone or "combustion chamber" as they insisted on calling it, Greebo committed the kind of social faux pas that you just cannot get away with at school. He ran away crying.

Mickey pressed on. In his bedroom-cum-workshop-cum-pirate radio station, he built a two-staged whopper out of Calor Gas cartridges and aluminium tubing, and it looked seriously scary. His guidance system, he boasted, would be one of the local church bells which we all knew had been stuck in the "up position" since some nasty business in the Great War. We didn't doubt his technical prowess, we had spent many an evening in the past listening to Pirate Radio Mickey, until Her Majesty's Government kindly put us out of our misery by shutting him down.

By now, the entire project was strictly unofficial. It had been months since they had closed down Science Club after That Nitro-Glycerine Thing, and no-one had dared something so wonderfully dangerous since then.

Those of us in the know were given a time, date and location and met Mickey at his "launch silo", an old tunnel up in the woods near to school. We were amazed. He had rigged up a launch pad, and set up a control centre about fifty yards away, at the end of a very long wire in a ditch.

Mickey gave a short speech on how he was the future of the British Space Industry, and how we were a "bunch of ponces" for not believing he could take the project so far. Solemnly we counted down, and he connected the wire to the terminals of the lorry battery that powered the whole thing.

Nothing.

"Fuck!" said Mickey, and we all laughed at him for being a big cock.

He got up and followed the wires across the clearing to the launch pad.

He was halfway to his target when the thing went off.

It was most impressive. The rocket took off with a WHOOOOOSH and flew a good fifty feet in the air. We applauded and whooped. All well and good, but Mickey hadn't really worked out how to get the second stage going, and gravity took control of the whole affair. The monster started tumbling back down to Earth. Towards us. Bristol's loss was our ... err ... abject terror.

There were cries of "Oh shit!" and a general cacking of pants as we lurched out of the ditch in all directions. And good thing we did, too.

Brief chemistry lesson: There comes a time when setting fire to a gas in an enclosed space, that quantities of fuel and oxygen reach the correct proportions. It's called the flashpoint. When this happens, there is, to use the correct terminology, a fucking great explosion.

Mickey's throbbing monster hit the deck roughly where the six of us had been cowering just moments before. It lay there, glowering, a blue flame coming out of the nozzle getting smaller and smaller. Until....

BANG!

The gas canister went off. It wasn't a particularly big explosion, but it had the effect of rupturing the second stage canister, which went off about three quarters of a second later. My entire world went a beautiful shade of orangey-blue-yellow.

Words cannot describe the noise it made, but I'll give it a damn good try.

Take a deep breath and go:

T H W O O O O O O O O O O S S S S S S S S H H H H H H H - BLAAAAAAANGNGNGNG-eeeeeeeeeee!!!!", the last bit being the ringing noise that haunts you for the next two weeks.

Mickey shrugged.

"Same time next week, lads?"

No thanks, mate, I think I'll just slink home and drain the blood out of my ears, thank you very much.

Mickey surrendered. His granny sent him a small tin of soil, which got stuck in the post and arrived two weeks too late to use on the project. It didn't make any difference, he sat at home one evening and made up a comparative analysis off the top of his head and got a grade A. And while the rest of the class was moving on to the important subject of reproduction with the voluptuous Miss Shagwell, Greebo and Hackett were still up the school field throwing coke cans at each other.

Cream Crackered

"Can you eat three cream crackers in a minute without stopping to take a drink?"

That was the challenge offered by BBC's Nationwide programme, that bastion of early-evening viewing, news analysis and regular Nutter-of-the-Day spot. Today's nutter was a pub landlord who offered that very challenge to his customers, charging them a quid a time for the privilege of taking part, with the lure of a tenner if they succeeded. Not many did, and the landlord looked like he was well on his way to his first million.

It certainly grabbed the imagination. It was the "Did you see it?" topic in the school playground the next morning, and one of the kids whose mother happened to be a school dinner lady brought along several packets of Jacob's finest to spread the three-in-a-minute gospel, charging twenty pence a throw. He went home minted.

The craze, by happy coincidence, came just a couple of weeks before the school's Christmas Fayre, complete with crap Olde Worlde spelling, and the promise of yet another new car for the headmaster. Straight onto the bandwagon we jumped, and signed up for an exclusive three-in-a-minute stall. We were even given a whole classroom to run the stall, such were the expected crowds for the event.

Perhaps the organisers were blinded by the success we had had the previous year, when our stall had been one of the most successful there had ever been. The premise was simple. Two weeks before the event, we ran around the school taking pictures of all the teachers.

"It's for a project, sir," we said.

Then it was straight off to the darkroom to run off photographs of our esteemed educators. On the day of the event, the photos were mounted on a large board, and punters were invited to part with their money in return for the chance to throw darts at their weekday tormentors. Even after subtracting our - cough - expenses (do you realise how expensive photographic paper is?), the Head's new Toyota fund made more than three figures.

So, on with the crackers. We got a few tables, chairs and a jug of water in case there were any choking emergencies, and Ernie's mum turned up with a huge catering box of short-dated cream crackers she had got on the cheap from the wholesalers. We were ready to go.

The doors opened, the punters flooded in, and true to form, no matter how hard they tried, no-one was able to down the requisite three crackers to win the promised tenner. Even the school fat kid, Big Mac couldn't manage it, and by God, he tried enough times. Like the previous year, we took a fortune, even after the subtraction of - cough - expenses (do you realise how difficult it is to dry-clean biscuit-encrusted spittle out of your school uniform?) the school Toyota-purchasing committee were more than pleased with our efforts.

But there was one fly in the ointment. Did I mention that Ernie's Mum's huge catering box of cream crackers was absolutely huge? The box was like the inside of the TARDIS, and no matter how many you took out, it was still full. There was enough in there to feed an entire army, and even after a couple of hundred punters having a go on the game, with only three or four requiring hospital treatment, we still had about three million of the bloody things left. What, in the name of God, were we supposed to do with several thousand almost-but-not-quite out-of-date cream crackers?

Ju-Vid knew exactly what to do. His chaotic brain worked differently to ours. That's why, looking back from the relative safety of the twenty-first century, we always got ourselves into so much shit.

"Hey!" he said, "These things fly exactly like frisbees!"

And he demonstrated the fact by wanging one across the classroom. He was right. It DID fly exactly like a frisbee, right up to the moment it hit Cookie on the forehead and shattered all over the place.

"You git!" responded Cookie, grabbing a handful and chucking them back, scattering crackers across the room like a blunderbuss. Now, that looked like a good idea. All six of us grabbed handfuls from the box, and ducking and diving behind tables, we started full-scale cream cracker warfare. Other kids, attracted by the noise, joined in. And we charged them 10p a go.

Let us quietly close the door on the battle raging in Room Ten for a good quarter of an hour, while elsewhere the headmaster handed out raffle prizes and congratulated the pupils, parents and teachers for their generous support, quietly going through the 1981 Toyota catalogue in his head. People applauded, held their prizes proudly to their chests and began to drift off home.

Now, see the scene from the point of view of Miss Olga, the school's terrifying deputy headteacher, doing the rounds of the classrooms to make sure everything had been tidied away properly. Room seven - clear. Room eight - nice and tidy. Room nine - clear. Room ten. Room ten.

The door appeared to have a table pushed up against it, and there's rather too much noise going on in there to be healthy. She went back to the school hall and fetched Mr Quinn, our arch-nemesis, former boxer and fearful PE teacher. With one good hard shoulder barge the door swung open. Doom.

I don't think I really need to describe the scene to you. Six fifteen-year-old kids, assorted hangers-on, and an unlimited supply of cream crackers in an enclosed space. As the two teachers walked in, several of these crackers were still airborne, skimming through the air to join their wasted brethren lying several inches deep on the floor. They crunched underfoot. There was no point denying anything. Caught, as they say, like a Treen in a disabled space cruiser.

Quinny, the king of the imaginative and ironic punishment not only let the shit hit the fan, he also made damn sure we cleaned it up afterwards. This one broke all records. Not only did we have to clear up our mess, we had to stay behind after school until the end of term helping out the cleaners - not for the first time, either. On top of that, we had to write a 1,000 word essay on why we shouldn't waste food, which he promptly tore up in front of us without even a passing glance. Then there was the indignity of a midwinter cross-country run, thrown in because old PE teacher habits die hard.

That certainly taught us.

It was during one of these after-school do-all-the-hard-work-for-the-cleaners sessions that we made a terrible discovery. There, in room ten, pushed into an alcove and forgotten, was a half empty box containing about five million cream crackers.

"Here!" said Ju-Vid, "These things fly like frisbees!"

Lab of Doom

In the grim existence of youth in a Middle-England secondary school, science lessons were the highlight of the week. After the hard slog through dismal Maths, French, and English classes, we only had science, games and design to keep us vaguely sane. And sanity was the last thing that was going to come out of an hour and a half on the school playing fields. Our games masters brought us to despair with their maniacal love of cross-country running and no-holds-barred rugby; while our school's arts and design faculty was staffed entirely by misfits, outcasts and psychotic metalwork teachers.

Science it was, then. Our school invested a lot in the sciences, with a brand new Science Block heaving at the seams with enthusiastic staff and an explosive store-room. It was just a shame that the subject was taught so bloody badly. The teachers were, by and large, faultless. They struggled with a daft, confusing course, and tried their best despite the tools they were handed. And speaking of "tools", some of my fellow students weren't exactly top drawer material, either.

If you got a decent teacher, you were halfway there. We had three. For Physics, there was Mr Wilkes - a former nuclear scientist who built nuclear weapons shortly before all that trouble that came with his CND membership.

In Biology, there was the pneumatic Miss Shagwell, whose short, tight lab coats (I'm sure you're supposed to wear clothes underneath) were the stuff of many young lads' sleepless nights battling the evil pickle.

And in Chemistry, Dr Gilkes. He was... strange. Piercing blue eyes that could cut you in half. Unworldly mannerisms. He was always recruiting for Science Club, an activity which was clearly a front for an Illuminati-inspired takeover of the world using knowledge gleaned from brilliant young students.

His lab was The Lab of Doom, and we, dear reader, were his underlings, like Igor to Dr Frankenstein.

He stared at us with those cold, cold eyes as he handed us our assignments for the day.

"What are the properties of coal?"

Stupid bloody question. Set fire to it and it burns, end of story. But, in order to get an A grade in science, you had to go through the whole gamut of tests, with chemicals, microscopes, and when you really got bored, fire.

And that's what Graham, Tim and I did, at our workbench specially selected to be able to view Miss Shagwell's arse teaching biology to a rapt audience of teenage perverts through the partition wall. With our sample of black dust scraped up from the coal hole behind our house, we set to our task with grim determination.

Add water to coal dust. The water goes black.

Add potassium permanganate - the purple and seemingly harmless standby of the school lab - to coal dust. It goes black.

Add anything you can lay your hands on to coal dust, and bugger me rigid if you don't get a test tube of black liquid.

It was no good. This day in the lab was going nowhere fast, and only Miss Shagwell's rear view could save us from insanity. Thirty minutes in and we hadn't even set fire to anything, let alone cause a window-shattering explosion that would close the school down for another week while they had the structural engineers in.

Tim summed up our feelings for the whole sorry affair: "Sod this for a laugh."

We piled up the remains of our coal dust on an old tin lid perched on an asbestos sheet, and properly attired in lab coat and protective goggles, Graham trained a bunsen burner on it. Wussy orange flame, two minutes. Nothing.

Okay, highly inflammable coal dust, if you want to play it that way, we'll give you the high-powered blue flame and see how you like it. So we did. It glowed a bit, but nothing.

Now, in retrospect, the following might be seen as rather fool-hardy, but with Dr Gilkes elsewhere trying to keep the matches out of the hands of our differently-educated classmates, there was no one to tell us the grand act of folly we were embarking on.

Two bunsen burners. Then three. Full heat. Not a hint of a flame. The odd crackle maybe, but the raging inferno we expected was simply not happening. The tin lid, however, glowed white hot and started to melt.

What was happening, however, was that the concentrated heat of three burners going at full-throttle on one spot on the asbestos was causing it to expand. And expand it did. The only trouble with that was that the cooler parts of the mat were quite happy as they were, and didn't have much truck with this trying-to-get-bigger thing. The hot bits were quite insistent, and godammit, their atoms were going to jig about like buggery if the cold bits wanted to or not.

After a full five minutes of not paying attention to our all-to-bleedin'-obvious fate, our attention had wondered. No longer were we waiting for the raging inferno that was never going to occur. Miss Shagwell had turned to write something on the blackboard next door, and we were enjoying a rather fetching profile, resembling a contour map of the Brecon Beacons.

BLAMMO!

Actually, it was louder than that, with a ringing in the ears to follow.

BLAAAAAAAAMOOOOOOO!!!!!-eeeeeeeee

There was an explosion of coal dust and white-hot asbestos that has probably shortened my life by a good five years. The tin lid scythed through the air and embedded itself in the side of my fake Adidas bag (All Day I Dream About Sex), sending up black clouds of smoke as it burrowed its way through the melting plastic.

Tim, Graham and I stood there in stunned silence as twenty-five pairs of eyes trained on us. Dr Gilkes calmly strolled over and flipped off the gas supply. We looked at each other. Smothered in coal dust, we looked like the Black and White Minstrels, and the removal of our lab goggles just made us look even more ridiculous.

Miss Shagwell stifled a giggle and went back to her blackboard, still wobbling in a rather suggestive manner from barely suppressed laughter. In fact, everything she did was suggestive, even, it turns out, laughing at poor, victimised students.

From the back of the lab, some of our classmates started to laugh, and if this was an episode of The Simpsons, Nelson Muntz would have chosen that exact moment to go "Ha Haa!"

"Well," said Dr Gilkes "that'll teach you."

Teach us? Teach us?! Surely that was HIS job. We nearly had our heads blown off, and as we spoke, structural engineers were being called in to remove splinters of asbestos from the fabric of the building. And worse, Miss Shagwell, the object of our youthful desires had laughed at us. Crushed. Totally and utterly crushed.

The next science lesson, I kid you not, was entitled "The Properties of Human Blood." And yes, blood was spilled. Everywhere.

Pomagne

What in the name of Bacchus was Pomagne all about then? For the uninitiated, Pomagne was some kind of sparkling pear-flavoured fizzy thing pumped up with donkey flatulence that came in champagne-style bottles, pre-dating alco-pops by several decades and designed to look sophisticated.

In all my years as a committed boozer, I never, ever saw it in the shops, but they gave away crates of the stuff at school and village fetes up and down the country. There must be warehouses full of Pomagne that the manufacturers can't shift, instead offering it up to Round Tables, school fundraising committees and bottlers of paint stripper on the cheap just to cut their losses.

The Win-a-bottle-of-Pomagne game was an annual fixture at our school Christmas Fayre. You bought a ticket, the Pomagne guy spun the arrow, and if your number came up you won a bottle. Eight to one chance, simple as that. For the princely sum of twenty pence, you could get your grabbing teenage hands on three quarters of a litre of nine per cent proof sparkling pear flavoured wine substitute, and the powers that be were none the wiser.

"You are over eighteen?" asked the man with the terrible facial hair.

"Oh, yes," we lied through our teeth.

Kids won gallons of the stuff, and soon a drinking den was set up in an unused classroom, where dozens of eleven-to-sixteen year-olds spent the afternoon getting completely and utterly shit-faced. As you can imagine under these circumstances, there was vomit. Lots of it. While some kids were quite content to sit in a corner, clutching six bottles of their booty, taking generous swigs before lapsing into unconsciousness, others began to sing, fight, and go on drunken tours of the school, pissing into bins and trying to round up players for "the world's biggest game of strip poker".

Safe in our den of vice, we knew we were safe from the powers of teacherdom, just as long as no-one spilled the beans. And nothing could possibly go wrong.

The big, stinking splat of dung against ventilator came during the Grande Olde Christmas Raffle draw - the climax of the whole event, where, as usual, some four-year-old speed demon would win the first prize of a motorbike and a set of steak knives.

Benny stood at the front, clutching his tickets in his left hand, half empty bottle of Bulmer's finest pear-flavoured sparkling wine substitute in the other. He swayed slightly as if blown by a gentle breeze.

"And the second prize winner," announced the Headmaster, rummaging in the barrel of carefully folded tickets, "is....."

We never found out who won the second prize.

"Blaaaaaaaaaaargh!!!!!!!" said Benny as fruit-flavoured vomit surged all over Bull's feet and legs.

Shocked silence.

"Sorry sir," he said, and for good effect, "Blaaaaaaaaaaaargh!!!!!"

An all-teacher hit squad turned over the Kids' Speakeasy, where the World's Biggest game of Strip Poker had just reached a crucial stage. Bleary-eyed and retching pupils were led away to an uncertain fate, the local casualty unit, and in one case, the fire station. The head put a ban on anyone even mentioning the whole affair at school the next week. So everybody knew about it, then.

At the following term's Summer Fayre, I won six bottles of Pomagne. The Speakeasy was in the gym store room. I can't remember who won the strip poker this time, but I did get a whole week of detention instead. Arses.

Guns

When I reached the ripe old age of fifteen, I signed up for the Air Cadets. The "Spacers" are essentially a youth organisation run by the Royal Air Force to get kids interested in planes, flying and the military life, in the hope that they'd sign up for a career. They let us have real uniforms, free flying lessons, and if we were really, really good, guns.

We had our own drill hall in the centre of Henley-on-Thames, which we were forced to share with the army cadets, a bunch of long-armed mono-browed troglodytes with all the intelligence of a bread roll.

The Drill Hall used to be the town's police station. The old cells for housing prisoners were still there and used as stock cupboards; you could lock people in for a laugh and leave them there the whole night, their screams echoing down long, abandoned corridors, falling on deaf ears.

The commanding officer was a crumbling old relic of the old-style air force. He had actually served with my grandfather during World War II, and spent many happy years dropping red hot British steel onto the Bosch, and as far as he was concerned, he was still doing it. Only from behind a desk hundreds of miles and four decades away from the action.

But the guy who really ran the show was Warrant Officer Simmons. He was old-school RAF too, with a huge handle-bar moustache and rock-hard. Strict wasn't the word of it. If your hair was too long, your uniform was wrong or if your boots were dirty you were for the high jump. But he was one of the lads too, keep on his right side and he was a pleasure to be with. He taught us cuss-words and insults we never knew existed. He taught us how to make the officers' lives hell with "saluting traps", and he also taught me how to shoot the bollocks off a fly from three hundred yards.

Hero.

Every other weekend we piled into an RAF bus and head up to the air station at Benson where we shot at things. The only problem was the weaponry. They gave us old Lee Enfield rifles which had (and I'm not kidding here) seen action in the trenches of World War One. There was absolutely no subtlety about them - they went off like cannons and kicked like a mule, and you'd be nursing a bruised shoulder at the end of the day. I saw with my own eyes one particularly stupid kid from Slough squadron (and Jaysus, did they have some thickies on their books) trying to hold the weapon in front of him like a pistol. His first and last shot of the day caused a recoil which broke his nose. How we laughed.

All that was to change in the early 80s. The British armed forces switched over to the much-maligned SA-80 rifle, a weedy little thing made out of plastic, tinfoil and lego bricks. This left them with a huge pile of unwanted Self Loading Rifles and ammo. The best idea the Ministry of Defence ever had was to give them to the cadet corps. It was a massacre. I fired so many rounds in a two month period, I actually qualified as an RAF marksman, along with a number of my comrades. But, you know me by now, there would be a price to pay...

The SLR is semi-automatic. Instead of creating a bastard great explosion and a donkey-kick like the old weapons, it used the gasses to eject the old cartridge and load the next one. All you've got to do it pull the trigger and rat-a-tat-a-tat, you get an impressive shower of empty shells flying out like the scene at the end of Rambo II. A twenty-round magazine would disappear in seconds and then they'd let us have another go. Smashing.

Walken, bless him, tried his hardest, but the words "safety catch" and "assault with a deadly weapon" were a foreign concept to him. He was only about four foot something (and four foot across - he was like a walking, talking cube), his rifle was only slightly smaller than he was. He lived in the local boarding school for "problem" children, mainly because his parents were sick to death of him trying to kill them. We named this school, rather cruelly, "The Blob Farm" as they kept sending us recruits on the misunderstanding that we were in dire need of fresh psychopaths. Now, it turned out, it was our turn to feel the wrath of Walken.

"WALKEN!" bellowed our hero WO Simmons "POINT YOUR WEAPON DOWN THE RANGE!"

"What's that sir?" he said, swinging round, the lethal end of good old Belgian steel sweeping an arc in front of a terrified crowd of spectators, who, as a man, dived for cover.

I remember the next comment as clearly as if it were only yesterday.

"HOLY FUCKING CHRIST! HE'S TRYING TO KILL US!"

Walken turned full circle, and just in time, too. His finger tightened round the trigger and a hail of bullets ripped up the range, shooting up turf, stones, bits of wood, anything in its deadly path. One bullet had ricocheted off something solid (and yes, they really do go pyang-whoo-whoo-whooo like they do in the movies) and thudded into the wall inches away from where Phil's head had been moments earlier. I am reliably informed that he "shat his pants". Join the club, mate.

The firing stopped. Empty cartridges tinkled onto concrete. There was a deathly silence. The smoke cleared, and we all staggered to our feet in a daze. Out of twenty rounds, nineteen had flown off to all corners of the range and back again. The twentieth had scored a perfect bulls-eye on the target. Walken put his weapon down and shrugged.

"Sorry."

Simmons went volcanic. Gentlemen, welcome to Swearing 101.

The funny thing was, not long before this little episode, a fellow spacer called Sergeant Marcus Sergeant had taken a pot-shot at the Queen during the Trooping of the Colour, and got himself banged up for five years for treason. After that, they decided we couldn't be trusted with firearms, and they wouldn't let us have guns for AGES.

Sick

Being a teenager in the Air Cadets was ace. Her Majesty's Government paid out thousands and thousands in taxpayer's money to give us guns, summer camps, free flying and tenpin bowling. And guns. It was all in a good cause, I suppose - the whole idea was to get lazy, stupid, TV-obsessed kids off their backsides and get them ready for a career killing people

As it stands, I can still get a mirror shine on even the dirtiest of boots armed with nothing but a small rag and a spoon. If there's ever a call for that kind of skill in the cut-throat world of international communications, I'll be quids in.

So, thanks to the Royal Air Force's desire to rope us all in as potential fighter pilots, they did their best to chuck us on as many planes as they could. We were even allowed to take time off school to visit air stations, an unexpected perk that made us the envy of classmates who thought we were all uniformed ponces.

We were regularly carted off up to RAF Benson or RAF Abingdon where we met 6 Air Experience Flight and their collection of antique Chipmunk trainers, which was a basically an excuse for retired fighter pilots to throw a tiny plane about with an increasingly green-looking kid in the back.

Chippy flying was this: skill. Unfortunately, we were made to sit through a dire safety film which told you what to do if the plane crashed (die, basically) and then sit around for hours on end waiting your turn and stewing over your fate. Then, you were strapped into a parachute which made you walk like a monkey and thrown into the back of a plane that was built in the late 1940s.

The pilots were psychopaths. They'd had a long, varied, but insufferably peacetime career in which they'd been on endless exercises in their multi-million pound fighter jets, and had never, ever seen action. And now the RAF had spat them out at the other end and they were reduced to flying spotty kids about in a single-engine trainer that had cost two-and six from a jumble sale. Payback time.

The bastards threw those little planes about like there was no tomorrow. Loops, rolls, some impossible stunt I have only ever seen duplicated on a computer game, and that ended up in a messy exploding fireball. You'd spend half an hour alternately hanging from your seat straps or zooming head-on towards an ever enlarging landscape, the tiny engine screaming like a German Stuka bomber, before pulling up at the last minute. You could see people on the ground pointing and running in terror as we'd hurtle towards them. I'm sure I once heard the pilot screaming "RAT-A-TAT-A-TAT-TAT-A-TAT you bastards!" at one stage. It was like "633 Squadron" all over again.

Unfortunately, there were casualties. The lads would stagger from the plane, still in a parachute-induced monkey walk, clutching bulging sick-bags and vowing never to return. I spent the rest of the day on my back, while the world spun around me at an alarming rate. Some kind soul had left a bucket next to me "just in case", and boy did I need it.

Poor old Murza parted company with his lunch at the top of a loop, missed the bag entirely and filled the entire rear cockpit with diced carrots. The pilot continued with his routine, and by the time they landed, Murza was head-to-toe with vomit. After a quick wipe-round, the next poor sap was bundled in, and he spent the following thirty minutes trying to dodge carrots as they bounced around him from all angles.

It was brilliant. And we went back for more.

A single-engine trainer was one thing, but we wanted genuine operational aircraft. Our Commanding Officer found that all it took was a phone-call. Ring up an air station, ask if they were flying anywhere, and would they mind if they took us along too?

We soon made friends with 115 Squadron whose job was to calibrate runway equipment at all RAF bases. So on any given day, we could end up in Belfast, Gibraltar, Germany, or on one memorable occasion, Cyprus. They even threw in lunch and a spell in the cockpit. Anything, it turned out, to make their job more interesting.

However, it was when we were cordially invited to RAF Lyneham that it all went horribly pear-shaped. Lyneham is the home of the Royal Air Force's C-130 Hercules fleet. Big, noisy, bone-shaking transport aircraft. They're fine if you're one of the flight-crew as they've got a big, breezy and comfortable flight deck. For anyone in the back, though, it's worse than cattle trucks, and quite the worst experience of anybody's life. Margaret Thatcher once spent twelve hours in the back of one of these monsters en route to the Falkland Islands. Good.

We all bunked off school with the dreaded official letter and set off to meet our destiny courtesy of an RAF bus. It's a relatively long drive from Henley to the other side of Swindon, especially in a charabanc that's so old they have a man walking in front with a red flag. Stopping at Membury Services, we stocked up with all those things necessary for a schoolboy day out. Sweets. Loads of them. Walken, in true Ralph Wiggum style, ate the lot within ten minutes, and was looking distinctly green before we even got there.

Just to really stoke things up, we arrived at Lyneham to find that we'd been booked an early lunch - completely free of charge, courtesy of the British taxpayer - in the canteen. And it was a fry-up. Greasy eggs, bacon, sausages, the works, all washed down with acid-flavoured bromide-laced tea that only the armed forces can manage. With all this goo bubbling up inside, NOW we were ready to fly.

We were booked on Herky 218 for two-and-a-half hours of "Bump and Go". The pilot was going to spend the afternoon flying round and round in circles practising his take-off and landing techniques. And if that wasn't bad enough, the weather had taken a turn for the worse. We just KNEW what kind of flight this was going to be.

It was fine for the first hour or so. We took off, flew around Southern England for a bit and all took turns visiting the flight deck. The loadmaster also opened the rear doors so we could look out into 10,000 feet of sheer drop below us. That was good.

But before long, the pilot started his sequence of take-offs and landings. Bump. Go. Bump. Go. That was bad.

Some of the lads were beginning to look distinctly peaky. The loadmaster took the hint and started handing out bags, sick, for the use of. Jez was the first to go with a discreet little honk, closely followed by Alan. However, things were about to get hideously out of control. It was Walken. He'd stuffed himself stupid with sweets and fizzy drinks. Then he's gone back for seconds of the canteen fry-up.

"I'm gonna puke" he gasped.

"Sick bag! Sick bag!" we shouted over the roar of the engines.

But it was no use. He'd already dropped the bag onto the floor, and he was reaching the point of no return.

You may have heard the saying "You can't hold back puke".
And you can't.

Once it's on its way, you can't stop that bodily spasm that expels the contents of your stomach with great force. But top marks to Walken for trying. With his hands over his mouth, you could actually see his cheeks bulging as he gamely tried to hold back the inevitable.

And then came the explosion. Have you ever put your finger over the end of a hosepipe to make it spray? Well, that's what Walken did, only with a gutful of chunder. There was a veritable fountain of barf, cascading over everything in a ten feet radius. Projectile vomiting at its finest. I was the unfortunate soul sitting next to him, and took the full force of the blast. Several others nearby were also drenched, and the foul stench of spew filled the cabin.

There was nothing for it. Most of us were already feeling a little queasy to start with, but this was the final straw. I was the first to go, closely followed by several others as the foul-smelling cloud did its worst in a domino effect of diced carrots. Within seconds everyone had chundered, some into the bags provided, and at least one straight onto his lovely shiny boots.

Still feeling rank, and still scraping the remains of Walken's lunch off my uniform, I looked up to see the RAF loadmaster in fits of laughter at the cream of our nation's youth, slowly but surely puking for Britain.

We still had over an hour of this torture to go, and by the time we had landed and taxied back to the hangers, the cargo hold of the Hercules looked exactly like the kind of hospital ward Florence Nightingale did her best to eradicate during the Crimean War.

There were groaning bodies everywhere as we tried to shut out the full horror of the last two hours. One by one we all staggered out of the cargo doors, falling to our knees and kissing the ground. One can only assume that the Pope has the same pilot.

We vowed: Never Again. Everyone, that is, except Corporal Flynn. He was as happy as a sandboy, and had spent the entire flight joyfully putting away chocolate bars and the remnants of the flight crew's lunch. The bastard. And where is he now? The smug git ended up as a Royal Air Force pilot, who is, as we speak, making life hell for visiting Space Cadets.

A month later, we went back for more.

On football

In a moment of idiocy, I decided to put together a football team which I shall call Double Entendre XI. In the end I managed to get no less than seventeen players - past and present - to play for the filthiest team on the planet:

1. David Seaman
2. Danny Shittu
3. Rod Fanni
4. Raphael Scheidt
5. Berndt Haas
6. Nicky Butt
7. Nwankwo "Mr Sex" Kanu
8. Uwe Fuchs
9. Paul Dickov
10. Wayne Wanklin
11. Joseph Desire Hand Job

Subs:
12. Lopez Ufarte
13. Argelico Fucks
14. Tony Woodcock
15. Julian Dicks
16. Dean Windass
17. Joaquim Manuel Silva Quim

Manager: Stefan Kuntz

In an ideal world, they would all be playing at Young Boys' Wankdorf stadium in Switzerland in a filth-match against Peru's Deportivo Wanka. Sponsored, naturally, by Turkish bank Arcelik.

If I was Roman Abramovich, I'd stop all this mucking about with

Chelsea right now, and do my damnedest to make this happen. It would be this: aces. In fact, I'd have the players out on the park right now, practicing like ...err... buggery. I want to see Wanklin and Dickov lobbing Seaman on a regular basis, or you're not playing.

Glands

Regular readers of this column [or, if you are reading this in book form, you may even have taken in the previous pages] will remember that I spent my late teens as a member of the Air Cadets. This was a youth group run by the Royal Air Force, along the lines of the Scouts. Only without that dyb-dyb-dob nonsense or tying things to your woggle. Oh no! This was the real McCoy. They even gave us guns when they thought they could trust us. The fools.

We were stationed in Henley-on-Thames, a beautiful riverside town best known for its annual Regatta and the huge brawls between toffs, tourists and anarchists on Henley Bridge which marked the start of the boat racing. And Boris Johnson.

Winter times, we would be literally confined to barracks for drill nights. We'd make and fly model planes (you'd be amazed what you can manage indoors), use the radios, march up and down the drill hall, and fire the guns that the fools trusted us with.

On the long summer evenings, things were different. We had the town at our mercy, and we got out to play football, build rafts up by the river and have huge fights with the Sea Cadets. We marched around the back streets and generally had a Good Time. We always finished with a big parade outside the front of the building as the Union Flag was solemnly lowered at the end of the day.

This particularly balmy July evening saw us in formation on the parade ground at the front of the Drill Hall. Neatly lined up in our flights, boots gleaming and trousers neatly pressed, the Commanding Officer inspected his troops as part of the time-worn ceremony steeped in centuries of national pride. He exchanged a few words, read out a few notices and then turned to salute the flag.

It was then that a couple of the lads noticed we had a spectator in one of the old houses opposite the parade ground, just twenty yards away over the road.

It was the lady of the house, standing at the window, towelling herself down after a bath, completely oblivious to the testosterone-fuelled turmoil she was about to cause down below. Being a spotty teenager, you only notice two things in these circumstances, the left one and the right one. Brought up of a diet of Page Three Stunnas ("Busty Dusty gets 'em out for our Falklands Heroes" was one I remember from the time) and furtive school yard porn, we weren't disappointed.

Let me, dear reader, piece together my scant memories of our spectator's appearance. She was around forty, certainly no older, slim build that suggested that she worked out, certainly a bottle blonde and the biggest pair of top bollocks that any of us had seen on any woman, ever. And that included Darren who was a trainee fireman, and knew about stuff like this.

One by one, squadron members realised what was going on, and the parade became a sea of stupid grins and muffled laughter. From my position at the back, it appeared that the CO was saluting not the flag of our nation, so recently glorious in South Atlantic conflict against the Argentinean foe, rather a magnificent pair of 40DD bazongas in an upstairs window. I, for one, was on the edge, and it wouldn't take much to send me over.

It was at that moment she took her towel and gave both mammaries a vigorous, circular rub, ending with her giving both nips a little tweak. They wobbled like blancmanges in an earthquake, and from the looks of things, she seemed to find this most satisfying. That was it - even Mr Tipping, his salute already wavering, was now bent double with laughter, and we all followed suit. The entire squadron broke ranks, laughing, clapping and cheering.

Approximately 0.00027 seconds later, the accidental exhibitionist grasped that she'd been rumbled by a gang of unruly school-kids and their uniformed minders. She screamed. She dropped her towel, to reveal a bush that resembled a large, black fluffy poodle nestling in her lap, and whipped the curtains shut.

I told you she wasn't a natural blonde.

The applause was deafening, and lasted for several minutes, with several passers-by and Greasy Joe from the Chip Shop down the road forming a small, appreciative crowd for good measure. After we had all calmed down, Mr Simmons, our erstwhile Warrant Officer, made us all go back and do the parade again to "give the flag the respect it deserves", and we stood there while we went through a tits-free repeat of the flag-lowering.

Poor old Jez, who'd been on flag duty had missed everything, and had thought that we were laughing at him. He was even more upset when we filled him in with every single sordid detail of the episode at Greasy Joe's later, with a few extra details "she even winked at me" thrown in for good measure. Every re-telling got more and more lurid, and several weeks later I'm sure I heard a version that involved at least three lesbians, various sex aids illegal in the free world and the Kids from Fame.

The following week we turned up at the Drill Hall to find a "For Sale" sign on the house opposite. Can't think why. Mystery naked woman, we never knew your name. But thanks for the mammaries.

Haiku Corner

Buggering bollocks
I can't write sodding haiku
Total bunch of arse.

Grenade

One of the advantages of joining the Air Cadets, I found, was that you got to meet a better class of lunatic. I thought I was a pyromaniac, but Ally and Jim were a danger to society. They seemed to know all the best combinations of household chemicals for maximum results, they knew how to rig up all kinds of trip flares, rockets and things that went off loud enough to scare old ladies.

Jim also had a "mate", who'd just come back from hitching round Europe, and knowing his interest in the dark arts of exothermic chemistry, had got hold of a little present for him whilst in Spain. A Civil War vintage

German Stick Grenade. The genuine article, we were told. The lads soon found out it was a dud with none of ze banging-machen-werfer inside it, but they soon put that right with a concoction known only to themselves and certain Irish terrorist groups.

A small knot of enthusiasts were invited up to the woods around Sonning Common to take a look. And what a bunch of tin-pot idiots we must have looked: combat jackets, Dunlop Green Flash plimsolls and chunky push bikes.

We gazed on the Wehrmacht's finest weaponry in awe before strutting round the wooded clearing with jerky goose steps, shouting out "Gott in Himmel, Englander" and "Achtung Spitfire" to anyone who thought it was funny.

"Achtung!" shouted Jim, as he lobbed the grenade into the centre of the clearing.

With cries of "Fookinhell!" we dived for cover, fully expecting red hot shards of metal to fling themselves towards us.

"Relax, relax!" says Jim matter-of-factly, "You've got to pull the pin first", as we sheepishly picked ourselves up off the dirt.

There then started a game of chicken, where someone would chuck the bomb in the air, and we all legged it, still acting the idiot, shouting "Die Englander Pig Dog!" from the safety of the trees.

"You lot think you're sooo clever", beamed Ally, nonchalantly pulling the pin out of the grenade. It took him a full second to comprehend what he'd done, whereupon his jaw dropped, and his arms and legs all decided to move in different directions.

"Throw it you twat! Throw it!" Jim finally yelled from about fifty yards away, hands over his private parts to save them from shrapnel wounds.

So he did, with all the effort that his jellified arms could muster. It hit a tree with a hollow CLUNK and bounced back to land at his feet, the astonished look on his face giving way to one of desperation.

Galvanised into action, we did what any true coward would do: "Fookin' leg it!" came the cry, and we took off for the safety of the road, our bikes, Jim's house, anywhere that was a long, long way away.

As I ran, I was aware of the words "OhshitOhshitOhshitOshit" getting closer and closer. It was Ally, who had finally got both his legs working again, and pumped up on adrenaline rapidly overtook the lot of us and disappeared into the distance.

Seconds later, there was a WOOOOMPH as the thing went off, and a warm glow lit our backs momentarily. Bits of wood, leaves, pine cones, stones and the odd lump of twisted metal rained down onto the clearing. It wasn't a big explosion by any means, but it would have been enough to leave Ally in pieces up a tree somewhere.

Sheepishly, we headed back to the scene of the crime. There was a small crater, ringed by burning undergrowth.

There was also a blue flashing light. God knows how, but someone had called the Police.

"Now lads, what's all this about an explosion in these woods then?"

I must admit, it all got a bit out of control from here on in. We sold the copper a cock-and-bull story about how we were building a den up in the woods an' climbin' some trees an' stuff when all of a sudden, like, we heard an explosion, up in the sky, like, and God strike us down if we're lying sir, a meteorite landed right near us. Look at the crater, sir, just here. Amazin' sir. Couldn't believe it. Is there a reward?

He stood. He looked. He stuck his pen in the hole surrounded by charred grass. He took some notes, and the next day a load of hairy scientist types turned up in a white van and took away all the molten metal bits and some stones. The miracle of the Sonning Common Meteor even made the Henley Standard, a group of mystery schoolboys were feted as heroes, but by then we were far too busy hiding from the authorities under our beds.

As far as I know, the "meteor" is now sitting in a museum or laboratory somewhere, or at the very least has been carted off to that huge warehouse in the final scene of "Raiders of the Lost Ark" where it can do mankind no further harm.

What an evil web of lies we lead. The Man's bound to find out sooner or later. Might as well be now.

Wrong Funeral

Roger's dad died.

Roger's dad was a lovely bloke, but smoked like a chimney, and alas, this was to be the end of him. A charitable type, he helped out at our Air Cadet squadron, teaching the lads the ins-and-outs of engineering, the meaning of hard work and the definition of a choice few words into the bargain.

One day, his heart decided that he'd had one fag too many and he keeled over and died, roll-up still sticking out the corner of his mouth, the poor old bugger. The only consolation was that he didn't die at work. He was a bus driver.

Still, we were invited to pay our last respects at his funeral, and seeing as he was an instructor at the space cadets (a name given to the ATC by regular Air Force crew, as "they do nothing except take up space"), it was an all-uniform job. Black armbands, the works.

We got time off college, got changed in the back seat of my clapped-out Renault 4 (a major achievement of contortion that hinted at a future as a circus act) and headed off to Bracknell Crematorium, officially the most depressing place on Earth. It's like regular Bracknell - which is depressing enough - only with the addition of gravestones and a wrist-slashing Garden of Remembrance to distinguish it from the rest of the town. There is an Army shooting range just behind the ovens. Once in, you're unlikely to leave.

We arrived there in good time, joined up with a few of the other lads and a sombre officer corps, black arm bands making us look like the Hitler Youth on a social call. As casually as you could among the fake plastic flowers of a municipal crematorium, we mixed in the waiting room with tearful friends and relatives, making small talk about "such a wonderful person" while we waited for Roger and his mum to arrive.

And boy, they were taking their time, probably taking the bus driver's prerogative of turning up when they felt like it. In retrospect, the funny looks we got from the assembled friends and relatives should have told us everything was not quite as it seemed.

With the polite cough of a man used to working with the recently deceased and the near-dead, some bloke in a black suit ushered everybody from the waiting room into the chapel, and the coffin was carried in and placed on the dais.

Still no sign of Roger. The vicar started the service, and it was only when he referred to the deceased as "she" that the alarm bells started ringing. We thought we knew him pretty well, but we would have noticed if Roger's old man had been a woman.

The eulogy was a clincher. "Call her mum, gran, or just plain Shirley..."

"Oh bollocks!" cried the Commanding Officer just as the opening bars of "The Lord is my Shepherd" rang out on a Bontempi organ. Bollocks indeed, the entire congregation turned and stared as one, the impostors unmasked.

We legged it. I'd like to say we crept out like stealthy ninjas into the night, were it not for some thoughtless bastard scattering the pews with heavily embroidered prayer cushions exhorting us to "Praise Him!" and reminding anyone who noticed that "He is Risen!"

Ian the Shed, tall and gangling, was the first to go down, like a big ginger tree in a gale; the rest of us bundling over him like a horde of mad Belgians on It's a Knockout, it was clear he wasn't going to be risen for quite some time.

As the singing started, all dignity was lost.

The Lord's my Shepherd, I'll not want - "Get your foot out of my face."

He makes me down to lie - "You bastard, that hurts!"

In pastures green; He leadeth me - "Get your hand off my arse."

The quiet waters by. - "Christ on a bike, who's farted?"

We hid in the Garden of Remembrance, cremating a few cigarettes and swearing too much in the presence of the recently scattered, until an hour later, Roger arrived for his old man's funeral.

"I did tell you they changed it to THREE o'clock, didn't I?"

"Oh yeah, yeah. We went to the dress rehearsal an' all."

Shirley, wherever you are - we're really, really sorry.

Wales

You're a student, and only one thing matters in life. Drink. Lots of it, and preferably as cheap as possible. So it was a throwaway remark by Clive that started it all off.

"Do you know how cheap beer is in Wales?"

We didn't. He told us. We went to Wales on holiday.

The whole affair was planned like a military operation. We were to take the train to Merthyr, and walk up through Wales, climbing over three of the biggest mountains we could find. It would be a healthy two weeks of hiking and camping, set off with the desire to get rip-roaringly drunk whenever the opportunity presented. We bought piles of military-style dehydrated meals, and meticulously planned our route down to the last footstep. It was going to be hard work, but fun. You heard me: FUN!

It was late July when the six of us took off. Two hippies Steve and Martin, two slobs myself and Clive, and brothers Pat and John.

It was a blazing hot day when we finally got to Merthyr in the late morning, real T-shirt weather. It was just a shame we'd dressed for a crossing of the Antarctic. Our packs were so heavy with food, clothes and tents we could barely lift them, let alone walk. Then there was the small matter of the route march to the youth hostel near Brecon, about fifteen miles away. After about thirty minutes of trudging through the heat, we had reached the cemetery on the outskirts of Merthyr, half dead with exhaustion, more than willing to join the inhabitants.

Words cannot express the hell of that day. But I'll give it a damn good try with "Bloody fucking awful". We arrived about seven hours later, having taken a pointless so-called short cut across country that had got us hopelessly lost 400 yards from our goal, sweating like pigs and about ten pounds lighter.

You think THAT was bad. You should have seen dinner. It came out of a vacuum sealed bag marked "risotto, just add water".

We did.

We got cement.

Cement that would block up our collective arseholes for weeks to come. We had bags and bags of the stuff too. They looked like torn up cardboard and became known as "Ratpacks", on the assumption that only a rat would eat them. Or worse still, that was what they were made out of.

The next morning we dragged ourselves out of bed, hopping around on blistered feet. We had a mountain to climb. The idea was that we'd climb Pen y Fan, go over the top and arrive in Brecon in the late afternoon, happy wanderers singing the joys of summer. Bollocks to that – far too much like hard work. Up the mountain with minimal gear and back down again, and stuff those plans we'd spent weeks putting together.

With the sun still pelting down, it was a hard old slog up the mountain. And what did we do when we got there? Admire the view? Slap each other's backs on a job well done? Nope. We threw stones down the side to see how far they'd roll. I had the find of the day - a large round boulder, about the size of a basketball and weighing about fifty pounds.

"Hey guys! Look at this!" I shouted, heaving my find over the edge. I fully expected it to fall about twenty yards and stop. Instead, it shot down the mountainside like shit from a goose, gaining momentum as it went. About 1,000 feet below us there was a squad of soldiers - almost certainly SAS recruits - on a mountain route march. Like a silent movie, we watched in horror as one of them pointed up the mountain at the guided missile approaching, and they scattered in all directions, quite literally for their lives. We hid.

For a full five minutes, the boulder of doom thundered on. At one stage it ripped through a flock of sheep, miraculously missing every one of the panicking beasts. Then it chased a horse for a good hundred yards before slamming into a dry stone wall, sending shards of shattered rock in all directions.

I was in fits of laughter at my achievement. The lads weren't. Steve the hippie, despite thinking the law was Babylon itself, was all in favour of handing me in to the police if I'd had killed anyone, and continuing the holiday without me. The others were in full agreement, and Pat and John already had me in an arm-lock, just in case the SAS decided to come up the mountain to sort out their attackers.

"You TWAT!" was the politest comment that the usually laid back Martin offered, though he was finally beginning to laugh by then. Back at the hostel, I was put on ratpack duty. For ever.

That night, exhausted, we decided that the over-optimistic itinery was going in the bin. Huge, boring slices of walking were cut out, replaced by bus and pub. The next morning, we flagged down a bus outside the youth hostel which dropped us in Rhayader, cutting out three day's hard slog on the roads.

Ah, Rhayader! A crossroads, five churches and more pubs than you could shake a shitty stick at. We pitched our three tents at a ridiculously cheap camp site populated by a bunch of snotty kids and carnivorous sheep, cooked another meal of shredded cardboard and hit the town. Village. Whatever.

"Six pints of your finest, Landlord!" shouted Pat, who when not eating cardboard usually existed on a liquid diet. "That's me sorted, what are you guys having?" Years later, when he finally got a job, he asked that his pay-checks be sent to a pub in Farnborough "to cut out the middle man". He eventually developed an allergy to Guinness, which forced the brewing giant to lay off dozens of workers as a result.

I have to admit that we got very, very drunk. Outstandingly so. There were more pubs in Rhayader than seemed physically possible and we tried them all. All I can remember of this night is the fact that one pub was SO full of young ladies desperate for our attention, they were spreading themselves across the pool table while Pat and Clive were trying to line up a shot. Even if they were naked and holding up signs saying "Get it here, you foul-smelling English studs", we still wouldn't have been interested. I look back on that night with a certain amount of shame.

However, I couldn't help thinking that they would have been more than a little disappointed when an invitation to "come back to my place" meant a reeking sleeping bag in a field full of hippies.

We eventually regained consciousness the next afternoon. Steve had somehow come into possession of a tap, so presumably the centre of Rhayader was on the verge of flooding. The whole town knew there were six English idiots nearby who had spurned the advances of their local slappers, and were now hell-bent on washing the place into the Irish Sea. We had to get away, and fast before the baying hate mob caught up with us.

With heads pounding, we struck camp and ambled for two miles up the River Wye towards our next objective, a youth hostel halfway up a mountain in the middle of nowhere.

We never made it. Each step was a sickening lurch in exhausted hangover-land. We broke through some trees to find a beautiful bend in the river, completely secluded from human contact. Sod the hostel, this was real Marlboro country, only without the cancer sticks. We're going to live like cowboys, true heroes to the last. We're going to sleep on the dried up river bed on the inside of the bend with a whopping great camp fire to keep us warm. It would rule.

There were one or two details us ignorant, drunken townies failed to take into account...

1. The dead sheep lying fifty yards upstream in the river whose "crystal clear" waters we were so readily drinking from.

2. Lighting a fire directly onto a dried up river bed of large pebbles does tend to make the stones explode with extreme sleeping-bag-burning force.

3. When it rains heavily during the night, dried up river beds have a tendency to become raging torrents.

And that's what we found out. Come dawn, all six of us were cowering in a hastily erected two-man tent, beating off half the sheep in Wales with a stolen tap as they tried to join us in the only piece of shelter for miles around. See? The females of Wales were throwing themselves at us, and we still didn't get the message.

Later that day we reached the Youth Hostel. It was from another world. The only water they had came from the previous night's rain. They didn't have any electricity either, and all the light came from olde-worlde gas lanterns. All very nice, but even halfway up a mountain in Wales it's not what you'd come to expect from twentieth century civilisation. Another meal of shredded cardboard, and after the best part of a week on the road, it emerged that only one of us had managed a crap. Outside, the natives were building a wicker man.

Grimly, we struggled on. Walk. Bus. Pub. Walk. Bus. Mountain. Pub. Train. Pub. Walk. Bus.

Soon, we found ourselves at the foot of Mount Snowdon, the tallest mountain in Wales. We'd planned a simple ascent up the Watkin Path, which was a fairly gentle uphill stroll until you reach the last few hundred feet. Then, it turns into a wall of rock that saps any energy you may have had left. At least we were no longer carrying cardboard food rations, and we were pretty much used to our backpacks by now. From flabby townies, we had become rock-hard, hard-drinking adventurers.

As it turned out, it was a nicely leisurely first couple of hours to the summit before the path suddenly lurched up on the steep final ascent. Then, in the noon-day sun, it was a killer. We scrambled up as best we could, the only thing on our minds was a pint in the bar on the mountain summit.

"I hope it's still open by the time we get there" I mused.

"No sorry mate, it's just closed" came the reply from some joker going in the opposite direction.

That was far too much to take. "If it is", I said, "I'll come after you and rip your bloody head off and use your brains to paint my house".

Nervous laughter.

I was rabid and only half joking, and it took the rest of the guys to physically restrain me from carrying out my drink-crazed threat.

In the end, there was no problem with the bar, which probably saved Mr Smart-Bastard's life. The problem lay with the quality. Fizzy keg rubbish. The lads were outraged, but they drank it anyway, and we passed the time watching some idiot accidentally drop his rucksack down the side of the mountain. It was very much like the earlier Boulder of Death episode on Pen y Fan, except with this person's entire worldly goods. Luckily for him, it caught a sheep square in the side, saving him a trek of several miles. The sheep was OK, and spent the next few minutes savaging the rucksack until it was a mass of clothes, sheep shit and saliva. How we laughed.

All we had to do now was get off that mountain and get out of Wales. Easier said than done. The six of us arrived in Bangor-on-Dee of a Saturday afternoon just as it was closing. What we didn't know was that this part of Wales is VERY religious, and closing meant CLOSED. Everything. Even the station, and we'd missed the last train until Monday morning.

The worst bit was, and we didn't know this either, that after two weeks on the road, we smelt funny. Sure, we'd washed at some stage - if your idea of washing was jumping into a river fully clothed seven days and two mountains ago. And no-one had the front to come out and tell us. We were students. Personal hygiene was for people with jobs.

So, there we were, trapped for two days in the most closed town in the world. What could six foul-smelling students do with themselves to pass the hours? The youth hostel took one look at us and told us they were "full" and politely let us sleep in the grounds, but come Sunday we were on our own. Of course, it wasn't all doom and gloom. There was always the streets.

Idea! We'll go to church! The local clergy would take care of us, paupers that we were. Free bread and wine, too. Didn't Jesus say something about providing food and shelter to strangers?

Two minutes later, and we were back on the streets again on the sharp end of some of the hardest vicars known to man. They threw us out because we scared the old biddies who were now cowering in the vestry. Come on, Jesus had a beard and hung around with blokes that stunk of fish, and I bet he never got thrown out of church.

By a stroke of luck we found a tea room that was open for the Devil's service on a Sunday. It was full to the gills with happy customers partaking in tea and cake. But not to us. "Sorry, we're closing", said a waiter with a clothes peg on his nose. Several elderly customers, I noticed, were already wearing gas masks.

We took the hint. In the end, we managed to beg some food from the back door of a restaurant like a bunch of tramps, which was, in effect, what we had become. Monday couldn't come fast enough, and bright and early we were on the first train out of there.

Funnily enough, for a Monday morning commuter train, there were an awful lot of empty seats around us.

However, we were totally unprepared for a smart, clean shaven young man to come and sit among us.

"Sorry mate, that seat's taken."

"Whaddaya mean 'taken' you bastards?"

It was John. He'd had a wash and a shave. Even his own brother hadn't recognised him. When I got home, my dog chased me out of the house. I had two baths, and my clothes actually walked their own way to the washing machine, where they dissolved into a brown sludge.

As far as I know, there are still court orders barring me from Wales. Lovely place. Smells funny.

Chemistry

You've got to hand it to my teachers. They always tried to innovate and make our school experience different from other run-of-the-mill schools. OK, in the case of the luscious, pouting Miss Shagwell, it basically involved wearing as little as possible and shitting [*Author's note: this is one of many spelling mistakes in this volume which I have decided not to correct for purposes of unintentional hilarity*] on her desk with her legs apart, but you get the idea.

In the science labs, they really wanted to do things differently from the traditional, and frankly boring, learning-by-rote that was a curse on the modern system. So they went mental and abandoned the tried-and-tested route of the core sciences Biology, Chemistry and Physics in favour of a hotch-potch of half-baked ideas called "Integrated Sciences".

We wasted a lot of time drawing leaves, "identifying patterns", comparing colours of stuff in test tubes and heating up even more stuff that didn't do anything terribly exciting, while kids at other schools were doing things the old-fashioned way. And the right way, as it turned out. Our entire course was, I found out far too late, a load of wanky bollocks.

So when I reached college to study for my A-levels, it transpired that I'd spent the last five years of my life doing absolutely nothing; and of chemistry in particular, I knew precisely squat. I swiftly came to the conclusion that anything above a fail grade would be a triumph. Dr Lawson knew that I was a kill-or-cure, giving me a list of books, which stacked on top of each other, were about three feet tall. They contained words like "valances", "ionization" and "dielectric constant". I was doomed.

For the next two years Dr Lawson crammed seven years worth of knowledge into my head, until the blood came out of my ears. I knew absolutely nothing about the theory of chemistry, and struggled with all the simple stuff my fellow students took for granted. When it came to practical work, thanks to my teenage years of setting fire to things, I found I had a natural talent, and that would ultimately save me from failing the course.

It all hinged on the final A-Level exam that June. The written paper, as I suspected, had been an utter nightmare, but I managed to bullshit my way through it and hopefully get a grade. Any grade. I wasn't going to be particular. Anything higher than an F would be just dandy.

Then came the practical test. We were given quantities of chemicals we were asked to identify, find atomic weights, do strange measurements with mass spectrometers and arcane stuff that may or may not turn lead into gold.

Silently, grimly, we set to work. Add a bit of acid, test for fumes. Heat it up, check for colour changes. All well-drilled and things were going well.

Things would have been absolutely peachy if I hadn't tried to sneak a peak at Joanne Sutton's arse at a crucial moment. I was heating up some almost random concoction of dangerous chemicals over the blue heat of a bunsen burner. Just one little peak. Just one little twitch of the hand at the wrong moment. Excuse: I was eighteen years old. Girl's arses were important then. As arses went, Joanne's was a denim-clad peach.

WOOF.

Flames shot out of my test tube and spread over the bench in a way you only ever see when a car blows up in an action movie. A great gobbet of burning goo fired out of the end, arced through the air and hit Dr Lawson squarely on the back.

His lab coat was now on fire. Oh, how we laughed.

Dilemma. This was an exam, on which the futures of a dozen young people depended. You're not supposed to speak. So is it the done thing to tell the invigilator that you've just set him on fire?

With smoke and eerie green flames now wafting up his back to his shirt collar, I thought I'd better risk it.

"Errr... Dr Lawson? Fire?"

He sprung into action, grabbing the lab's fire blanket and dousing the flames that were playing across the workbench. My answer paper had a lovely antique-style burnt fringe to it, which would certainly add some gritty realism for the examiner.

"No sir, it's you."

The flames were right up his back and you could smell singed hair. If he didn't know he was on fire by know, he must be made out of asbestos.

At last, he twigged, ripped off his lab coat and we took turns stamping on it. The green sticky stuff got stuck to his Hush Puppies, and carried on relentlessly burning, melting the sole of his shoes as he finally beat the flames out.

There was a stunned silence as everybody else turned and stared at the tableau unfolding in front of them. Dr Lawson stood there, a plume of smoke rising from his head.

Joanne Sutton stared at me with a look which said "you utter, utter spastic", and another arse was lost to me for eternity.

"Well don't just stand there," said Lawson in his broad Northern tones "You've got an exam to pass."

"Burns easily with green flame," I wrote. "May be Copper based."

In the middle of August, my grades flopped onto my doormat. Mathematics: D. Physics: D. Chemistry: E. Result! By today's lax standards, those would equate to straight A grades and I would have made it to Cambridge to chum it up with Stephen Hawking. That's what I call a lucky escape.

Golf

Golf! I quite liked the idea of golf, if you forgot the bad trousers and the natural association with chinless silly buggers. My Grandad, being the life member of a noted course in Northern Ireland, coaxed me into taking up the game, and I took it up with a gusto. I'm still not that bad with my mashie niblick out on the Weymouth pitch and putt, but back in my teens, it was a steep learning curve.

Large metal clubs? Small round projectile weapons? Entrusted to me by unsuspecting parents? Were they mad? I mean, what possible damage could I do?

I'll draw a discrete veil over my dad's greenhouse. It was a one hundred per cent fluky accident. All I was doing was practicing my short game up and down the garden, aiming for the washing line pole. One tremendously skilful shot actually hit the target, but with a little more power than intended. The ricochet resulted in subsequent loss of pocket money, and a ban on playing round the house. My Uncle Mick (one of those people who cannot drive past a golf course without slowing down to a crawl whilst saying "Oooh! Golf!") practices by chipping balls over his house. Woe betide anyone coming up the driveway.

It was decided, therefore, that I should go on a golfing holiday. Not only that, my parents could kill several birds with one stone by sending me over to Ireland to stay with my golf-mad grandparents and have me out of the house for a couple of weeks. They even gave me spending money. Lots of it, and my green fees were covered for the whole holiday. They even laid on a golfing partner - a local kid about my age named

William by his none-more-Orange parents. I promised to be on my best behaviour. As if I would let them down.

It was ace. I would meet William at nine in the morning, and we would go round the course again and again until we were dizzy. Sometimes we'd even manage to complete a hole without hacking it to pieces. William even managed a hole-in-one on the short fourth - a shot that went in off a tree, but as there was no adult member around to witness it, the feat existed only in our twisted memories. To celebrate, we fished a load of old balls out of the pond and took turns at whacking them from the sixth tee into Belfast Lough, no more than thirty yards away.

I had recently become a New Romantic, discovering the delights of the mighty Ultravox and Depeche Mode. I hefted my clubs round the course in the full outfit.

"That long black coat of yours," said Grandad, "Is costing you two shots a hole."

Yes, but dammit, I was the coolest kid on the course. Not for me the tartan trousers and the Pringle jersey! It was black, black, black, but I did spare the old man's blushes in the clubhouse by going light on the make-up.

On July 29th 1981, William and I had the entire course to ourselves as one Charles Windsor tied the knot with a certain and not-bonkers-at-all Diana Spencer. We went round four times and then hogged the snooker room until we were kicked out at closing time.

But fifteen-year-old William had more than one love. He loved his golf and his snooker, but more than both he loved Mary Donnelly. Mary was the seventeen-year-old daughter of the club captain, a glorious young lady of those certain proportions that they only make in Ireland, who made William walk like he had two overripe plums dangling between his legs.

Which he did.

She was a golfing goddess, whose very presence on the course would leave William a quivering mess, desperate to impress his true love with his prowess on the greens. It would have been easier, in retrospect, just to ask her out.

With Mary and her old man waiting behind us, William teed up to drive off the first. A bag of nerves, he focused on the ball, Mary's chest, the ball, Mary's legs, the ball, his balls and then back on the ball again. With a silent prayer, he let fly with a mighty not-quite-in-the-manual swing and thrashed the ball straight down the middle of the fairway.

In his dreams.

In fact, the ball flew fifty yards straight up in the air, perched at the top of its arc, and landed three feet away from his feet, taunting him with the words "Stolen from Downpatrick Driving Range".

Clenching and unclenching his fists, a man defeated, he let his true love play through. Whether this was to hide his embarrassment, or just to watch her arse was never made clear.

We watched them disappear down the first fairway. Her dad hit a sparkling drive, and she followed suit, both finishing off with respectable par fours. I could watch her bending over to pick her ball out of the hole all day, and I did. Then it was our turn. I got there in seven. William, still shitting bricks, finally holed out for twelve after playing bagatelle with a few trees, a rabbit hole and a water hazard that no-one had noticed before.

Onwards to the second.

My drive bumped and rattled up the hill, a whole fifty yards, with a huge divot of grass managing to go further. With the object of his affection just reaching the green, William managed to keep the ball on the island and hit one right up the middle. We strutted after our balls.

Another three scuffed shots and we were within a hundred yards or so from the green. A couple of halfway decent, if rather weedy, hits would see us within chipping distance, so we went for it. William did exactly that, and scooped one into a bunker some twenty yards short.

Then it was my turn. I addressed the ball, swung, and fully expected to top the thing and see it scuttling along the ground, yard by yard, on its merry way to the target.

Except I didn't. I caught it full on the meat of the club, and gave it a mighty thwack that would have had Nick Faldo in orgasms.

One thing rapidly became clear - there was no way on God's Earth that my little white ball of fury was going to stop before it hit the green. It was going like the clappers - a greenhouse killer, if you like. And right in its path stood Mary and her scary dad, the club captain who drove a huge Volvo and probably ate fifteen-year-old hackers for breakfast, using their smashed golf clubs as a toothpick.

"FORE!" I shouted.

Except it came out "........shit......."

"FORE" shouted William.

Except it came out "Get out the fuckin' way!"

They didn't get out the fuckin' way, and the ball bounced once and caught Mary's Dad right in the back just as he lined up a birdie putt.

The world stood still. Nothing happened. The ball seemed to stick in the middle of his back, like it was glued there. It dropped onto the green with a barely audible thud. Then, like a grand old tree succumbing to the woodman's axe, Mary's Dad keeled over forwards onto his face, his putter pinging away, bent double by the impact of body and ground.

Oops.

"FORE!" I shouted, rather too late.

For such a calamitous faux pas, things turned out rather better than expected. Despite our initial plan of running away and joining the Navy, we decided to peel the poor bloke off the second green before he damaged the grass in any way, as fatal injuries notwithstanding, it was very poor form to annoy the green-keeper.

Mary's Dad was rather forgiving about the whole affair, and let us join him and Mary as a foursome. This was a suggestion that turned poor William's game from just about passable to the equivalent of a hundred monkeys with a hundred toy golf clubs. Eventually, they'll come up with a round of golf, but you'll get a whole lot of shit before you do. All he wanted from life was a twosome behind the gazebo on the fifth.

The only words he ever spoke to her were "Can I polish your ball?" while standing by the washer on the eighth tee. She politely declined, and inside he died. Her ball remained unpolished, and he eventually became a nun, such was the depth of his shame.

On the other hand, she said to me "You're quite the golfer", and she was allowed to come round to my grandparents' house - as the captain's daughter - for Sunday tea; and I accidentally got to see her arse when the door of the downstairs toilet swung open at an inopportune moment. I gave her my phone number. She never rung.

William hated me.

I told him about her arse.

William hated me and tried to force a pitching wedge down my throat.

On Philosophy

This week, I have busied myself with questions of a philosophical and scientific bent, and for good reason.

Saturday 7th August 2004 was an auspicious day in the Duck household. The first ever asking of that greatest of philosophers' questions in our home, a question first put by Aristotle to Socrates in 487BC, and pondered by the finest minds of humanity ever since.

This is a question that has defined the very shape of our world, the fragility of the human psyche and has caused the rise and fall of great empires. Not just a question. *The* question.

Did not Our Lord ask this of Judas Iscariot at the Second from Last Supper? A question asked, forsooth, by Lady Macbeth of her husband in Act II Scene I of The Scottish Play; revisited as part of Abraham Lincoln's famous Gettysburg Address, a theme eventually taken up by Martin Luther King in his stirring "I have a Dream" speech. And now, with our lives at a crossroads, our very future in the balance, it was the turn of Scaryduckling.

So it goes:

"Are you a Benny tied to a tree?"

I answered, naturally, in the negative.

Scientists and thinkers have struggled with the Benny Controversy and its implications for humanity for decades. In his now famous experiment into Benny Theory, Erwin Schroedinger demonstrated that the very act of ascertaining whether the subject is tied to a tree or is a Benny on the Loose causes the so-called Deacon Field to collapse, risking widespread contamination with Benny germs. Because of the dangers, the Schroedinger's Benny experiment is never likely to be attempted.

Albert Einstein spent many of his later years pondering this so-called Loose Benny problem. In an elegant solution proposed in his "Special" Theory, he realised that the curved nature of the universe allows the subject to be simultaneously on the loose **and** tied to a tree. The implications of this proved devastating for the people of Vladivostok, when in 1954 an uncontrolled Benny leak at the city's naval dockyards left several square miles completely uninhabitable, and still contaminates the population today.

Indeed, much modern thinking in the field of quantum mechanics is based around theories of multiple dimensions, parallel universes and free-radical Benny particles, where all solutions to the Loose Benny Problem can exist, including the so-called Humphries Dimension, where scientists theorise that there are no trees and is populated by nothing but Bennies on the Loose. However, as Schroedinger's Benny points out, merely attempting to view these events may even bring about the end of our universe through a destabilizing of the time-spazz matrix.

Professor Stephen Hawking has neatly sidestepped this problem and the potential threat to our existence posed by a rampaging critical mass of Bennies by instead devoting his energies to an entirely different question. Hawking boils it down to a succinct four words in an updated edition of his classic "A Brief History of Time": "Have you got Skill?" Alas, even Hawking's enormous intellect cannot answer the unanswerable, and we must resign ourselves to the fact that Bennies will always be on the loose. And they've got African Bum Disease.

Surfing

Surfing! The ancient battle between dude and sea. Ever since the aborigines jumped up on a dead kangaroo* and rode the wave back to shore, mankind has embraced this most noble of past-times like a favourite son that hasn't washed for a month. Famous surfers include that fella off the opening titles of Hawaii 5-0 and ...err... Keanu Reeves.

Surfing. It's ace.**

Newquay is the surfing capital of the universe, apart from all those other places like Hawaii and Australia. It is also the holiday destination for every tosser on the planet who seem to think it's the coolest place in the world. Which it isn't. As a veteran of Cornish holidays (I've only got to go there for the next three hundred years to qualify as a local), you soon appreciate that the nearer you get to Newquay, the higher the wanker quotient.

127

So why in the name of God did we decide to visit Newquay? Ah yes, I remember now. We thought it would be cool to go surfing. It could only end in tears. In fact, I could guarantee it.

Fistral Beach, then, is a long, windswept curve of golden sand with some of the finest surfing waves in the country. I stood there, shivering in my Marks and Spencer bathing trunks while my brother negotiated the old getting-changed-wrapped-in-a-towel stunt, the traditional on-holiday contortion mastered by hapless Britons on the beach since the beginning of recorded history. At last, we were ready, handing over a sizeable deposit to the muscular and tanned board hire bloke.

"Strewth!" he said, spotting two skinny nerks trying to join the in-crowd, "You two fellas know how to use these things?"

"Yes", we lied. We'd seen Hawaii Five-O, "Piece of piss."

Out on the brine, the experts were cutting up the water like old pros. And unlike these total no-hopers, we were taking the dog with us too.

So, out onto the waves we went, paddling our boards out ever deeper until we were at the point where the waves were just starting to break. Time to fly.

There were girls watching. Real-life surfy girls with proper lady-bumps, on the prowl for roughly-hewn surfers. People like us. Rarr.

With a swift paddle, I launched myself onto a wave and I was away. Now to find my feet.

Hup!

Splash.

Arse-over-tit.

It was at this point that we both became conscious of the fact that this surfing lark may be rather more difficult than it appeared. In the next two hours, I spent approximately ninety minutes with my head under water, drinking South West Water's finest sewage outfall, something which would only worry me for the next few days.

Then, finally, with a shout of triumph, I was finally up and standing, surfing the waves like a true star. Then I realised I was in about three inches of water with the tailfin wedged in the sand. Bumflaps. But it was a start.

My confidence increased, and fairly soon, I could ride a wave, fall off and look like I knew what I was doing. Time, then, to go for The Big

One. I'd go out with the big boys and ride one all the way back to the beach, and I too would attract girls, get a great tan, and if I was really, really lucky, chest hair.

Then, it came.

Like that huge wave at the end of Point Break, it was a monster. I turned the board, and looked along the line of surfers, all ready for the ride of their lives. It hit. We paddled. Three - two -one and HUP! Onto my feet and riding for the first time ever - I was a real surfer! King of the World!

For a whole twenty-seven nanoseconds.

With a blood-curdling scream I looked down into the valley of doom, and was flipped head first into the drink, taking huge gulps of shit and tampon-strewn water.

At this point in the tale, there's one thing you should know about surfboards. They come with a little velcro strap on the end of a long elastic. You put the strap round your ankle, so when you come off, you don't have to spend hours chasing after your board. This little device saved me hours of frantic wading up and down the beach, but it was soon to have its awful revenge.

"Spang!" went the elastic band, as the board was swept away from me.

"Spong!" it heaved as it reached full stretch.

"Spung!" it went as it accelerated toward me at a rate of knots.

"JESUSFUCKINGCHRISTMYARSE!" I shouted as the sharp end of the board caught me squarely up the rusty sheriff's badge.

Not on either cheek, but right up the hole. A perfect bull's-eye.

That was it. I was getting out. The surf bums were openly laughing at me. And worse, so were girls.

"Hey!" said my brother, "You're bleeding!"

He was right. The board had split my trunks clean in two, showing my bleedin' bleeding ring-piece to the entire beach.

Only one thing for it. Clench the buttocks and make for the hills as best you can.

"Fun?" asked the board hire dude as I gave him his evil bit of wood back.

"Yes", I lied.

"You do know your arse is bleeding," he observed.

Yes, I knew.

"And there's a big split in your trunks," continued the graduate from the University of the Bloody Obvious.

I'm pleased to report that it stopped bleeding eventually. However, at three o'clock the following morning, the gallons of ingested sewage struck back.

It was a camping holiday.

I was in a sleeping bag.

With an aching ring, which was about to spend the next thirty-six hours on fire, squirting brown windsor soup through the eye of a needle.

The camp-site toilets only had Izal shiny white paper.

Fill in the blanks for yourself.

Worst. Holiday. Ever.

* May not actually be true.
** No it's not, it's shit.

Behind the Sofa

Two words: Gay Daleks. And I'm not just saying that because Russell T Davies of "Queer as Folk" fame wrote the Dr Who comeback. Some of my best friends are stereotypes, after all. But think about it of a bit. I've always though the whole concept was a bit suspect. You never, ever see female daleks, do you? All those butch, manly pepper-pots cooped up in a spaceship together, plotting the downfall of the galaxy under the command of mad scientist Davros, a confirmed bachelor if ever I saw one. There's an awful lot of pent-up aggression in that set-up that's just got to come out somewhere.

"OOH. I'LL. SCRATCH. YOUR. EYES. OUT."

Perhaps that's why they're so angry. Alienated from an ...err... alien culture with no concept of gender or sexual equality, they're thrashing out at society in the only way they know how. Maybe, and I'm prepared to be corrected here, there ARE female and itty-bitty kiddie daleks out there, living in happy family units in heterosexual harmony, going on day trips to the dalek equivalent of the Lakeside Shopping Centre. It's just that they're not scary enough for The Doctor and K-9 to battle to the death.

"DAD. DAD. TABITHA. KEEPS. TRYING.TO. EX-TERM-IN-ATE. ME."

"TOBY. STARTED. IT. HE. KEEPS. POKING. ME. WITH. HIS. PLUNGER."

"RIGHT. THAT'S. IT. DON'T. MAKE. ME. STOP. THE. CAR. AND COME. BACK. THERE."

"NOW. YOU'VE. GONE. AND. ANNOYED. YOUR. FATHER. THAT'S. THE. LAST. TIME. WE. TAKE. YOU. ANYWHERE."

Come to think of it, I'm having difficulty imagining how daleks would "get in on" in the first place, be they gay or straight. They just don't have the equipment for it, unless those bobbly bits have some function they've never told us about.

"OH. LUCINDA. YOU. HAVE. SUCH. A. BEAUTIFUL. EYE. STALK."

"OH. GREG. THE. WAY. YOU. THRUST. YOUR. RAY. GUN. MAKES. ME. FEEL. WONDERFUL. INSIDE."

"FANCY. COMING. UPSTAIRS. FOR. A. QUICK. ONE."

"WE. CAN'T. GREG. EVERYONE. KNOWS. WE. CAN'T. GO. UP. STAIRS."

"OH. BOLL-OCKS."

And don't get me started on the Cybermen.

The Way of the Exploding Fish

WARNING: "The following paragraphs contain scenes of fish filleting which some readers may find disturbing."

Fishing. What the bloody hell is that all about? Crap, that's what.

You sit for hours on end next to some poxy lake on the half chance that some fish will be stupid enough to bite the hook you've left lying around for them.

My brother loved fishing. Matt next door loved fishing. Whole swarms of kids who also loved fishing would descend on the gravel pits of a weekend, grasping rods and green boxes filled with maggots. My dad was yet another fishing nut, and virtually threw me out of the door with a rod in my hand so he could enjoy a quiet kid-free weekend. I wasted hours waiting for something to happen. What a waste of life. I want it back.

I soon found out that I wasn't the only kid forced down the lakes against their will. After approximately ten minutes of tedium, I gave up altogether and went for a walk, where I found kindred spirits wishing they were doing something, anything more interesting. Matt, it turned out, despite his faux enthusiasm for the hobby, was one of them and would do anything to slack off. We also found John and Squagg, victims of their parents' desire for a quiet Saturday. Will, on the other hand, loved fishing. He had all the gear, several rods, keep net, landing net, stool, and a little tent thing, all guilt presents from his absent dad. He represented everything we hated about fishing. He had to die.

He also had one gadget that immediately caught our eye. A ground bait catapult. It was a genuine catapult that you used to fire off handfuls of maggots into the middle of the lake to attract the fish. It didn't take us long to see that this had possibilities...

"Dad? Can I have some money for a ground bait catapult?"

CH-CHING! Sorted.

Next weekend we went to the lakes suitably armed. Catapult. Marbles. Large stockpile of French bangers purchased on a recent trip to Calais, huge double dose of maggots straight out of the vending machine at the garage. How many customers mistook it for a coke machine and got a wriggling mass of bluebottle larvae? The mind boggles. And who, in the name of our lady of donkey poop, had the job of keeping the monster topped up?

And so it came to pass that after a token ten minutes of fishing (total catch, as usual = sod all) we'd had enough and went in search of Will. And sure enough, he was in is usual place just below the weir, all his gear laid out nicely, set for a day of rollercoaster excitement that is coarse fishing.

Pang! The first handful of maggots was shot out of the catapult and caught Will square in the back. The wrigglers bounced off his parka coat, and in a rather pleasing result, several ended up in his lunch box. By firing into the air from under cover of bushes, we found we could simulate a rather pleasing heavenly shower of maggots coming in from all directions. How we laughed.

It wasn't long before we were back, pelting him with maggots, marbles and bits of mud, but the novelty soon wore thin. There's only so much unanswered cruelty you can hand out before you get bored.

It wasn't long before we came across Lewis. Lewis was our friendly local psychopath, who was made to go fishing in an attempt to calm him down. It was not, however, a complete success. Lewis was only interested in fishing for pike, the fishy equivalent of the football hooligan, which he then proceeded to whup over the head with a stick to kill them.

"Hey lads!" said Lew, "Look what I've got!"

It was a whopper of a pike, about two feet long, huge spiky teeth and stone dead, something to do with the club hammer lying on the ground next to him. At a guess.

"D'you want it?" he asked.

A plan formed in our heads. An evil one. Of course we wanted it. We paid him in maggots, sweets, marbles and French bangers. He was pleased. What we did next was neither big nor clever, and fishy rights activists will hate me for it. But...

After a few minutes spent "preparing" the fish, we returned to Will's fishing hole. Needless to say, the Firework Code never warned us about sticking bangers up a dead fish's arse. So we were in the clear, then.

"Hey Will! Look what we've got!"

"Wow! That's a beauty! Can I hold it?"

"Of course you can mate, of course you can. Could you weigh it for us while we're here?"

Instructions for Blowing Up Fish:

* *Congratulations for purchasing this Semtex Primed Explosive Fish! This fine piece of equipment will give you several seconds of enjoyment if used according to the manufacturer's manual.*

* *Light fuse sticking out of pike's mouth with "pretending to look hard" cigarette cadged off Lewis.*

* *Hand over fine, yet dead, aquatic specimen to unsuspecting victim.*

* *Stand well back.*

* *Spend a couple of minutes filling out guarantee card.*

* *Laugh like a bastard.*

I should, at this point, tell you that French bangers are nothing like the girlie ones you buy in the shops in England in the run-up to Bonfire Night. These ones are about four to six inches long, an inch across and look exactly like a stick of dynamite as purchased by Wile E Coyote from Acme. They also produced a bang to match. In short, they were evil.

"Yup", said Will, "she's a real beauty. Six pounds at least..."

There was a less-than-muffled explosion as Pikey went off in a shower of fish bits. Will took the full force, falling off his stool to land on his arse in the lake, legs flailing around madly.

"You bastards! Just wait till I tell my mum!" he shouted through a goo-splattered face.

He didn't need to. In one of those turns of fate that could only happen in a not-made-up-at-all tale such as this, the Bailiff chose this very moment to come round to check our fishing licences. And face facts, he didn't like what he saw. Especially if your professional career is dedicated to stopping pimply thirteen-year-old youths sitting up to their waists in the drink, covered in fish guts and holding onto the smoking tail end of a recently deceased fish.

That rather-too-familiar quote that was the bane of my life: "What the bloody hell's going on here?"

It was a fair cop. The Bailiff gave us a right old bollocking and took away our fishing permits, telling us never to show our faces on "his" lake ever again. Gutted, I don't think.

As small victories went, we had managed to get out of the weekend fishing chore for once and for all, and there was nothing our parents could do about it. Nothing, however, could have saved us from the onslaught we got from Will's mum later that day. There is just no defence against a mad forty-something battleaxe with a grudge. Especially one armed with half a fish and right on her side...

Will, if you're reading this, we're really, really sorry*.

*Lie

Aerosol

Let us begin with The Swedish Chemist Shop Joke:
A man walks into a chemist shop in Stockholm.
"Good morning," he says, "I wish to buy some deodorant."
"Ball or aerosol?"
"Neither. I want it for my armpits."

The street where we lived in Twyford always seemed to be in a state of flux. Some of the houses were owned by British Airways, and they rented them out to staff to keep them local. Most of the time, however, there were always a few left empty, and this gave us the chance to do what thirteen year old kids loved to do: doss around on someone else's property.

Me, my bruv, neighbours John and Matt were rather too adventurous for our own good. We'd all been told by our parents to a) stay away from those empty houses ("They belong to somebody and they'll be cross"); and b) never play with fire ("Don't come running to us if you end up engulfed in a ball of flame").

Already this tale has an air of inevitability to it.

Matt's garage was a treasure trove. He was the last to move into the estate, and his parents had filled the garage with boxes of stuff from their previous place in London. Matt's dad was a do-it-yourself freak years before it became fashionable to knock your house about until it screamed for mercy, and one of these boxes was filled with aerosol cans of paint and all kinds of dodgy chemicals with great big red warning signs on the side. Naturally, we got to them before he did.

At this point, I'd like to blame television entirely for what happened next. One of us had seen a James Bond film where Sean Connery kills a deadly snake with a blast from an aerosol can sprayed over a lit cigar. It produced a flame several feet long and looked dead cool. We had the goods. We had to try it.

The garden at number twenty-seven was ideal. It was a corner plot in a dead end, so none of the other houses overlooked it. And it had been empty for months. We didn't have cigars, but we had a cigarette lighter "liberated" from an ashtray at the village hall. But first things first - it was

135

dark and getting cold, so, hearing our most primitive of instincts, we lit a nice big bonfire from scrap wood and warmed our bones.

Then it was time. Matt flipped the lighter on, and John hit the button on the first can. There was a loud "**PHWOOOOOUM!**" and a sheet of flame shot out a good five feet, singeing Matt's hair and eyebrows. Wow. We all had a go, and with expert manipulation of the flame and using a rolled up newspaper instead of the fag lighter, we found we could have four flames on the go at once.

It wasn't before the first cries of "Achtung Flammenwerfer English Pig Dog!" were heard and attempts were made to set fire to each others' arses. It seemed the right thing to do at the time, and hardly anyone got killed.

Equally impressive was finding that one of the tins contained some kind of foam which was, happily, "WARNING! HIGHLY FLAMMABLE!" We could spray a message on the wall and set fire to it before it evaporated. Three of us were rolling on the ground in hysterics, watching through tears of laughter as Matt set fire to the word "FUCK" in six foot high letters.

By this time, we were getting through aerosol cans at an alarming rate, and our stash of a dozen cans of highly flammable paint stripper was running out fast. What I didn't know was then as each one ran out, Matt was chucking them onto the roaring bonfire to be devoured by the flames.

The label on each and every one of these cans reads: "WARNING! Pressurised contents. Do not puncture or burn, even when empty". And we were about to find out why.

BOOOOOOMPH!!!!!!!! The first can exploded in a ball of flame and shot out of the fire like a rocket, missing my head by inches and clattering onto the nearby garage roof.

BLAM! WOOOMPH!!!! BOOOOOOMPHA!!!! One by one the cans went off, and we were literally running for our lives. Smouldering metal and plastic was raining down around us as we hit the street, meeting our neighbours running the other way to find out what the bloody hell was going on. The two elderly lesbians at number forty were convinced it was the Blitz all over again, while the ex-copper three doors down from me suspected rogue IRA dissidents.

Our parents, however, knew the long-and-the-short of it, as we were betrayed by our guilty faces and the unused aerosols still in our hands. Dad dragged us home with the classic "small boy side-hair tweak" (extremely painful), and once again we were sent to our rooms, grounded and banned from doing anything exciting or interesting, ever.

Two weeks later, buoyed with the joys of throwing dangerous things onto bonfires, we threw a half-full five litre oil can onto a raging conflagration on some local waste ground and didn't hang around for the end result. That one made the local paper.

Firestarter

Every year around the 5th of November, the village of Twyford holds its bonfire carnival in memory of some poor Catholic bloke from York who had horrible things done to him in return for his botched part in trying to blow up the King and his Parliament. A fair exchange all round, I suppose, giving us English Protestants the chance to set fire to stuff, totally legally, for several weeks a year. Poor Guy Fawkes. Lucky old us.

The carnival is a torchlight procession of decorated floats from the station to the recreation ground, where there's a fairground, the mother of all bonfires and what is reputed to be the largest display of fireworks in the south of England.

The bonfire is what can only be described as a towering inferno, built over several days from railway sleepers, wooden palettes and all the trees within a five mile radius. You can feel the heat of this conflagration over one hundred yards away and it burns all night to the sound of local teens puking up over the side of the fairground twister.

The following day was always very different. Where there were several thousand people the night before, the Sunday saw several dozen kids meandering round the Rec looking for dropped change while the fairground folk slowly took their machines to pieces. The largest crowd was always around the embers of the fire; which the night before had been the size of a house, now reduced to a smouldering pile of ash and still pumping out tremendous heat.

There were dares. On pain of being called a poof, you had to walk across the flames, hoping beyond hope that your flares wouldn't catch fire. On reaching the other side, you were formally inducted into the hard lads' club, while the trembling pooves on the other side still had to face their ordeal. Those who had made it were easily identified. They were the ones with smouldering trouser hems, smoke still rising from the soles of their melting Dunlop Green Flash plimsolls.

But the real fun was to be had with the stuff you could throw onto the fire. There were heaps of torches which had made up the torchlight procession the night before, great long things dipped in wax that stoked up the fire nicely. We would also throw on great armfuls of rubbish, which the Great British public had thoughtfully left behind; and when the flames were really licking up round our ears, singeing the fluff off our parka coats, on would go the first of the fireworks, because we were a big bunch of stupids.

Gaz, one of the tougher kids in school had brought his own supply, which he ladled on liberally. Within seconds, it was like a war zone, as we dived for the cover of our bikes, hedges, other kids, anything. A rocket fizzed past my head and exploded halfway up the only tree for miles around. I still swear to this day that it actually parted my hair, leaving a frazzled streak across my scalp. An inch lower and I would have grown a third eye socket.

Fireworks, we all agreed, were stupid. Anyone could throw a firework on a bonfire for an easy laugh, and besides, we were rather attached to our facial features rather than risk having them blown off by a passing air-bomb. We would, it was decided, use our imaginations.

"Meet you back here in twenty minutes."

And what an arsenal we collected. Every single bin, shed and garage was raided for every last aerosol can, paint tin, and anything marked with those wonderful words of wisdom "Keep out of direct sunlight, do not burn or puncture." Wise words indeed. There would be no puncturing. Plenty of burning.

An experimental can of underarm deodorant was cast onto the flames. Minutes later, there was a satisfying explosion, and the Great Smell of Brut wafted round the park. This was good, and was immediately followed by a shower of cans as everybody flung their booty onto the fire. The resulting cacophony was something to behold, and I'm pleased to report that there were only minor shrapnel injuries and very few burst eardrums.

Then Gaz came back. He had just one item for the fire. It was a one-gallon Castrol GTX oil can. You should understand that is wasn't one of those plastic wussy things you get these days. Cold steel. About to get very hot steel. Straight onto the flames it went.

"Errr, Gaz mate?"

"Yuh."

"Was there anything in that can?"

"Yuh. A bit."

"How much?"

"About half."

"Oh shit."

We watched as the can developed an ominous bulge. We backed away slowly. The bulge got bigger, until the can was almost twice its original size.

"Lads," suggested a mature yet rather frightened voice, "I think it was time we legged it."

We legged it.

BA-LAAAAAAANG-NG-NG-NG-NG-NG-NG!!!!!!!!!!!

The fireball was a good thirty feet across, and the heat-wave knocked us off our feet. A rather pleasing mushroom cloud hung over the recreation ground. Several of the fairground people could be seen running around in wide-eyed panic, still clutching their oversized spanners. As a matter of fact, several of us kids were running around in wide-eyed panic too, as an explosion like that could only mean one thing: trouble. At the very least, a visit from the local Plod; at the very worst - parents.

No pack-drill, no questions asked. Home, and blame somebody else.

When the coast had cleared, and the bomb disposal people had gone away, we went back to survey the wreckage. The fire still burned, and would do for at least another two days. Of the oil can there was nothing except a small crater in the ashes.

"Hey lads," said Gaz.

"What?"

"My dad's got another one in his garage...."

Salvation
I'm beginning to worry about Nathaniel, our local Jehovah's Witness. For years he's ploughed a lonely furrow outside the den of iniquity that is Blockbuster Video in Weymouth, trying to spread the word to an unlistening congregation. I saw him, bright eyed and bushy tailed first thing the other morning, accosting old dears coming out of the Post Office and chasing frightened holiday-makers into Boots the Chemist.

"Jesus thinks you're special," he said to me.

"Ooh, ta very much," I replied, well pleased that at least somebody in the world likes me.

Then I got thinking about it. Did he mean I was "Special" special, or "Special Bus" special? If it was the latter, I would have willingly gone back there and biffed his lights out and forced him to eat his satchel-full of Watchtowers, cold and without sauce.

I needn't have worried. As I went back the same way just before lunchtime – and somewhat richer after selling my bike to the suckers at second hand shop – the heat of the day and a myriad of rejections was already taking their toll. The eyes were wide and wild, the carefully slicked back hair was all over the place, and the joy of Christ's love may have ebbed away somewhat.

"OI! YOU! JESUS SAYS YOU'RE FUCKING SPECIAL!"
and
"TAKE A PISSING WATCHTOWER OR I'LL STICK IT UP YOUR ARSE!"
and
"YEAH? JESUS MAY LOVE YOU BUT I THINK YOU'RE A BUNCH OF WANKERS!"
Pray for him. Or not. Your call.

Paper Round

I was fourteen years old and stony broke. It was no good - fifty pence a week pocket money just wasn't doing the job for me. After all the necessary expenses - 2000AD comic, a quarter of sherbert lemons and a bob or two for the jazz mag fund, there was precious little left to pay off the school bully.

Faced with poverty, I had to get a job. I took myself down to the local newsagents and begged them for a paper round. They told me to bugger off.

A couple of weeks later I got a phone call. It turned out they no longer wanted me to bugger off, and they had, in fact, the highly prized vacancy of delivering newspapers to the citizens of Twyford. 50p a day, take it or leave it, sonny. I took it.

It turned out that the Peppall Twins were moving house, so I got one end of the London Road, and my brother got the other, nicer, end. I'm not saying that parts of my round were rough, but the tarmac road actually ran out halfway, and you would often approach some of the council's finest housing across lawns several feet deep in burned out cars, abandoned Wankel rotary engines and dead postmen.

I'd get up at six in the morning, cycle down to the shop, run round the houses as quickly as possible, get home by seven and do my homework before going to school. This got me a) paid and b) evenings to myself. Sorted.

Fridays were the worst, though. That was the day the Maidenhead Advertiser came out. For a town where precisely nothing happened, they certainly managed to fit a lot into the newspaper - about one hundred and twenty pages of it, in a volume that would make JK Rowling blush. You couldn't even fold it in half, let alone make it small enough to fit through a letter box. The miserable buggers on my round, too lazy to go down the shop and buy it for themselves often got their copy one sheet at a time. And while I was struggling with that lot, it turned out that my brother's round had a punter who had his porn delivered with his morning papers, fuck my luck.

My round had the unfortunate effect of bringing me into contact with Walter, the school drongo. Walter (pronounced with your tongue pressed firmly against your lower lip), was an obnoxious little turd, who could often be seen wandering the village, lost in a daze, reading "Commando" comics through broken National Health glasses; and dressed in his Army Cadet uniform, the only outfit he possessed outside of his school clothes. He lived with his mum and his nan, two enormous, frightening women, who would often wade into fights to defend their son's honour, which was bloody, often, and reminded one of Norwegian whalers flensing their catch of blubber.

I had to deliver the Daily Star to his house, perhaps the most forbidding in the whole village, and every morning I had to endure the sight of Walter's mum, with a face like a melted owl, getting dressed in the living room window. In retrospect, she was probably trying to tell me something (that something being "Hey! Look at my immense tits and big, fat arse"), which has left me scarred for life. She was enormous, even through the wrong end of a telescope she would loom over you like something large and loomy, and possessed a voice that was perfectly suited to warning ships off the rocks at Beachy Head. I reached a deal with the milkman where we'd meet by the gate and "do" the house together. Safety in numbers, as it were.

One day, Darth who ran the paper shop (I never found out his real name - he wheezed and groaned like the Dark Lord of the Sith through years of Capstan Full Strength cigarettes) announced that Walter (pronounced with your tongue pressed firmly against your lower lip) would be starting a paper round. He got Pennfields, the next road along from my round, and perhaps I'd like to show Walter (pronounced with your tongue pressed firmly against your lower lip) the ropes?

No. Fucking. Way.

I showed him the ropes, like a good boy, and the complaints soon started rolling in.

His second week on the job, if things weren't going badly enough, it snowed. About six inches of the stuff, and blowing up a horrible Arctic blizzard, so my brother and I left our bikes at home and walked to the shop. The whole affair took an hour longer than usual, but we got round done and earned our precious fifty pence for the day. Riches. Walter (pronounced with your tongue pressed firmly against your lower lip), on the other hand, brought his mum's Raleigh Shopper bike (extinguishing for once and for all my desire to be reincarnated as a womans' bicycle saddle), and spent the next twenty minutes carefully rearranging the newspapers in the basket on the front while we warmed our bones in front of Darth's ashtray. Then he got on his bike, cycled a full ten yards up the road and fell off, flat on his face. Newspapers exploded across the road, and whipped up by the wind, flew in all directions across the High Street and over the Post Office.

We laughed.

"Didn't hurt," Walter (pronounced with your tongue pressed firmly against your lower lip) said defiantly, blood running down his chin.

Darth went ballistic. He was so cross, he nearly dropped his cigarette. Walter (pronounced with your tongue pressed firmly against your lower lip) sheepishly picked up what was left of his papers, and disappeared into the blizzard, rounding up loose lifestyle sections and Daily Mail health scare specials like Captain Oates on his last fateful walk into history.

The next day, it rained. Buckets and buckets of freezing cold rain. We had our bikes, our waterproofs and our special thick plastic newspaper sacks to keep the newsprint nice and dry for our friends, the paying customers. Walter (pronounced with your tongue pressed firmly against your lower lip) turned up in his Army fatigues and his mum's Raleigh Shopper with the wire basket on the front, still filled with what was left of the previous day's newspapers, which he had diligently rounded up, and taken home to dry on the radiator. He piled the new day's papers on top and spent another twenty minutes carefully rearranging them while Darth watched, shaking his head at the shop window, a sprinkle of fag ash giving a cheerful Christmas effect to the scene.

Then he got on his bike, cycled a full ten yards down the road, and fell off, his glasses skidding under the wheels of a passing car with a sickening crunch.

We laughed.

"Didn't hurt," Walter (pronounced with your tongue pressed firmly against your lower lip) said defiantly, blood running down his chin.

The papers spent another day drying out on his radiator, and were delivered the next day. I should know, as I had to do it, as Walter (pronounced with your tongue pressed firmly against your lower lip) had got the sack for being "a useless - wheeeeeze - tart". After protracted negotiations with Darth, during which I genuinely thought he was going to die, I was offered an extra pound for the honour of both rounds. I should have held out for two - I was virtually chased off the estate by irate punters who thought I was to blame for a week's worth of newspaper buggery.

I had the easy end of the deal. Walter's Mum (pronounced with an air of abject terror) went down the shop and ripped Darth limb from limb, before rushing home to try and shag the terrified bloke who'd come to read the gas meter. Over the next months, I saw enough quivering flesh and brassieres constructed by the best of the British shipbuilding industry to last a lifetime, and all for fifty pence a day. Friends, desperate for any naked flesh at all, thought I the luckiest kid in the world. Au contraire.

The milkman, the postman and I still meet at the same victim support group. We're getting there.

Part III: The serious bits

"In which Alistair Coleman writes a short story on the subject of human rights which he thought was rather good, and is rather less dull than you'd expect."

The Re-educated Man

Samuel Aruna had many secrets.

A journalist, Samuel heard things that weren't meant for his ears, or ears outside a tight circle of people with a compunction toward violence. Samuel knew this, knowing when to keep his mouth shut. His job at Young Africa was too important to him and kept his family fed. With basic needs to fulfil, you cannot lose them through a loose tongue.

Samuel knew how the powerful silenced people. He knew who top politicians were sleeping with. He knew which companies paid governments for contracts, how much everybody got as kickbacks. The trick was listening to secrets, and keeping your damn mouth shut. If you must tell somebody, or more fool you, if you want to put it into print that the emperor's naked, do it so that nobody knows who that let the rampaging tiger out of the bag. People with a compunction toward violence tend not to possess a sense of humour.

Samuel's biggest secret was this: diamonds. Diamonds in Sierra Leone, a small, violent county on Africa's Atlantic coast. A former British colony rich in gems, poor in humanity. War followed government followed murder; and always they fought over diamonds. Sierra Leone's accursed riches. Fight on the wrong side, make the wrong alliances, open your mouth to the wrong people, and they come for you in the night. They wouldn't kill you, not the first time, simply relieve you of your hands. Then, you beg for death.

Aruna had spoken to enough people, some with hands, some without, to know who was emptying Sierra Leone of its wealth, filling pockets and safety deposit boxes with riches traded in the murder of entire villages. Individuals, corporations, governments.

The West, Samuel surmised, is not as civilised as it pretends. In fact, they are as cruel as any dictatorship, role models for corruption and self-aggrandisement. Years of colonisation and oppression taught the Third World everything it need know about the First, and they copied it enthusiastically.

The second thing Samuel recognised about the First World is that it knows the exact worth of the private citizen: nothing. The individual amongst millions matters not, can be made never to have existed at all. If he has no property, no money, no voice, then he is nothing. No-one will miss him when he is gone, for soon they may be gone too. A first World attitude learned in the Third, especially when the worthless stands between the corrupt and a diamond mine.

Samuel knew names. He knew why, where, how and how much. He knew about the razing of a village to end any question of who owned certain land - and hence, mining rights. He knew which corporation owned the mine, how many they had killed to purchase it, and which people they paid money to. Not for their silence, but for their continued government support, and it suited to keep them in office.

He also knew the value of not telling these secrets. He told no-one else, not his wife, children, friends and certainly not colleagues. Life was a struggle, circling round the need to provide for his family in times of little or no money and the knowledge that whatever happened, he lived in a world of little opportunity. At least he had a job, better off than the hundreds he saw, homeless, destitute, on the streets everyday. By keeping quiet, he could keep it, along with his hands and his life.

He didn't even trust himself to keep his secret. It was kept, in his own code, in a book marked "Accounts", inside a cashbox, locked inside the bottom drawer of his desk. But today, he arrived at his desk in an upstairs room at Young Africa to find the drawer open, the cashbox smashed and the book gone.

His stomach tightened. He knew what was going to happen next. He sat at his desk, phoned his wife, knowing that the call was certainly being monitored by a third party, and told her that his work would probably keep him away for some time. She wasn't surprised, even with the nervous tremor on his voice - he had worked away many times before, and was used to his absence. They had agreed a code-word in case this very scenario occurred: "Uncle George sends his regards". In his intestine-knotting panic, he completely forgot about imaginary Uncle George, and Marion would never know.

Samuel waited. It was still early. He liked to be the first in the offices, giving him the chance to work without disturbance, and the opportunity to be home early to shop, cook for his family. His family came first, the job merely a means of providing for them, with the risks that entailed.

Journalism is a dangerous profession. Not as dangerous as, say, a fire-fighter, a police officer or deep-sea fisherman. But none of these jobs entail bringing down the wrath of so many people as the result of writing, speaking, searching for truth. In a typical week, fourteen journalists are arrested and thirty assaulted as a result of their work. One journalist is killed every week; while papers, radio and television stations are closed down, censored, bullied and threatened daily.

In some countries, particularly in Africa, journalists suffer harassment, assault and prison simply for petty criticisms of their esteemed leaders. Elsewhere in the world, this kind of name-calling is called satire. Where Samuel grew up, it's called treason.

"Don't shoot the messenger" is a well-used phrase. But why waste a bullet when you can beat him to death after a campaign of intimidation, violence and torture? The powerful say they like truth and equality. In reality, this is mere lip-service to public expectation, where their truth is preferred to that told by an inconvenient, independent media. To stifle free thought, criticism, dissent is to own the minds of the people. To ensure opposition is silenced is to secure power and cement the status quo. Lessons from the First World taken up in the Third. McCarthyism - the climate of fear when political opponents and so-called free press are too cowed to speak, finds an eager audience wherever power needs to be secured. The people are told what makes them happy, and in turn, they are happy with what they are told.

This is the world in which Samuel Aruna worked, and he knew that he must pay the price.

"Mr Aruna? Would you step this way?"

Two men, both suited, neither armed, stood in his office doorway. He stood and followed them out of the building.

"Your cell-phone, please", he was asked on the stairs, and he surrendered it meekly. When asked, he also gave up his wallet. Outside was a dirty white delivery van, like thousands in the city. No windows, dirt smeared over the number plate making it impossible to read. A hand guiding him by the elbow, he stepped inside, sat on the floor and took a last look at daylight before darkness enveloped him.

They drove.

The journey lasted for some time, yet Samuel was sure that they never left the city. They had crossed at least one bridge, taken more left and right turns than he could remember, and just as he thought he knew where he was, in a throng of voices, car horns and squealing tyres, the van pulled off the road and they sat motionless for several hours. He considered hammering on the walls, shouting and screaming until somebody came, but he feared that this someone would be armed and show no pity in silencing him.

Woken by a bump in the road, the van was moving and Samuel was now hopelessly lost. They drove for some time - minutes, hours, Samuel couldn't tell - and he urinated in a corner and wondered if he might eat.

The van stopped. The sound of shutters rolled down. Voices outside. The doors opened into the half-light of ...where? He was indoors, but no windows, only the large shuttered door that filled the whole of the far wall, olive green paint all round, a dim bulb in the ceiling. He was led, silently by his captors, who may have been different men by now, still wearing the same suits, down more drab corridors until they reached a cell.

This was different. White walls, white floor, steel door painted white, lit by a bulb high on a white ceiling. No windows. No way of telling day from night. No way of seeing outside. He was being erased. He couldn't see outside, outside couldn't see him, outside didn't care. Death.

A bedroll and a blanket lay in a corner. Next to that, some sort of chamber pot. Grounds for optimism, even if the threadbare mattress was flecked with bloodstains of a previous inmate. They intended to keep him alive, for now at least, even if the pot indicated he might not leave the cell for the time being.

At first, Samuel paced the room, like Papillon in solitary confinement. Six paces end-to-end. Four paces side-to-side. Jumping, he couldn't reach the ceiling and its merciless white light and small grill which he took to be a ventilator, but equally a means of spying on him. The door had no keyhole on the inside, just a spy-hole near the top, and a slot for meals near the bottom.

His assumptions were right. For several days, he saw no-one, just a hand pushing a tray of barely-edible food through the slot, and a stern voice asking to empty the pot. In the meantime, Samuel slept, paced the room, sat in contemplation, all under the glare of the relentless white light which was never switched off.

He calculated three, maybe four days, but he could have been wrong. He had no way of telling the time, no way of reckoning how long he slept or how regularly his meals were appearing. Apart from the pisspot-emptying guy, he heard no-one else. No guards. No other prisoners. Starved of sunlight, day and night became mere abstracts. There was only awake and asleep, alive and dead.

On the fourth or fifth day, the door opened for the first time. He was led from the room by a guard. He may have been a soldier, but wore no identifying patches on his olive drabs, and the dim light of the corridor hid his features. Samuel was allowed to shower and given a change of clothing - a t-shirt and a pair of fake Adidas jogging bottoms. Then he was led back to his cell. Past his cell. Down the corridor to another room. Behind a table sat the two men who had taken him from his office. After days of reflection, going over every detail of his arrest, he could recognise their faces anywhere. Mr Black, and his good friend and colleague, Mr Black.

"Good day, Mr Aruna," said the man on the left as Samuel was seated in a chair opposite them, "My name is Mr Smith, and this is Mr Kabbah. We'd like to ask you a few questions about the contents of this notebook."

For the first time, Samuel saw the cashbook on the table. His death sentence. Seated at a lower level than his interrogators on a beaten wooden-backed chair, Samuel felt like a schoolboy being told off by his teachers, sitting high-and-mighty, up there in their smooth, padded stainless-steel office chairs.

"It is mine," he confessed.

"We know that," snapped Kabbah, "We also know the contents. A rather childish code, and then a simple matter of translating the resulting Krio dialect. Do you think us stupid?"

Samuel Aruna's heart sunk. He may as well have written the whole thing in plain English. It would have been less of a secret then. Secrets are best not kept, or better still, forgotten.

"You do realise that this book means a lot of trouble, Mr Aruna. For you, for us and any number of people. Please think about what you have done. We will speak again."

The interview lasted less than two minutes. As the cell door locked behind him, he noticed a pad of paper and a pencil on his bedroll.

"For you," Kabbah's voice rang through the spy-hole, "Write your confession. And do not try to kill yourself."

Samuel managed a smile. They wanted him alive, at least for now. They still have a use for him. He knew not to get his hopes up. Reprieve was by no means a certainty.

He wrote.

He ate.

He filled his pot.

He slept.

He dreamt of meeting Marion the first time in Freetown.

He woke to boots kicking his face, abdomen, arms, leg, groin.

He defecated in his jogging bottoms.

He cried, slept some more, but did not dream.

In the morning - assuming it was morning - he was allowed to wash the blood and shit from his body and given fresh clothes. Smith and Kabbah did not see him that day, or the next. His notepad and pencil had disappeared.

The next time he slept, men came to his cell. They did not beat him. One stubbed out a cigarette on his arm, another on his groin. A third man raped him while the other two held him down.

Handcuffed and manacled, a bar between the two making it impossible for him to stand straight or sleep without contorting his body into impossible positions, he was left for days.

Noise. Rock music, white noise, the theme from Sesame Street, the roar of aircraft were piped into his cell for hours at a time. Whenever he slept, he was kicked awake. His food became less palatable and less frequent. He was no longer taken to shower. Instead, a fire hose was fed through the food flap and he was sprayed with cold water, and left to sit shivering under the pitiless white light.

"Sunny day, sweepin' the clouds away...."

Aching, he was left alone, for a day, two days. His head spun with fear, pain, fatigue. He would tell his captors anything, admit any crime, take any punishment just to see the sun, breathe fresh air, see Marion again. But would his confession damn him or give him life? As he sat, head in hands, in the corner of his white cell, he prayed for death's swift arrival. It would be release, for this was not humanity.

Death did not come. Only painful sleep.

He was kicked awake. Had he slept hours, minutes? He couldn't tell. Two men stood above him, their features ghoulish silhouettes against the cell lighting. Not suits. Uniforms.

Wordlessly, they hauled him to his feet, and led him, half stumbling in his manacles, from the cell. Down the corridor, past the interview room and into a dimly lit hall that may have been a gymnasium. The two men let go of Samuel's elbows and he slumped to the wooden floor on his knees.

A gun cocked.

"Say your prayers."

Say it isn't true.

Say you'll do anything.

The grain of the wooden floor. The cobwebs on the metal grill covering the light high up in the ceiling. The brush strokes making up the lines of the basketball court. The stains of blood and vomit on the front of his t-shirt. In his final moments, his senses took everything in.

Cold metal against the back of his neck.

A click.

Laughter, cruel, ugly laughter before being dragged, legs barely functioning, back to his cell, where he was flung into a corner in a sobbing heap.

"We can do this any time. One day, the gun will be loaded."

The cell door slammed shut, leaving Samuel on his own, vomiting, reaching until nothing was left, urine staining the front of his trousers. Tomorrow. Next week. Every day may be the last, except there were no days.

"Come and play, everything's A-OK."

They came again. In the middle of the basketball court, they made him kneel, and he heard the focussed explosion of a shot, the heat of the round and a ringing in his ears that blanked out everything except for the knowledge that the pistol was loaded with blanks, and the men's laughter was even more raucous than before.

"Won't you tell me how to get, how to get to Sesame Street."

Alone. No food. A tooth found on his bed roll. Blood in his urine. Only the dreams. In the minutes he was given to sleep, only the dreams offered escape.

A lizard on a rock. A sunlit, slow-moving river. A leafless tree, standing on its own in a field. A mask. Large, wooden, carved, decorated in gold, round screaming mouth with painted gold lips. His arms held down as it was lowered over his face, screaming and writhing silently as he tried to turn his head away. The smell of aromatic oils rubbed over its surface, the roughly hewn wood inside the mask, coming closer and closer. Change the face, change the man, change the mind. Wake screaming, screaming. The music is still there. The light is still blinding.

"Wooah we're halfway there... Wooah Livin' on a prayer."

Mr Kabbah came.

Dark suit, grey tie.

"You will come with me, Mr Aruna. It is time."

Samuel did not follow.

"Mr Aruna, do not play games with me. You will come."

Samuel turned to face the wall.

"I have killed more important men than you, Mr Aruna."

"Tell me," said Samuel, "Why are you so afraid of truth?"

"We are not, Mr Aruna."

"Then why am I here?"

"You are here to learn what truth is, Mr Aruna."

"And who are you to teach me?"

"Come now, you know you are in no position to ask that question."

"Yet I ask. Who are you to tell me who is the liar and who tells the truth?"

"We are, Mr Aruna, the ones with the money. The guns. The power."

"But when that power is challenged, you do this to men?"

"Such is power, as you know. I am sure that in your career you have seen this many times."

"You know that already."

"Ah yes, your book of codes. A veritable tale of woe, no?"

Samuel turned to face his captor, anger etched onto his face.

"I have seen more men killed by people like you that I care to count. Not just men. Their wives, their children. And to perpetuate what? A system that takes without asking? A system that leaves the poor to die? A system that lashes out at those who dare to question it? I ask you, do you sleep well?"

"I sleep very well, and I will tell you why. It is because of people like me that millions wake up in the morning, go about their lives and are able to do the same the next day and the next. It is people like you that question everything, make people unhappy, upset the balance of their lives. People are happy with what they have."

"Even those you have killed? Are they happy?"

"How do you know they are dead, Mr Aruna? Show me these dead people."

"I have evidence."

"Show me."

Samuel stood, hunched in his chains and followed Kabbah from the cell. Outside, a guard released him from the cuffs and manacles for the first time in ...when? The skin where they had been was red with blood and ached to the touch.

They walked in silence down the dusk of the corridor until they reached the interview room. Mr Smith was sitting behind the table - black suit, dark blue tie - flipping through Samuel's notebook whilst referring to a small sheath of papers beside it.

"Ah! There you are, Mr Aruna. I was getting rather worried. I trust our men didn't treat you too badly."

"Hm."

"Discipline can be a problem with enlisted men, but what can one do?"

Samuel considered his options. In the face of probable death, he had escaped relatively lightly. "I have no complaints."

"I'm glad to hear that," said Smith, "Sit down and let us talk."

"I have already spoken to your friend."

"So I gather," said Mr Smith, nodding to a TV monitor over Samuel's shoulder, showing a view from the air duct in the ceiling of his cell. "You have been the model guest."

"Prisoner."

"Guest. You may leave at any time."

"Then I shall..."

"...but only after you have answered our questions."

"I have nothing to answer for."

"But you have. Let us see for ourselves."

Mr Smith rifled through the papers on the desk, until he reached a page heavily annotated in red ink.

"There is much to read here," he said, "but this story about a so-called 'massacre' worries us. Tell us about it."

Samuel told what he knew. How people had worked this land for generations. How the land was theirs by right. How men, sweating in business suits, had come one day by helicopter and offered to move the people there somewhere better. A town.

Then he told them how the people had refused this kind offer - this land was all they knew, this was their ancestors' land, and leaving it would betray their people, their ancestors' memories and their descendants' birthright. They would stay. The men in suits went away, but returned a few days later, offering new land and US dollars. The people told them to leave. They were not going to abandon their land. We are not savages, we have no need for your bribes. But construction men were already arriving, digging at the land with their machines, felling trees, building roads.

The men in suits went away again, and did not return until the local people were gone.

"Gone?" asked Mr Smith.

"Gone," said Samuel.

He told them of the day the men with guns came. They killed the local people who refused to leave, and the construction workers moved in even before the bodies could be removed. The men in suits returned, for they had their diamond mine.

"That is a fine story, Mr Aruna. Perhaps someone might want to make it into a film someday?" said Kabbah.

"It is the truth."

"Who says?"

"A survivor."

"Ah yes, so it says in your codebook." said Smith, looking at another heavily annotated page of notes. His finger was on a name, circled in red pen. Underneath Samuel could make out the word 'Expedited'. "We checked this 'survivor' out through the contact details you helpfully left us. There is no such person."

"I have met her."

"There is no such person."

"I have recordings my interviews with her."

"You are mistaken. There are no tapes. There is no such person."

"Photographs."

"No photographs. Perhaps you are confusing this person with someone else you have interviewed? Quite understandable under the circumstances. This..." Smith looked at his notes, "...Rosemary Diallo never existed."

"The massacre..." protested Samuel.

"...never took place," finished Kabbah, in a manner suggesting that this matter was now closed.

"The people?"

"They were moved. They agreed to new land, farm machinery, money, houses. They are happy. That is the way of the world. Everybody wants more."

"This is the truth?"

"Yes it is."

"Whose truth?"

"There is only one truth, Mr Aruna, as you well know," said Kabbah.

"Your truth is a lie."

"Prove it. Our truth is the one people believe, therefore it becomes the truth. No-one will believe you, Mr Aruna."

"And if we were to fly into the interior of Sierra Leone?"

"If you could even get the UN to fly you, you know what the situation is like outside the cities. You must be pretty foolhardy to visit these places."

"But if we did?"

"We would find happy people farming the land, Mr Aruna. They will be pleased to talk to you about their new life."

"And they will tell me there was no massacre?"

"Of course," said Smith, "They are now our people. They will say what they are told. Sierra Leone may not be a large country, but there is more than enough to get lost in. How will you know you are even in the right place?"

"So this lie becomes the truth?"

"You must understand, Mr Aruna, this is not about a few peasants. This isn't even about this diamond mine you are so keen on. We cannot let you stir things up," Kabbah explained.

"So there are interests?"

"Ever the journalist, sir," said Smith. "You understand this - we allow people like you a certain leeway. Small triumphs extracted from OUR truth. It keeps you happy, it keeps the public happy knowing there is an inquiring press, and it keeps us happy knowing you are as harmful as a fly on a cow's back.

"But every now and then, you think you have come across your Watergate, but we cannot allow this to happen. People like you need putting back in line. And interests? Yes, indeed."

"Who?"

"You expect us to answer that, Mr Aruna?" asked Kabbah, "We are the ones questioning you."

"It makes no difference now," said Smith to his colleague, "he is in no position to tell anybody."

Samuel shivered.

"You see, sir, you have upset many people. Our backer himself has contacted us directly. He is very worried what this can do to our country's reputation. There is a great deal of money at stake in this project. Government money, foreign money, large corporations. They don't like to be linked with murder, sir, and that is precisely the accusation you are making. Your lies have upset a lot of people."

Samuel had no idea that his story had gone quite that far up the food-chain. Now he understood why he was in detention. It wasn't just company money at stake; a billionaire's stake in some construction conglomerate, his was a story that could destroy many people, himself included. And family, friends, colleagues. Retribution would not finish with his body being found on a street corner, the victim of a violent street robbery.

"Time to choose," said Kabbah.

Time to choose. Truth. Lies. Truth. Their white lies. Their truth.

"Is there a choice?" he asked.

"Sir," said Smith, "there are always choices. You must choose what is best for everyone. You may even get to live with it."

Let the lie live and learn to live with it. Sacrificing yourself for a story that will never be told, noble as it sounds, is not even the smallest of victories. There are times when two and two must be made to equal five.

"Your nose is bleeding," said Kabbah.

Samuel dabbed the blood with the front of his t-shirt. His nose now bled regularly, several of his teeth wobbled in his mouth, and the ribs on his left side ached when he moved.

"Choose, my friend," Smith urged.

For emphasis, Kabbah stood above his prisoner.

Two plus two. Makes four.

For emphasis, Kabbah let his jacket fall open to reveal his service revolver in a shoulder holster.

"Choose," said Smith.

Two...

Samuel chose.

"Your truth," he gasped.

Five.

Two smiles.

"An excellent choice, Mr Aruna," said Kabbah, "we knew you would see it our way."

Samuel was led back to his cell. As the door locked behind him relief, hatred, confusion, fear overtook him. What was to come? Surely, they couldn't release him with this knowledge in his head? One word, and the house of cards would come tumbling. But then... he was one man. A man discredited, against the entire machine. One word, and it would be death. He did the only thing he could do. He slept.

The men came. He was dragged from his cell, legs thrashing behind him, screaming, to the gymnasium. He wouldn't kneel. He had told them everything they wanted. He had nothing else to give, they had taken it all. Not just his secrets, his dignity, his humanity, his mind. Now his life.

A boot in the back of his calves and he was on his knees. The same boot in the small of his back and he was spread-eagled on the floor. Cold metal to the back of his head, a final cry for mercy escaped his lips as a pathetic whimper. No longer a man, just an animal for slaughter.

A flash of light, a moment of pain.

He awoke with a jolt. His hair was thick with his own blood where the butt of the pistol had clubbed him unconscious, a numb pain in the back of his head. In his left hand was his codebook, exactly as he had locked it away in his cashbox all those days - weeks? - ago. As worthless as a child's dot-to-dot book now. Plausible deniability, the government machine's word for barefaced lies, was against him. The warning was clear: you're a lucky man, Mr Aruna. Open your mouth, and you'll find a gun barrel inside it. He didn't need further persuasion.

He was in the back of another van. It may even have been the same one that picked him up. Windowless, it was too dark to tell. All he could feel and hear were the bumps in the road, the muffled beeps of horns and rumble of traffic.

The van stopped.

The doors opened in a blinding gush of light.

The morning sun.

Two pairs of arms pulled him out of the back on left him staggering, shielding his eyes.

Two sets of doors slammed shut, and the men Samuel had never known, never met, disappeared.

The van pulled away, losing itself in traffic. Samuel Aruna found himself, alive, tattered, exhausted outside the offices of Young Africa just off Queens Boulevard. A couple of miles away, the entrance to the Midtown Tunnel, and beyond that the towers of Manhattan. Samuel Aruna looked up at the building. He wasn't ready to go back there and start his new career towing the party line, that could wait. Samuel Aruna went home.

New York didn't care, either.

Up the Congo

The almost entirely serious piece that I vowed I'd never put in a book. So, here it is.

The Foreign Office told me not to go to Brazzaville. So I went anyway. How stupid was that?

If you don't know what I do for a living, it is this: I'm a Technical Operator-cum-Journalist for a large media corporation, researching and receiving foreign TV, Radio and press for various large government organisations. The proposed trip to Congo and Nigeria was to research their local media outlets, buy newspapers and generally find out what's on the radio and TV there and in the surrounding countries. Easy.

It all went horribly wrong the moment I reached Heathrow Airport. I got there on time, which was about the only thing that went right that week, and it was downhill from there on. British Midland don't let you book your luggage in early, so as a result you have to join a mad last-minute scramble and the poor staff on the check-in desk are totally deluged by passengers. The flight was to Paris, but I was connecting there for Douala in Cameroon and then on to Brazzaville.

"Can I book my luggage through to my final destination?" I asked, hoping to save a lot of grief in countries that speak French and wave their arms at you.

"Ummm....Errrr...." she replied.

"No problem", said her supervisor, leaning across the workstation and typing in the airport codes. I watched as my case, all my clothes, my drugs, my wash kit, my camera and most of my technical equipment disappeared down the ramp. Never to be seen again.

It was in Paris that I came across my first African queue. The Cameroon Airlines flight was called, and everyone and their dog bundled for the gate. No-one ever queues in Africa, it's every man for himself. Priests, nuns, little old ladies, all elbowing their fellow passengers out of the way. It's not as if anyone's going to be left behind, it's the principle of the thing, you **must** get there first and watch, laughing as everyone else struggles. I got quite good at it. I soon learned that people will go to any lengths to be the first in the bundle, even going as far as forming an orderly queue...

The words "We will start loading the plane with families and the disabled first" actually mean "Every man for himself". All of a sudden everybody has a family, or failing that, a limp. Even the clergy (no flight in Africa goes without at least one priest, nun or mullah for moral and gravitational support) are in on the game. "Hand luggage" is also a very loose term, meaning anything from a chest almost the same size as the passenger down to, in one case I witnessed, a bucket of lard.

After a six hour stop-over in Douala ("The armpit of Africa - hot and sweaty" according to my Lonely Planet guidebook, and who was I to argue), the real fun started - Brazzaville Airport.

Let me set the scene: Congo had recently emerged from a civil war. It's dangerous, and the FCO discourages Britons to travel there and I can see why. The place is a dump, run, as far as I can tell, by the police, the army, miscellaneous people with guns, and anyone else who fancies chancing their arm with the unsuspecting traveller.

I approached the immigration bundle with passport and landing card in hand, hoping to get through at the first attempt. In most of my fellow travellers' cases, money is changing hands. Except when I got to the barrier, and there was no way I was getting through. All my papers were in order, but for some reason, Mr Bastard decided to intimidate me. He wasn't interested in a small financial gift either, trying to get something more out of me, as he knew I must be in the Congo for a reason, and therefore I must have more than a few francs to give him. My passport disappeared into a plastic bag, along with those from a few other unfortunates. On this guy's whim, I was in the shit.

It's then that Bernard showed up. He's the driver that I'd had the foresight to book from the hotel. We wait until Mr Bastard's back is turned, steal my passport back, and we run for it, laughing like idiots in our moment of triumph.

It's then that I find my luggage hasn't arrived. Dejected, I fill out a lost luggage form for the Air Afrique office, but I'm not hopeful.

I arrived at the hotel completely knackered after 24 hours travelling only to find the survey turning to shit already. I still have enough equipment in my hand luggage to work with, but crucially, I have no reference material, no spare clothes, no anti-malarial drugs, and the one thing I really want to do is brush my teeth. I spend the whole week remembering with a groan what's gone missing. Camera... groan ! Spare glasses... groan ! Socks... groan ! Hairbrush... groan ! The list was endless, but don't tell that to my insurers.

Tuesday morning.

I got up, dress in the same fetid clothes and go down to the foyer for my breakfast. It was crawling with troops, armed with a variety of pistols and AK-47s. It turned out that the army used Le Meridien as the married quarters for its officers, but I could never get used to sharing the lifts with a crowd of heavily armed guys in dark glasses.

On closer inspection, I also note that the rather spectacular cut glass patterns in the floor-to-ceiling mirrors gracing the reception are caused by bullet holes. And the rather interesting concrete mouldings are in fact grenade scars. Charming.

As all my drugs were missing in action, I was utterly terrified of getting the shits. I know the food is flown in from France twice a week, but my breakfast still consisted of a pile of toast and boiling hot black coffee.

Now to face the main problem - I fly out on Friday, I am in a country where men sweat for a living. I need clothes.

No problem, it turned out. Four of us - myself, Bernard, and some hired goons drove to the market and I pick up some shirts and jeans, a toothbrush and shaving gear. I'm a bit of a novelty, and the sight a local in a Man United shirt has me in fits of unexplained laughter. Back at the hotel, I report my bad news back to HQ and get on with the survey. I bought some newspapers and find to my horror, in the sports pages, one of the local top Congolese teams resplendent in their brand new Man United kits. Is there no escape from the army of Satan? The girl in the hotel newspaper kiosk tries desperately to get friendly with me. She's either after a chance of a free passage out of Brazzaville, or maybe it's my fetid, unwashed animal magnetism - either way, the advice of an older, wiser colleague is ringing in my ears: "You can catch it shaking hands with a vicar out there." I vowed to spend the rest of the week hiding in my room.

Then, just as things are going well, one of my teeth falls out. Marvellous. Just what you need 5,000 miles from a decent dentist. Still, another trip out to the Red Cross pharmacy landed me a packet of Larium and I no longer have to worry about getting malaria. I also see, joy of joys, a guy in an Arsenal shirt. The faith is reaching Central Africa, crushing the forces of darkness before it.

My case, it turns out, has been found. In Angola. Easy mistake to make if you're Mr Damn Fool at British Midlands who thinks he knows airport codes off the top off your head. TAAG have a flight to Brazza Thursday. I go back to the madhouse of the airport to find it, but surprise, surprise it's not there. My flight out is Friday, and I'm determined to be on it, case or no case. The survey done, the boredom is killing me.

So next day, I settle the hotel bill [finding, amongst other things, that a fifteen minute phone call to my boss had cost 95 pounds!] and head for Maya-Maya airport. Again. Another sweep through the offices, but no case, but unfortunately for me, I'm now known there as "The White Man With No Luggage". I'd spare you the horrors of my checking in for my flight back to Douala, but good grief it was awful.

The following people expected (mostly took) small bribes: Three guards at doorways leading to the departures desk. The check-in, the departure tax (receipt given!), the glowing old man operating the terrifying x-ray machine, the little old fella who was in two minds as to whether my hand luggage was too large, the lady at the door to passport control, passport control, the man at the door out of passport control leading to the departure lounge, the two guys searching the hand luggage outside the departure lounge, the guy doing the body searches outside the departure lounge, the guy guarding the door to the departure lounge, and the policeman who had accompanied me through the airport, obviously telling all his mates in Lingala that I was a soft touch with a big roll of currency. Some of these people may even have had jobs there.

Okay, for "departure lounge" read "store room with a few benches". Myself and about 100 other people were stuck here for two hours, no refreshments, no toilets. Then, another African bundle through a tiny door, out onto the airfield and onto the plane. Not for me though.

"Mr Coleman", says a voice (in fact, it is pronounced 'Collie Man', something I've got used to on my travels), "We have found your bag". I turn to see a beaming police officer. I follow him, like a big twat, to an office.

Wrong!

I realise too late that neither he nor his colleagues had ID badges.

The first one punched me. Someone else clubbed me over the head. I got the message, there is no case, they just wanted money, the pistol being brandished towards me and the hefty looking chaps with AK-47s underlining their point. Luckily, I split the rest of my cash and travellers cheques to other parts of my person and hand luggage. They get 1,100 dollars and let me go.

Simple problem: I can stay behind and complain, or quietly get on the plane and leave. Complaining would mean missing my flight and being stuck in Congo until Monday. My passport having been stamped "departed" would cause no end of trouble, as would accusing the police of robbing me.

I got on the plane, puke up somewhere over Gabon and keep my mouth shut.

One connection later and I'm in Lagos, fully expecting more airport chaos. Murtala Mohammed airport has a reputation of being one of the most corrupt in the world, but to my surprise, I sail through with no problems, even quicker than Heathrow. A new government cleaned the place up, and it was almost a model of efficiency. The road to the city can be a bit hairy, so I was met by a driver who has a way with street hawkers and conmen. He drives at them at 70 miles per hour. Ayo and his Mercedes demonstrated how hairy it is by driving at 95 mph the whole way in the dark, lights off and leaning on his horn. He's brilliant, and I tip him handsomely and promise to employ him as my personal driver for my entire trip.

Gone midnight, thoroughly pissed off, my head hurt, so I just fell into bed and sleep. Next morning I ring, in turns, my wife and my boss telling them that this trip has turned from shit into utter, utter shit. Within an hour, there's a ticket waiting for me at Murtala Mohammed for that night's departure to London.

With a day to kill, I go see the hotel doctor and get my head looked at. There's a bump, I'm still dizzy, but no real damage done. Then I take a swift look around, though not straying far from the hotel..

The only problem is the currency. Changing a $50 travellers' cheque into Niara for a bit of spending money, I found the largest bill they have in Nigeria is a 50. Fifty dollars works out to about 5,000 Niara, so you can imagine the size of the wad I was presented with. Nevertheless, this provided plenty of "small change" to give to people, even going as far as getting someone to carry my hand luggage for me at the airport, as the weight of it (a sports bag containing amongst other things, the world's heaviest laptop) had left me decidedly lop-sided.

The trip back to the airport was an education in itself. Ayo was his usual lunatic self, as were the usual crowd of minibuses packed to the gills with passengers, even hanging out the doors, riding on the running boards, whilst hammering up the motorway. Three-up on a moped was not unusual, and not a helmet in sight. All of a sudden, nine o'clock at night, right in the middle of the motorway, a traffic jam. It's where the minibuses that drop their passengers off at the shanties stop and do their trade. And as we crawl by, there are crowds of people doing their best to make a living by the roadside, selling anything they can. But there's no threat, no barely suppressed violence, unlike my experiences from another country, just people selling anything they can lay their hands on. Poor me, I must be a millionaire to them.

And then... it's onto a plane, lovely cuddly British Airways, Shakespeare In Love for the in-flight movie, a **complimentary pair of socks** (you don't know how much this means to a man who has washed the same pair in his sink every night for a week), and home at six the next morning.

So, Africa on two shirts, two pairs of trousers, two pairs of underwear and one pair of socks. It can be done. Just listen to the Foreign Office next time. And oh yes, in case you **are** wondering... **no** they do **not** drink Um Bongo in the Congo. However, they do drink Vimto in the Cameroon, but they haven't quite got round to writing a catchy advertising jingle for that one yet.

Postscript: I read with interest news stories about fierce gun battles round Brazza early in 2002 in which "armed militia groups dressed as airport officials" were all but wiped out by Congolese army units following an uprising of guerrilla groups. That's karma in action, folks.

Part IV: The Boy who never grew up

"In which the idiot reaches adulthood, but is unable, for some reason, to leave childish things behind. With hilarious results."

Wedding From Hell

I remember that day well. It still comes back in nightmares. Big, vivid, full Technicolor nightmares with added blood, swearing and violence. It was ace.

It was the occasion of the marriage of my old Uncle Pete (aged fifty) to Brenda the twenty year old local bike he'd got up the duff following a late-night knee-trembler in the office stock cupboard. Something that happens all the time if you read the letters pages of the right magazines ("Dear Fiesta, You won't believe the most incredible thing that happened to me at work the other day…").

The big day came right at the peak of a fantastic inter-family feud and everybody present hated everybody else. All the signs were that it was going to be a classic and it didn't disappoint. I only went out of a misplaced sense of family loyalty (and to make up the numbers if it went off).

The wedding itself was half an hour of barely disguised threats in the church as the two families pointed accusingly at each other:
"Cradle-snatcher"
"Slag"
"Dirty old man"
"Money grabber"
From that charming little affair, we repaired to the second part of the day's proceedings. The reception was done on the cheap at a local youth club - in fact, the same youth club that I had almost razed to the ground in the summer of 1976 (see "Bottle of Fire" elsewhere in this volume).

Everyone on the top table went up to the buffet and cleared the lot, with Brenda, not known for her sylph-like appearance, going back for seconds before anybody else had even got firsts. If she had been present at the Feeding of the Five Thousand, at least 4,000 would have gone home hungry, and Jesus would have got a terrible write-up. In the end, the gannets left a lettuce leaf and two sticks of celery for the other guests, who, sensing a siege mentality, took turns to sneak out to the local fish and chip shop (see "Mao" elsewhere in this volume).

From start to finish, it only took two hours and thirty minutes for it all to go pear-shaped. Somebody stood on somebody else's foot. Somebody refused to apologise. A punch was thrown. It missed, and caught granny on the side of the head.

"You fooker!" shouted granny and let fly with her handbag. It caught Uncle Billy on the nose in an eruption of blood and snot, leaving granny looking like an Andy Warhol original.

"You bitch!" shouted Uncle Billy, spraying blood and snot over everybody in a six foot radius, managing to get in a hefty kick at the handbag swinger, but only connecting with a table leg, hurling drinks across the room in a pissy yellow shower.

Then, like that famous film of the Siege of Stalingrad, the two armies came together in a rain of blows, kicks, scratches and a rain of cheap keg beer.

The disco played on.

"Karma-karma-karma-karma karma chameleon..."

The police arrived to break it up, leaving only two totally committed young ladies grappling in the middle of the dance floor to the entertainment and amusement of all present, the man from the mobile disco stepping over the rival bodies as he carted his equipment back to his van.

Hours later, people were still coming back from the chip shop wondering where the hell everybody had gone.

It was my best night out ever.

Rubber

I made a solemn vow to Mrs Duck that she would never appear in one of my stories. So, here it is.

When we were first going out together (bless her, she called it "courting", though we never once ended up in front of a judge), she and I became regulars at The Swan public house just outside Reading. She liked it because it was a nice country pub, not too far from home with a nice atmosphere. I liked it because the landlady had the biggest pair of knockers I had ever seen, ever.

One Friday night, things were going particularly well, and it was becoming increasingly clear that my luck might be in (with the soon-to-be Mrs Duck, not the landlady, I should point out). Like Tom Sharpe's Zipser in Porterhouse Blue, it dawned on me that I had been caught short in the Johnny department, and that I might need rubberised protection of some kind. The kind they dispense from the everlasting chewing gum machine in the gents' lavatory.

I headed for the bog, pretended to have a piss while the last punter finished off, and turned my attention to the machine. It had that funny ha-ha graffiti on the front: "For refund, insert baby". I was totally out of babies, so I put my pound coin in the slot.

I pulled back the drawer. Nothing. Peering up into the mechanism, I could see the pack of three trying to come out, but somehow it was caught in the gubbins. I pushed the drawer back slowly, hoping that my bounty might fall through, but it snapped back shut before it had the chance.

Bugger.

I tried again with my last pound coin. I opened the drawer, and it was still empty. The packet was almost, but not quite, coming out. It simply needed a little encouragement, and by God, gravity would do the rest.

Reaching inside, I gave it a prod with my finger. It moved, but still no dice. So I gave it a firm push. It disappeared back up into the machinery and the drawer snapped shut. Straight onto my finger.

And here was my predicament: I was trapped. In the gent's toilets. With my hand stuck inside a rubber johnny machine. Try explaining that one away.

For what seemed like ten minutes I turned my finger this way and that, pushed, pulled, twisted and shook, but I was stuck fast, and if anything it was getting worse.

Then: woe! Footsteps!

Someone was coming down the corridor towards the gents. I was trapped. Laughter, ridicule and slow embarrassed death was only seconds away. Something had to be done, and quick.

With one foot halfway up the wall, I let out a silent scream and gave

167

one final mighty tug.

There was an audible CRACK! as my finger freed itself and I staggered backwards across the bogs, regaining my composure just in time for the landlord to come in for a piss.

"Alright there", he said.

I wanted to say "Actually, no. The machine's eaten my money, and now it's just tried to kill me and I've only just escaped with my life."

So I said "Alright Dave" instead.

That final blood-curdling tug actually broke my finger, and killed of any desire for after-hours activity. I was so embarrassed about the circumstances that I never told Mrs Duck about it, and only saw a doctor the following Thursday when the pain got too much to bear. Even then I told him that "I slammed it in a door", which wasn't too far from the truth.

You are the first person I've told. Go gently on me.

Up on the Roof

The one thing about living in a block of flats is never having to worry about the roof leaking. Yes, you do have to live with the people upstairs having a pet elephant, and the bloke downstairs having a predilection for thrashing, noisy sex at three in the morning, but as Paul Weller says, that's entertainment. So, when we finally moved into a real, live house, the first thing that happened was the discovery of the Great Lake of the Back Bedroom. Arses.

Like a complete tit, I had bought one of those lovely looking chalet style houses. You know the type - the ones with the flat roof where the bedrooms stick out for a nice Swiss mountainside effect. A flat roof where water settles in great pools, leaking down onto the foolish inhabitants below. And guess who had to go up there and fix it? Double arses. Supersized.

Brother-in-law very kindly lent me his longest, springiest ladder; and terrified, I started my ascent towards doom. I hate heights. I really, truly hate them. It's not the fact that I'm so far up, after all, I've safely stood on top of the Eiffel Tower with no problems; it's the knowledge that with one slip, I could end up looking like someone from those industrial safety videos they insist on showing at work.

Whimpering, I reached the top, and immediately found the problem. Water had collected on the roof, and instead of flowing off into the guttering, had leaked through some loose flashing around the chimney and into the house. No problem - straight down to B&Q for all the bits, and I was straight up there fixing the roof like an old pro.

Feeling particularly bullet-proof on this glorious summer's day, I stood up to admire the view across the rooftops and gardens of my new street. And that's when I saw Laura for the first time. My heart skipped a beat at this vision of womanhood. Gods, she was ugly. And naked. We had moved next door to the Munsters' Naturist Colony.

"Hello," she said, looking up from her book.

"Bwaargh!" I replied, clinging on to the TV ariel for dear life.

"You just moved in then?" she said, scratching the stretch-marks just above her fanny.

"Bwaargh! Yes, last week. Help!"

She then proceeded to engage me in conversation for no less than twenty minutes; me on the roof, shouting replies to the banshee sprawled butt-naked on a sun-bed next door. A perfectly reasonable conversation, held at one hundred decibels, with me trying not to shout out "For God's sake woman I can see your nadge! Put it away in the name of sanity!"

It was at this point that her husband Roger joined her in the garden. Naked as the day he was born, except for a rather ill-fitting hair-piece, and hung like a donkey. If he wasn't careful, he could have somebody's eye out.

"Roger," said Laura, pointing skywards, "This is our new neighbour, Scary."

"Bwaargh!"

In the time-honoured tradition, I made my excuses and left; choosing to jump thirty feet into a flower bed rather than waste two terrifying minutes on the ladder, sustaining only minor injuries. When I finally reached safety, Mrs Duck was quick to ask me about my first encounter with the people next door. I told her. She was not impressed.

We lived there for seven years, and credit to Laura and Wiggy, they never once mentioned the nudity thing in polite company. I, on the other hand, was unable to engage them in conversation without the fear of being bludgeoned to death by a giant toupeed trouser snake, and told everybody on the street. They needed to be warned. Ugly people in the corner house.

Lucky Bag

This is one of my favourite tales of woe, and the one journalists always seem to ask me about in interviews. They always ask the same question: "Have you had your vasectomy yet?" and the answer remained, until one foul, sunny and extremely painful day in August 2005, a very firm "NO".

The year was 1997. Mrs Duck and I sat down and earnestly decided that we had had enough Scaryducklings for one lifetime, and that, for various practical reasons, I should go and have The Snip.

I would present myself at the hospital and allow a perfect stranger to cut a hole in my ballbag and do strange, unnatural things with my plums until they didn't work anymore. It seemed totally fair at the time, after all Mrs Duck had gone through the pain of child birth twice AND endured a lifetime of marriage to me.

Following a visit to the doctor (who actually tried to talk me out of it), I put my name on the list, and waited, knowing full well that such was the state of the Health Service, it would be upwards of two years before they got round to me. Six weeks later, I got a cunningly worded letter asking me to present myself at Battle Hospital in Reading, and don't forget your gonads. Arses.

Despite my morbid fear of blood (my own) and incredible pain, I bravely faced up to my ordeal. I am, after all, the son of a doctor and a nurse, so what did I have to worry about? An entire lifetime of regular supplies of "The Lancet", the journal of the medical profession, for starters. Every month it would flop through our letter box, and every month I was introduced to a new kind of skin condition, hideous disease or bizarre injury, all in glorious Technicolor. It put me right off following in my father's footsteps, and I have steadfastly pursued a career path that has taken me as far away from these knife-wielding goons as possible. And now I was going to let one of them loose on my bollocks. Doom.

Bright and early I awoke on that Monday morning. I showered. Then I shaved. And shaved again, a process done with the utmost care so as not to cut any more holes in the scrote than was absolutely necessary. All this was done in a bathroom resembling Piccadilly Circus, with people from a five mile radius bursting in to use the lav, surreptitiously checking out how I was getting on with the 'nads.

With the kids packed off to relatives, I took the short journey down the road to the Battle Hospital. It was deserted. Not a soul to be seen. Like the Marie Celeste, there were signs of habitation, a half drunk cup of coffee, a coat on a hook, but no-one present. Eventually, after a search of the hospital's empty corridors, I collared a passing nurse and asked where everybody was. She told us.

It was Monday morning. Princess Diana had forgotten to do up her seatbelt during a frenzied Saturday night in Paris, metamorphosing from "Sex-Crazed Royal Tart flounces round Europe's capitals with Egyptian Boyfriend" in the early editions of Sunday's papers to "We'll Never Forget You, Princess of all our Hearts. Oh, and Dodi as well" by the following lunchtime. The entire hospital staff was allowed the day off to go and have a good cry over it.

"Even Dr Norris?" I asked.

"Especially Dr Norris", she replied, "Though I suspect he'll be remembering Diana with eighteen holes of golf."

It was all the excuse I needed. I took to my heels and ran, Mrs Duck struggling to keep up. I got out of the hospital building, and kept running until I reached the car. My gonads were safe. Dr Norris was hacking about with his mashie niblick on the golf course instead of hacking away at my crown jewels, which was a situation I could live with for the rest of my natural life. I jumped into the car and sped away, never to return. Except to go back and pick up Mrs Duck.

After all the national grieving, the crying, the media hyperbole and the fucking awful Elton John song, I feel the time has come to finally pay my respects to Her Royal Highness Princess Diana of Wales, who died saving orphans, poor people, kittens an' stuff:

"God bless you, Your Highness", I say, "You saved my bollocks."

A fitting tribute to a great, great woman. It's what she would have wanted.

Fiesta

It is my long-held theory that anybody who has ever made a living from writing, has, at some desperate stage, accepted cold, hard cash in return for the production of filth, penning dirty letters for top-shelf magazines. It stands to reason – you've decided to make money from the literary arts, and in any business you've got to start at the bottom. Literally.

For example:

"She gasp'd as she layde her eyes on mye thynge" : Chaucer, letter to "Wenches" magazine

"In the seventh civilisation, cross-eyed with lust, they wrote a fourth law of robotics": Asimov, opening paragraph of the unpublished "She, Robot"

"Now is the winter of our discontent, made glorious summer by that red hot divorcee who lives next door. She's always giving me the eye, and I was certain that she'd go for a 'hump' in more ways than one": Shakespeare, Richard III

"Twas brillig, and the slithy toves did gyre and gimble in the wabe: Her mimsy was all slither'd bare, and I couldn't believe it when she suggested her best friend join in too!!!": Lewis Carroll, Jabberwocky

"Suddenly Winston Smith began writing in sheer panic, only imperfectly aware of what he was setting down. His small but childish handwriting straggled up and down the page, shedding first its capital letters and finally even its full stops: 'Dear Fiesta, There's this girl at work called Julia who's been giving me the eye. I thought I had no chance but one day after the two minutes hate she...'": George Orwell, 1984

"The LORD said unto Moses

"If a man marries both a woman and her mother, it is wicked."

And Moses said unto the LORD

"Excellent!"

And the LORD sayeth unto Moses

"No, you bloody idiot. I'm saying it's BAD."

And Moses said again unto the LORD

"Too bloody right it's bad, you won't believe the amazing thing that happened to me the other day. I was alone in the tent and the wife's mother came round to muck out the donkeys. I never realised how sexy she was until I saw her with that shovel…"

And the LORD shaketh His head and goes off to find another chosen people." The Book of Leviticus

"And then, she done a poo": Anon

Q E blummin' D, as they say, but not in the letters column of Knave.

And from my loyal band of readers, who prove on a regular basis they can be just as manky as I am:

"Annual income 20 pounds, annual expenditure 19.19.6, result sixpence to spend on marmite, rubber bands, bootlaces and four hours with that lusty trollope next door." Charles Dickens, David Copperfeel (Vicus Scurra)

"Call me Ishmael. Some years ago -- never mind how long precisely -- having little or no money in my purse, and nothing particular to interest me on shore, I thought I would sail about a little and see the watery part of the world. It is a way I have of driving off the spleen, and regulating the circulation. Whenever I find myself growing hard I wander down to the less salubrious parts of town, behind the coffin warehouses where the ladies of the night gather. There I seek Mistress Betty or Lady Wilhemina, pull out my pistol and lay loose a volley of essence upon the white-capped smoothness of their rounded buttocks." Herman Melville, Moby Dick (Balders)

"TO CONFINE OUR ATTENTION TO TERRESTRIAL MATTERS WOULD BE TO LIMIT THE HUMAN SPIRIT. SO HAND ME THE KY JELLY, HOP ON, AND LET'S GET COSMIC BABY." Stephen Hawking, A Brief History of Time (GW)

Then.

We.

Did it.

Lots.

Harold Pinter (SeanDubh)

"The past is a foreign country, they do things differently there. Doggie-style, for starters." LP Harley, The Go-Between (Katherine)

"If your enemy is secure at all points, be prepared for him. If he is in superior strength, evade him. If your opponent is temperamental, seek to irritate him. Nip in through his back door and do his wife on the kitchen table" Sun Tzu, The Art of War (Angus Prune)

"Harry and Ron clutched their magic wands as Hermione's robe fell to the ground." JK Rowling, the as yet unwritten Harry Potter Book Seven, where they're all 18, obviously (Misty)

"Piss IV: The Curse of Piss"

Drink! The curse of the working classes, and I should know as I've mixed the two. Frequently.

Back in the days between leaving college and finding a real job, my friends and I drunk like those proverbial fish. Unfortunately, our local also did a rather fine range of chocolate-flavoured desserts, all served from a refrigerated cabinet mere feet away from our favourite table. It was a recipe for disaster.

A good session would involve between six and eight pints of the late-lamented Eldridge Pope Royal Oak ale, a crate of dry-roasted peanuts and at least two of those gateaux that come in boxes saying "Serves Twelve". There were six of us. In two years I put on three stone, and if I got drunk enough, you could roll me home.

It didn't take me long to work out that another few years of this would leave me looking like a professional darts player, shopping for clothes in places like "High and Mighty" and "Vince's Lard Boy Emporium", so I bravely knocked the juice and cake on the head for a bit, took up cycling and eventually restored myself to the picture of slightly chubby health that I am today. Oh, but there were blips. Big blips. Like the last day in my first job. I'd tell you about it, if I could remember what happened, but I'm pretty certain that vomit was involved. But the Big One was the Christmas party for my first real job outside the fluffy world of Her Majesty's Civil Service. A night I would live to regret.

In all the time I've been in this job - some sixteen years at the time of writing - our department has been an all-male affair. We've had a whole two-and-a-half women - two genuine and rather dedicated ladies and a pre-op transsexual - and the rest has been Bloke City. At one stage there were over sixty of us, a great festering pool of testosterone, locked in a compound somewhere in the South Oxfordshire countryside. And to quote Jeff Goldblum in Jurassic Park, "Drink will find a way." And so it did. Christmas came, and Bob organised a party. In a pub.

You could tell in advance what kind of evening it was going to be. Someone had hired a minibus to get us all home. Naive young chap that I was, I thought that this was because the pub was in the middle of nowhere. All well and good - but I hadn't realised that half of my twenty quid for the sit-down meal was actually going into the world's biggest bar tab, which we all put another tenner into on arrival.

We ate. We drunk. We arranged a good old-fashioned lock-in with the landlord. We drunk some more. Just before midnight, a taxi came to take some of the lads for their nightshift. We drunk to their good health. And drunk some more. I think you're getting the picture now. Drink was involved. Lots of it, and the greatest sin of them all - we mixed ale with spirits with wine with something green and even more beer. At some point (and this is always the telltale sign that you've gone too far), we started singing. Songs about an Eskimo called Nell and "stupid dicky-di-dildos".

It was around this point that things became blurred. I remember stumbling out into the cold night air, finding a seat on the bus, and then the torturous route home with frequent stops to let people off, either for a much needed piss, or simply because we had accidentally ended up at someone's house. With more than a little luck, I was eventually turfed out at the end of my road, and I staggered up the two flights of stairs to my flat.

Mrs Duck hadn't bothered to wait up. I shut the front door as quietly as I could, managing to disturb everybody within two hundred yards. I fell over in the dark. I said "fuck", realised I had said "fuck", giggled, and realising I was giggling, said "fuck" again. I went into the bedroom, where Mrs Duck was now awake and asking me in a rather pointed manner if I knew what the time was. I told her I did, it was nearly one o'clock and that I "really, really, really loved her." She was unimpressed. Some people just have no sense of humour. I fell into bed, and sickly, spinning darkness took me. For a bit.

I woke. The room was still spinning - violently so, in fact - but there were more pressing matters to attend to. Eight pints of heavy, a bottle of wine and lord alone knows what else had gone in at one end, and now they wanted out. Quite urgently. I staggered out of bed, and eventually made it to the bathroom. Whipping out The Mighty Mallet, I let go with what was surely going to be the greatest piss of my lifetime.

My fuzzy ball of contentment lasted all of three seconds. A light came on. There was a shriek of surprise and alarm. I was not in the bathroom. Oh no. I had taken a wrong turning and I was still in the bedroom. What I had taken for the cold porcelain of the toilet was, in fact, Mrs Duck's dressing table, now a streaming river of piss and resembling the back step of a pub at closing time.

Fair play to her, she didn't beat me up or anything, for she knew one thing I didn't. My Christmas presents were hidden under that table. So, on Christmas Day that year, I received my most prized possession ever - a signed photo of the entire 1989 title-winning Arsenal FC squad, with little yellow wrinkles round the edge.

Damn you beer, why do you treat your old friend like this?

The next day, I had to go to work. They were feeling particularly generous that day, and I didn't have to start until lunchtime, but I still sat at a workstation in the corner and did the absolute minimum that my presence required. On the way home I bought myself a catering pack of Resolve and - by way of apologising for the Night of Piss - Mrs Duck a fluffy duck called Wello. It was the least I could do. She cut his beak off and threw him out of the window.

There is a strange epilogue to this tale which would not look out of place in a special pissed-up edition of The Fortean Times:

Just before Christmas, I ran into my drinking buddies Pat and John, sipping orange juice and lemonades down the Old Devil, eyeing up the contents of the refrigerated cabinet longingly. Like me, they had sworn off drink for the week after their office Christmas parties. On the same night I had rendered Mrs Duck's hairdryer inoperable (simultaneously solving the problem of what to buy her that year), John had staggered home drunk from his party, taken a wrong turning, and pissed out of the bedroom window into the street below. Pat, on the other hand, had also taken a wrong turning, gone downstairs, got hopelessly lost and was discovered by Mrs Pat relieving himself in the corner of the kitchen. Heroes to a man. Up and down the country, AT THAT EXACT TIME, wives were catching their men folk urinating in unusual places. They never showed that one on The X-Files.

As one, we took the drinkers' vow: "Never, ever again." Not until the next time, anyway. Gateau was served.

Leaving Do

Dave was a jockey. He came down from Liverpool with a talent for stealing the hubcaps off horses and got a job in one of the famous stables at Lambourne in the Berkshire Downs.

It soon became apparent that this Stable Lad had one handicap - in the world of horse racing, small is beautiful, and this jockey wouldn't stop growing. He blamed hormones. We blamed the jockey's curse: pie retention. Any horse he got onto would scream for mercy and run slower and slower before stopping, resigned, outside the knackers' yard. Dave was asked to hang up his shit-shovelling shovel and was shown the door.

And that is how Dave left the world of gee-gees behind him and ended up bored out of his skull in the same office as me at the Ministry of Agriculture Cow Counting Department.

The Horses, however, were never far from his mind. On a typical day, you'd find him at his desk, hiding behind a huge pile of files, on the phone to his bookies, a copy of the Sporting Life sitting in his lap.

In a fit of anti-gambling fervour, we eventually confronted him over his habit.

"Dave," we said, "You're wasting your money on the nags, you'll end up in mounds of debt."

"Oh yeah?" he said.

"Err... yeah."

So we kept a tab on his gambling habits. He ended the month seven hundred quid up, and handed in his notice.

"It's no good lads, this isn't the life for me. I'm off to see the world."

He worked off his notice period, his feet getting itchier by the day, racking up even bigger wins on the gee-gees, while selling off his huge record collection to pay for his world tour, mostly to me.

And so, come his final day, he sprung a surprise on the rest of the office. He'd put three hundred quid behind the bar at the Reading Hexagon, and anyone who would like to come and help him drink it would be more than welcome. It was a no-brainer. Spend a Friday afternoon writing letters to Irish beef farmers in a dull concrete office block, or get stupidly drunk in the cultural hub of the Thames Valley. Mine's a large one. A very large one.

The Hexagon is actually a theatre. A horrible concrete theatre of absolutely no character whatsoever, whose annual highlight is Keith Chegwin doing the Christmas panto. It did, however, have one redeeming feature. It was the bar closest to our office. And as news of Dave's generosity got round, the place was stuffed with civil servants happily knocking back free booze.

The place was heaving, and pretty soon it was nigh on impossible to move. A trip to the bar could take up to twenty minutes, so we ordered three rounds at a time. With the amount of alcohol being consumed, it was inevitable that sooner or later somebody was going to need to go to the toilet for the fatal first piss of the session.

And that's where the trouble started. The toilets were a good thirty yards away across a bar full of tightly-packed and gently swaying civil servants taking time off from their cow counting duties. Dave, who'd been drinking since the place opened, was in no fit state to make the trip.

"Ladsh!" he slurred, "I needs a pish!"

Fair play to him, he made a brave attempt to force his way through the crowds, but the sheer numbers, the constant interruptions from his new drinking buddies attempting to wish him well and shake his hand, and his total inability to put one leg in front of the other soon saw him back at our table. A desperate man, he looked around for an alternative.

There was a pot plant. It was a big tub on the floor with a small tree, which may or may not have been plastic.

Dave looked at the plant. We looked at Dave. Dave staggered to his feet, his intention clear.

"Dave mate," said our boss in his scariest possible voice, "I would strongly advise you against pursuing that course of action."

Unfortunately, because it held far too many difficult concepts for the average drunk to comprehend, the boss man's warning had absolutely no authority whatsoever. Besides, how could you take the bass player from a Blues Brothers tribute band called Blooz Cruize seriously? This is a man who could recite the words to "Shake Your Tail-feather" in his sleep, and was therefore put in charge of counting cows AND pigs by the UK government.

Out came Dave's old man, and with a palpable sigh of relief he watered the plastic pot plant. He was lucky - such was the crush, the management didn't see what had happened. He slumped back in his chair to see our shocked faces.

"Where's me drink?"

The bar management had certainly missed Dave's golden shower, but other boozers had not. Faced with the same impossible task of reaching the Gents, they too followed their leader's example, headed for our corner and happily hosed away. After the fifth or sixth punter, a river of piss was now gently flowing across the floor in a miniature tribute to Wembley Stadium.

Then Dave dropped a bombshell. Literally.

"I need a shit."

We were mortified.

"No. Dave. Don't."

"Put your cork in."

"Wait until we get back to work."

"Don't even think about it."

"I can't look."

We looked.

Emboldened by his great liberating wazz and the example of his followers, Drunk Dave dropped his trousers and laid a hefty log in the plant pot. He was just wiping up on one of the plastic leaves, when he was grabbed from behind by two bouncers, and trousers still round his ankles, was carried through a crowd parting like the Red Sea to the door. Amazing, isn't it, what a half-naked drunk wrestling with two gorillas will do to a crowd.

What was previously a packed, noisy bar went deathly silent. People were already making for the exit. The manager was in apoplexy.

"That's it! All you Ministry people - you're all barred!"

Being just about his only lunchtime customers, we remained barred for a whole week.

Dave, as good as his word, went off on his world tour, getting as far as a potted yucca plant in an Australian bar before the money ran out. Within three months he was back at his desk, hidden behind a pile of files on the phone to his bookie. Broke as I was, I sold him his records back.

He is still barred from the Hexagon.

His poo, however, encouraged by its stunning theatrical debut, forged a successful career on stage and screen under the name Michael Barrymore.

Diet Club

The first rule of diet club: You do not eat all the pies.

The second rule of diet club: You DO NOT eat all the pies.

There was no denying it, Pauline was a big woman, and a career sitting in a civil service office counting cows wasn't exactly helping her lose the pounds, particularly as our office was directly over a Tesco supermarket and the lure of the daily cream cake run. To be honest, it was doing none of us much good, and the girl with the sandwich trolley was often lucky to escape with her life.

So, it was hardly surprising that Pauline should come in one morning with the news that her doctor had ordered her to lose weight. About three stone. And rather than having a spare limb lopped off, she was going to do it the hard way - by not eating and taking exercise. Was she mad?

Being civil servants with nothing to do except count the cars in the Tesco car park and work out the day's most popular colour, we jumped on this chance to do something - anything - like tramps at an all-you-can-eat dustbin.

We all took it terribly seriously, setting ourselves target weights, drawing up a hugely complicated graph, and laying out the rules of Diet Club in the best Civil-Servantese. I had a stone to lose, Mark two, and

Jeff, the skinny streak of piss, actually had to put on weight. Andy was excused because of his dicky heart, and was put in charge of liberating different coloured pens from the heavily-guarded stock cupboard to make the graph more interesting.

Andy was a militant vegan, recently made redundant from a health food shop. When he told the Job Centre this fact, they immediately found him employment at an abattoir, cutting up freshly slaughtered cows. The civil service was his second choice.

Monday was weigh-in day. You had to go down to Boots the Chemist, put your twenty pence in the electronic scales, and by the miracles of this modern microchip age, you brought the printed read-out back to Andy for verification and proper recording on the graph, which was prominently displayed on the wall, just under my Joy Division poster.

Jeff: "Who's this Joy Davison bird, then?"

In effect there was only one rule to Diet Club: don't cheat.

Monday mornings were spent swearing off the cake and squeezing the biggest log possible out on the toilet before lunch.

You wore your lightest clothes, even on the coldest, wettest of winter days, and we would all sit there, starving, waiting for lunch-time and the dash down to Boots for the computer slip of doom. All except Jeff, who would stuff his face stupid in front of us, while Andy stunk the place out with herbal tea.

The desperation on a Monday was palpable. Pauline steadily lost weight, while Mark steadily headed up the graph, and mine see-sawed up and down like a see-sawy up and down thing. The forfeits were enough to encourage steady weight loss - essentially being everybody's tea-making and paper-filing bitch for the whole week, physically restrained from spending money on the sandwich trolley.

Reports soon reached us that Mark was offering money to colleagues to act as ringers at his weigh-in, and come back with a slip showing a stunning weight loss. This, naturally, could not be tolerated, resulting in the severe punishment of hiding his cigarettes and getting the switchboard to bar phone access to the betting shop. Mark was a desperate man, and as we all know, desperation makes us take desperate measures.

It was three o'clock on Monday afternoon. We had all reported back from our lunch-time weigh-ins with a series of respectable results.

Pauline was particularly pleased as the weight was simply melting off her, straight onto poor old Mark. Just a shame he seemed to have left the office at one and rather neglected to return. Had he done a runner on us, the big fat bloater?

Security, ten floors below us, gave our office a call. Could somebody come down and vouch for a staff member who has mislaid his pass? Of course we could. I went. Anything to get out of real life work. And God, was it worth it.

There in the reception area was the security guard, a burly police officer and Mark, wearing nothing but his crusty y-fronts and a blanket.

"Yeah, he works here," I said trying not to laugh, "but usually he's got clothes on."

Poor, poor Mark. He got to Boots the Chemist, and desperation took hold of him. Spurred on by that TV advert of that fella taking his clothes off in the launderette, he put his money into the weighing machine, stripped down to his pants, and as the world stared, he jumped onto the scales for his best weigh-in for weeks.

When he stepped down from the scales to get dressed, he found that some joker had done a runner with all his duds. It was only a matter of time before there was this blue flashing light and an invitation to spend the afternoon in a bang-you-in-the-ass police cell, which he politely refused.

And there, standing by the lift door, was the head of personnel. He wanted answers to bloody difficult questions. Diet Club was officially banned.

And Mark. I let him have his clothes back. Eventually.

On Law

So what exactly, does the Master of the Rolls, one of Britain's top judicial posts do? The answer to this question is a simple one: The Master of the Rolls is a traditional post, handed down through the centuries to the most senior judge in the country, usually after a legal career lasting many years.

He has seen causes celebres come and go, criminals, traitors, politicians and has handed down judgements in some of the most important cases in recent years, and it is now time for him to take it easy.

The Master of the Rolls does one job and one job only - he is in charge of the lunch menu at the Old Bailey.

Top Shelf, or, Days of Chunder

On the Bath Road between Reading and the aptly-named town of Maidenhead (it's full of twats) lies the village of Knowle Hill. It is the home of a drinking establishment known as the Old Devil Inn, purveyors of strong ales, stronger spirits and artery-clogging pub food. We went there so often, that several of us seriously considered donating a defibrillator to the landlord for the inevitable day one of us had a heart-attack over a pint and cake.

Friday and Saturday nights - not to mention the odd Sunday and midweek binge - were spent in our favoured window seats knocking back the Royal Oak (original gravity 1054 - that's damn strong) and polishing off the pub speciality quadruple chocolate gateau and cream. At any one time there could be as few as four of us, or as many as ten, depending on money and alcohol poisoning status. I'm lucky to be alive.

But you know how it is with drink. You do stupid stuff, usually involving even more alcohol. All it takes is one loose comment, and your evening takes a turn for the worse, and there is nothing you can do from stopping it. And Pat made it:

"How many shorts do you reckon you can you fit in a pint glass?"

"Why don't we find out?" his brother John suggested.

Uh-oh.

"You know," said Pat, the connoisseur of the alcoholic art, "a pint of spirits is known as a 'Top Shelf'."

"How so?"

"Becausssse," he slurred, "You go along the top shelf of the bar taking one shot from each optic. Top Shelf. Shimple."

One thing led to another, and a brief inspection of funds indicated that we could quite easily afford such a drink, and one or two of us might even be persuaded to take a sip or two. Myself, already three sheets to the wind was minded to decline, however.

"Why, you chicken?"

"Because I'll fucking die, that'sh why."

"That'sh fair enough then."

We sidled up to the bar. Mike the Aussie barman gave us his usual "What are you mad Poms up to now?" look and we made the order with a feeble attempt to curry his favour.

"Top Shelf, please Mike. And whatever you're having."

"A what?!"

"Top Shelf," Pat repeated, pointing to the top shelf of the bar behind our able server.

Mike tried his best, but he was unable to pull the shelf away from the wall. So instead, following our directions, he took a pint glass and worked his way along, pouring one shot from each optic. It took eighteen, and cost somewhere in the region of twenty quid. These days, it would be nearer thirty.

"There you go chaps," he said, carrying the thing to the bar as if it was filled with nuclear waste, "Don't drink it all at once."

All of a sudden, it had lost its appeal. It looked dangerous, and smelled sickly. The whole idea would have died a death had a) we not already paid for the bloody thing and b) some German visitor to the pub not overheard the whole episode and announced that she wanted to take part in this (and I quote) "quaint old English custom." That would be the quaint English old custom of bowking large quantities of vomit into the gutter of a Friday night, then.

In the end, only two of the drunkards were up for it. Pat and Clive. Like troopers they gave it a go, both proclaiming that it was "bloody disgusting" and "which idiot put Pernod in it?" all the while staring at Mike, coolly sipping his glass of Diet Coke.

I will allow Clive to continue the story from here:

"I seem to remember I gave up somewhere around the 3/4 pint mark, or maybe a bit more. Anyway, I was slurred, sloshed, and barely capable of projectile vomiting into the pan in the bogs. Scary and John dragged me to the car park, as Pat said something like "Oi, not going to waste a good drink!" and downed the remainder. He then walked out the front door, and as the cold night air hit him, barfed all over one of the flower beds out the front. Oh such fun, at least neither of us were sick in the car on the way back."

Nope - they waited until they got back to Clive's house, where we witnessed a drunken zigzag sprint for the bathroom, followed by prolonged retching and the sound of heavy-duty redecorating. Clive's mum, used to these episodes on a near weekly basis, rolled her eyes in the now customary "He's done it *again*" manner.

Clive survived, but not without cruel, unexplained injuries - the price the casual drunk pays for his crimes against sobriety. Spotted in Budgens, he was, buying a bottle of Bushmills and some Preparation H. Hair of the dog, as it were. If the dog had a sore arse.

It wasn't over yet. Following the puking came an attack of the munchies. It was at that opportune moment that my brother turned up to give me a lift home.

He had wheels. His pride and joy was a clapped out Austin Allegro he had got cheaply from an elderly great uncle, and we would use it to go to the Chinese Takeaway in Twyford. We piled in, and amused him greatly with our repertoire of rugby songs on the way.

Who can failed to be amused by a rousing chorus of "I'm a stupid dicky-di-dildo!" from a bunch of drunks?

This island of drunken tranquility couldn't last.

"I'm gonna puke!" said Pat.

"GET OUT OF MY CAR!"

He did, staggering into the street and hurling all over the front wing of Nigel's Aggro.

"I'm gonna puke!" groaned John, who had not even touched the Top Shelf.

"GET OUT OF MY..."

Too late.

Fair play to John, he tried to wind down the window, only to find it would only go halfway. Isn't it amazing how vomit splatters, dear reader? There was puke everywhere, all over the inside AND outside of the car, and I'm sorry to say, most of the occupants. We stunk like a stairwell in a multi-storey car park, and being my mates, it was all my fault.

So, guess who, with a stinking hangover, had to clear the mess up the next day? As I hosed it down, I knew it was bad when I saw Dad's car floating into next door's garden on a tide of diluted vomit.

Most of it ended up in the windscreen washer bottle. It was the least I could do.

On tourism

Visiting London? This is all the information you'll need. Honest.

* 'Bobbies' - the British police - now prefer to be called 'Titheads', and have a secret signal that involves raising the middle finger of your left hand at them
* Why not visit the quaint village of Dagenham?
* At Windsor Castle there is a fifty pound spot prize for the first person to sit in the Queen's throne
* All taxis in London are free - just get out and walk away when you reach your destination. The proper name for a London taxi driver is a "sponger"
* The Tower of London has been moved to Swindon, which is walking distance from any West End hotel
* The National Gallery allows visitors to take pictures home with them - you don't even have to ask, they've got loads
* Changing the Guards at Buckingham Palace is made twice as good if you join in
* The Houses of Parliament have a fifteen minute "guest spot" which allows any visitor to get up and sing. 'Simply the Best' by Tina Turner goes down very well
* The police need as much help as possible with the capital's heavy traffic, and are always on the lookout for volunteers to direct traffic around Trafalgar Square. Just buy a helmet from any souvenir stall, and start work straight away!

Party

Steve had a moving out party. Despite falling out with the lanky git over those malicious "one bollock" rumours, I foolishly accepted his invitation. Turning up on my bike, I leant it against the skip outside his soon-to-be vacated council house and dived into the throbbing mass of humanity.

The skip, in retrospect, was a bad idea. People, turning up from miles around, drawn in by the thud of music and the waft of barely clad student, mistook the affair for a demolition party, and were setting about the place with a certain amount of gusto. It was clear, right from the start, that Steve was going to lose his deposit.

Not that I cared. This girl from college I had fancied for ages was there. Julia had come all the way from Bracknell just to be leered at by me. She had huge norks, a tight jumper and really, really tight jeans, and tonight would be the night that I would be the manly man and make my move. Right.

But first, a little drink and friendly banter to calm my nerves.

Then, another drink and a few matey laughs to calm my nerves.

And a calm to drink my nerves, buddy. Buddy-bud-bud.

And a nerves to ...err... yer me best mate, hic!

Cider.

Vodka.

Vodka.

Cider.

And this was proper scrumpy, from genuine, traditional plastic jugs with bits of tree at the bottom, not that fizzy crap I was forced to sell to winos in my Saturday job at a local supermarket for tramps.

With the party spinning, and the Frank Zappa classics "I promise not to come in your mouth" and "The Illinois Enema Bandit" ringing in my ears, I stumbled across the room to my beloved, perched as serenely as is possible on a beanbag in the living room. And I did exactly what any teenager would do after several pints of yokel-strength scrumpy and half a bottle of Russian paint-stripper.

"Awight Jooooliah!"

I grabbed her norks and puked down her front.

Putty in my hands.

I was hounded out of the party on a wave of disgust, stopping only to puke once more all over everybody's coats and jackets by the front door, and then onto two people scavenging from the skip in the front garden. I would be *persona non grata* round that neck of the woods for some time to come, and rightly so. I am still haunted by the look of horror on my beloved's face as I chundered booze and party snacks over her billowing cleavage.

I mounted my bike and made for home doing a whole 3 mph all the way, followed by the local plod, who was laughing too much to write me a ticket for being drunk in charge of a bicycle. Besides, I would only have added diced carrots to his freshly-pressed uniform. I was home by nine o'clock, much to the surprise of my parents, who were holding a rather posh candlelit soiree with a small group of friends and influential colleagues.

"Oh! Scary! Home already?" said my mother whilst passing round a rather pungent curry dish which my father had spent the best part of two days preparing.

"Uh," I said, "I don't feel too good."

There was a pause before I added: "Yaaaarch!"

All over the dog, who ate the lot and was soon as pissed as I was.

Thrown out of two parties in one night, and a hangover to match. The shame of it.

Meanwhile, in a council house in nearby Wargrave, my so-called mate Steve had taken pity on the love of my life, taken her upstairs, cleaned her up and had a go on her tits. Bastard.

Mao

"A revolution is not a dinner party." - Mao Tse-Tung, 1927
"Big bag of chips, please." - Scaryduck, 1982

Your conventional view of history says Chairman Mao died in 1976 after a long, distinguished life at the forefront of the Chinese Communist Revolution. That is, as we all know, a load of old cobblers. In reality, Mao Tse-Tung tired of running a country of one billion citizens and all their petty, personal problems, faked his death and ran off to run a fish and chip shop in the South of England.

Now don't get me wrong. He was a lovely bloke. You'd find it very hard to believe that this was the man who had led his people on the Glorious

Long March, had overthrown the corrupt government of Chiang Kai-Shek and saw his country re-born in the red-hot crucible of the Cultural Revolution. No wonder he wanted the quiet life. He cooked the best chips in Henley, too, as the long queues out of the shop door would testify.

With decades of Marxist-Leninist revolutionary leadership under his belt, it wasn't long before the other chip shops in the area withered under Mao's Great Leap Forward. Only the capitalist running dogs of The Brown Trout (its real name, I kid you not) survived, the long queues out of the door of this chip shop testament only to the fact that he cooked every single portion to order. One at a time.

We all loved Chairman Mao, and if he gave his Little Red Book of Fish Recipes away with every packet of chips, the entire population of Henley would have been card carrying reds by now, and not under the jack-booted powers of capitalist oppression that is Michael Heseltine and... err... Boris Johnson.

I actually went to college with Mao's son Andy, a youth who worshipped the music of Phil Collins rather too much to be completely healthy. He once filled an entire C-90 cassette with "Easy Lover", back to back, over and over to listen to in his car. This was shortly before I bludgeoned him to death with a frozen haddock. When pushed on the matter and threatened with the withdrawal of our trade for the pedestrian delights of the Brown Trout, he finally revealed the one great secret of the Chinese Takeaway.

"Andy," I asked, "When someone comes in and orders just chips, do you all come out of the kitchen holding meat cleavers and stare at them?"

"Yup. It's part of the job description."

"What do you say?"

"I go for the lyrics to 'In the Air Tonight'. My mum and dad run through the shopping list."

Rumbled. Phil Collins has a lot to answer for.

But it was dealing with Mao himself that caused the greatest problem. Great leader that he was, English was not his first language. He learned enough to serve the punters, and then stopped, causing no end of problems if you wanted anything more complicated than a pickled egg. Backed into a corner, he'd come out fighting with the only English phrase that came to mind.

189

"Sal'Vinegar?"

It became his catchphrase.

"Excuse me mate, can you change a tenner?"

"Sal'Vinegar?"

"Oi! The fruit machine ain't paying out!"

"Sal'Vinegar?"

"Do you do saveloys?"

"Sal'Vinegar?"

To the uninitiated, this could be confusing to say the least, and would sometimes lead to the poor customer fleeing the shop in terror at the barrage of requests for Sal'Vinegar. Being teenagers with a cruel sense of humour, and an embarrassingly old-fashioned concept of foreigners, we laid a trap.

Ian the Shed was new to the area. Shed desperately wanted to be our friend. We let Shed hang around with us on the proviso that he bought us all chips.

"Now, Shed", we warned him sternly, "this guy doesn't like having people take the piss out of him."

"Right."

"So, whatever you do, don't laugh."

"Right. No laughing."

Andy laid it on as thickly as he could: "Dad's very touchy about it. Don't laugh. He'll kill you."

"I get the message."

"Keep it zipped. Schtum. Especially when he asks you if you want salt and vinegar."

The trap was set. All we had to do was stand in the doorway. And wait.

"Five portions of chips, please."

You've got to hand it to Mao. He gave it his all.

"Saaaaaal'Vinegaaaaaar?"

Poor old Shed. He tried. God, how he tried. He bit his cheeks, tears streamed from his eyes, and his chest convulsed. But, sooner or later, he had to open his mouth to reply.

"Saaaaaal'Vinegaaaaaar?" Mao pressed.

He managed to squeak a meek "No thanks", before doubling up, the laughter roaring out like water from a drain.

Mao, bless him, had seen it all before and knew the rules of the game. He went for the meat cleaver and started shouting out his shopping list in Chinese.

"Three pints of milk!" he screamed, brandishing his weapon.

That certainly shut up Shed's laughing, as a look of fear invaded his face.

"Two loaves of bread and a packet of rice!"

Shed turned on his heels and scarpered from the shop, never to return.

"AND DON'T FORGET THE MARGARINE!" bellowed Mao after him, waving the meat cleaver around his head like a man possessed.

From respected world statesman who once told Richard Nixon to mind his step getting off that plane, to knife-wielding fish and chips magnate who, when pressed, could do a very passable impression of Cato from the Pink Panther, Mao Tse-Tung was our hero of the deep-fat fryer still going strong at the age of one hundred and nine.

And like the total hero that he was, Mao let us have our chips for nothing, and with as much sal'vinegar as we wanted. After all, as every good Marxist revolutionary will tell you: All property is theft.

During my researches for this piece, I have been told that Mao Tse-Tung had a penchant for de-flowering virgins, the dirty old sod. I bet they got free chips after. And a saveloy.

Blarney

Confession O'Booze: I'm at least 25 per cent Irish. Possibly more. And to prove it, I've done the going-back-to-my-roots tourist thing and kissed the Blarney Stone. An event which, in retrospect, explains a lot of things about the way I am now.

The Great Kissing of the Stone marked the halfway point in a pissed-up student holiday in Ireland, and the day we discovered The Worst Pub In Cork. No disrespect to the fair people of the city, but the whole place appears to be twinned with Portsmouth, only without the sailors; with public houses staffed by the East German women's shot putt team. In fact, Cork can be described by at least one of our party as "God, what a shit-hole. Worse than Catford."

Not many pubs either side of the water greet you with the words "Goddam it, you're a smelly, greasy fecker", so I suppose John had a point.

Disgusted with the fizzy keg beer and stone cold welcome in O'Bastard's Bar, we headed into the country and the fine surrounds of Blarney Castle. To the top of the crumbling Gormenghastian edifice we climbed, leaned backwards over the abyss and landed a big old smacker on the legendary stone. Moist, but no tongues nor genitals were involved.

On the way down we ran into a party of Wilburs - elderly American tourists, doing a tour of the "Old Country" in a large air-conditioned coach with "The Emerald Isle" written in green lettering on the front. This was the only time I have ever seen these words written down in all the time I've lived and holidayed in Ireland. Walking clichés the lot of them - flat-peaked baseball caps, plaid trousers and face-lifted wives. Easy meat.

"Top o' the mornin'!" we greeted them in faux-Irish accents, despite the fact that it was three o'clock in the afternoon. One of us at this stage may even have said "Bejebus" and "To be sure, to be sure."

Stopping for a rest, the Head Wilbur asked "Say, is it a long way to the top?"

"Miles," I lied.

"And then they hang you over the edge..." said Pat.

"...by the ankles..." continued John.

"...and there's no safety net," finished Clive.

The Wilburs just stared at us. They'd come all the way from Pigdick, Arkansas and nobody told them there was a higher than average chance of falling hundreds of feet to their doom. And the nearest vexatious claims lawyer was over 3,000 miles away.

"Do they..." started a clearly rattled Wilburette.

"...drop anyone?" Pat continued.

"That's right..."

"Hardly ever. No safety gear, but those old girls certainly have a strong grip, bearing in mind the arthritis."

Obviously, the stone's legendary powers were already coursing through us. Some of the Wilburs were already having second thoughts and were torn between completing their pilgrimage and fleeing to the air-conditioned safety of their Emerald Isle Express. Anywhere, in fact, that wasn't near these long-haired lunatics. Time, then, to twist the knife.

"Oh, it's all totally safe," said Clive, "except..."

"Except what?" gasped a Mrs Wilbur.

"They never wash the stone."

There was an instant, germ-free reaction.

"You mean..."

"You name it, they got it. Herpes. Hepatitis. Cold Sores. **AIDS**." The last was added with a completely unnecessary air of terror, striking horror into the collected Wilburs, like a huge pork sword to the heart.

"OH. MY. GOD. THAT'S IT!" screamed a Mrs Wilbur, "Come on Wilbur, we're leaving!"

There was a mild panic on the narrow spiral stairs as two dozen Wilburs in varying sized draw-string pants attempted a three-point turn and flee to some nice craft centre selling plastic Leprechauns.

Mission accomplished. How we laughed.

We went to the pub that night to celebrate our victory over the Great Satan, in a village with a donkey roaming up and down the main street, and a public phone box that invited you to press button A and button B to make a call. Unlike Cork, the welcome was warm, and the Guinness and fire-water flowed.

As we reached that point in the evening on the border between consciousness and the technicolor yawn, a local collapsed against the bar next to us.

"So, where've you guys been?" he asked, while gamely standing us all drinks.

"All over. Waterford. Cork. Blarney."

"Och, you didn't kiss the Stone, did ya? Feck, but them Yanks is fat daft buggers. Sweet jayzus they is, or oim the Pope's mother." Or words to that effect.

I appeared to be talking to another national cliché. Ireland appeared to be full of them today.

"Well..." I replied, expecting to be lectured on the pitfalls of the local tourist trap.

"You **do** know about the kids there?"

"No, but I've a feeling you're going to tell us anyway."

So he told us. The local kids, so the story goes, get pissed on tins of Heineken shoplifted from the local Spar market, break into the castle when the last tourist buses have gone, climb the three million steps to the top and piss all over the Blarney Stone. Regularly. Twice a night sometimes, in the knowledge that gullible American tourists would be puckering up to their fresh onion water the very next morning.

And we had kissed it.

And we had prevented gullible American tourists from doing the same.

Violated, that's how I felt, and worse, there was no wire brush available to scrub my lips and tongue. Only one thing for it - dilute the germs and flush them out of my system.

"Barman! Six pints of Guinness please!"

"Right you are."

"And my friends will have the same."

Cured.

Chicken
written by Nigel Coleman

A special guest story! This just proves that it does run in the family, and that I can handle tales of mirth and woe which are better than mine.

There are of course many advantages to be gained when moving in with your girlfriend. I won't list them here...use your imagination. But inevitably there is a certain amount of baggage that gets brought to the party. For example - and I'm expecting back-up here - every shit middle-of-the-road CD I've ever bought her (including that bald fuck Phil Collins) is now being played on MY sound system*. I'd have put a damn sight more thought into Xmas presents if I'd though we would end up shacked-up together. She'd have got Radiohead.

And then there is her horse.

Now don't get me wrong - her horse is a much-loved part of the family.

My daughters think it's the coolest thing on four legs, the girlfriend has doted on it since she was twelve (and yes, I know where your mind is going with this - Sandra is 38 now so pack it in), and believe me there are days in my job where I envy the life where you stand in a field and shit yourself without a care in the world.

The thing is, in the same way that I now can't avoid Phil Collins (unless I do some hammer drilling), I now am involved in the care of the horse. Going-down-to-the-farmyard-involved. Getting-your-car-muddy involved. Scraping-shit-off-your-Boss-trainers involved. And that's how I ended up entangled in the life of a chicken.

We were out shopping one Saturday afternoon when she asked me to detour to buy some 'feed' to put into the sharp end of said horse. I was always under the impression that she turfed it into a field every morning and it ate the grass, but apparently it eats 'breakfast'. You live and learn. Having loaded my beloved car with stinky bags of shit until the exhaust was dragging we set off for the farm where she pays for him to live.

Let me at this point put in a brief note about chickens. This might come as a shock to some people, but chickens are the most stinky, repulsive and nasty creatures to walk the Earth. Not only would they eat anything and everything put in from of them, they'd eat each other at the drop of a hat given half a chance. They're like rats with feathers and with more attitude. And what's with all that horrible red dangly skin stuff around their faces? It looks like they're all wearing Harry Redknapp's eyelids.

Anyway, when we arrived, the farmyard was covered in the little pecky tossers, which was a bit of a problem as I was buggered if I was going to heft the aforementioned stinky bags across the yard. I wanted to back the car up to the barn.

"Don't worry" she said, "They're not stupid. They'll move out of your way."

I backed the car up at 0 mph across the yard until I reached the barn. I then crippled myself heaving bags of stuff into the barn whilst she cooed and kissed the horse like a 'My Little Pony' advert (and incidentally, that's the mouth that she kisses me with...nice). When I was done, I noticed that the chickens where gathering around my car - and one of the fuckers even pecked the door! I ran at them shouting that piece of language that is internationally recognised in a way that the inventors of Esperanto can only dream of:

"Fuck off!"

Chickens shot off in all directions like a feathery firework. I check under the car to make sure that they'd all gone. Oh God, there's one still under there, next to my front wheel. Not moving, and its head's under my wheel. Bollocks.

I am of course of the opinion that all things horsey and farmyardy are her department, whilst cooking, eating, and manly DIY around the home are in my remit. I call to her:

"I've fucked a chicken...No, really...With my car. Help."

I move the car forward, to reveal a truly haunting sight. The chicken was squashed into the mud and its head and neck were at a really fucked-up angle. Its lifeless eye was staring up at me and we were just debating if we needed to let the farm owner know when it blinked at me! I nearly shat myself.

Oh great. Now we've got to wring its neck. Well, when I say we, I mean she...I'm not touching the thing.

"I knew it would be alright", she said matter-of-factly.

"You what?"

"It'll be fine in a minute."

"What do you fucking mean it'll be fine?" I whisper, fearing discovery by Mrs Farmer. "It's been run over!"

"No, it'll have had worse."

"Come again?"

"They always get trodden on - it'll be OK."

"It's not been trodden on though, has it?" I retorted, looking wildly around for signs of the chicken's owner. "It's been fucking parked on. By a fucking big German car."

She then proceeded to pluck Lucky from the puddle of mud (she made a loud squelch and left a perfect Kellogg's-like imprint) and carry her into the barn. I got my car keys out and flicked the mud out of its beak. It made some very odd noises while I had to run around aiming kicks at her concerned comrades who, unlike the solidarity and niceness shown in Chicken Run, were trying to eat their former friend.

On closer examination, I discovered a tiny droplet of blood on Lucky's beak. In other words, the sole visible injury that the chicken sustained after having an Audi parked on its head for ten minutes was a nose-bleed. A fucking nose bleed. It's still alive today, months after its amazing car park impression.

Oh, and do you know why it got run over? Why didn't the chicken cross the road whilst all of its mates sidled out of the way of imminent Goodyear doom? The poor twat only had one eye. Talk about survival of the fittest.

Why don't they make cars out of the stuff that chickens heads are made of?

* I draw the jury's attention to a copy of Michael Bolton - Timeless: The Classics found lurking in a CD rack during my brother's previous marriage. His? Hers? Planted by Jeremy Beadle? You decide. - Scary

An Apology

The management wishes to apologise to our fellow diners in the staff restaurant for the spectacle we caused during supper last night. We pledge that these scenes of riotous behaviour will not happen again. Perhaps a full and frank explanation is in order.

We were discussing recent book purchases, and my boss Swiss Toni admitted that he was now the proud owner of Roger's Profanisaurus which he had bought through Amazon (a snip at £7.99). In an in-depth discussion on the subject of this work of literary genius, Swiss confessed that he didn't know what "Rodeo Sex" was. So I told him.

Rodeo Sex, as I am sure you are all aware, is a derivation of the act of doggy-style coitus. Just as you reach the vinegar strokes, you say something along the lines of "Your sister likes it this way as well." The challenge is to see how long you can stay on.

I am afraid to say that this revelation caused a certain amount of food to be spat out, and scenes of a boisterous nature which cannot be tolerated in polite society. We'd particularly like to pass on our apologies to Her Majesty, we're pretty sure you'll be able to get the gravy off your regalia, ma'am.

Unlucky Duck, or, "Shitfaced"

Oh cruel fate, why do you taunt me so?

Have you ever have one of those unlucky Friday-the-thirteenth days where absolutely nothing goes right for you? Fall out of bed to be attacked by killer spiders in the shower, breakfast a bowl of dry corn flakes because the milk's gone green overnight, and trudge to work in the pouring rain, only for a car to get you by driving through a puddle just ten yards from the door? I do, all too frequently, and I blame it totally on the time I told Uri Geller to fuck off.

This was the day that I walked into a lamp post in full view of a bus load of school kids, and worse, in the company of a female work colleague who thought it was the funniest thing she had ever seen, and told me so in no uncertain terms. All I really needed, then, was for something truly unlikely to happen to me, like shitting on my own head, for example.

Lunch on this fateful day was chicken-flavoured grease and cardboard, a tribute to the chef's art of throwing random ingredients in the pot and heating it up until smoke came out. *(I can say this safely because the chef concerned is no longer with us. We have, however, been receiving a lot of "pork" products on the menu recently.)* Like a damn fool, and still smarting from my puddle, spider and lamp-post disasters, I found myself shelling out good money for this on the grounds that "you don't know where your next meal is coming from, chummy."

It tasted like it looked, and actually tried to make its own way back to the kitchen at one stage. So revolted was I by this crime against the culinary arts, I immediately dashed to the Gents, bent double, where I let fly with a brown laser of a turd that closely resembled a tin of oxtail soup with a dead rat in it. It stunk to high heaven - how unlucky could my day get? Answer: shitloads.

Still a bit queasy, I bent over to pull up my pants. As little white dots danced before my eyes, and a distant voice told me to "move toward the light", I lost balance and grabbed the first thing I could to prevent me from falling head first into the heaving brown mess in the toilet bowl. It was the toilet flush handle.

Alas, dear reader, the toilets at my place of work are nuclear powered, and so violent was the torrent, that I was caught full in the face with stinking brown splash-back from a range of no more than twelve inches.

I staggered around the cubicle in the final death throes of the Wicked Witch of the West, if she had her pants round her ankles and Dorothy had squatted on top of the cubicle and shat on her head, ruby knickers round her ankles. With the stench of crap now on a direct line to my brain, the final act of this story was not far away.

"Yaaaarch!" I shouted, "Rooooolf!"

Chicken-flavoured grease and cardboard vomit cascaded into the bowl, around the bowl, and I'm not ashamed to admit, nowhere near the bowl.

"Yaaaarch!" I shouted again, just for good measure. Somebody a couple of cubicles along shouted for me to keep the noise down, as they'd reached a vital stage in their crossword puzzle.

"Rooooolf!"

The whole cubicle now resembled an IRA dirty protest, and with only Cheapo Brand non-absorbent toilet paper to clean myself up, I knew I was trapped there for the duration.

Finally managing to get myself looking at least halfway decent, I staggered out of the cubicle and examined myself in the mirror. My brand new shirt (four quid, *Homme de Matalan*) was speckled with shit and puke. I was a distinctly brown hue, and looked like I'd been mud wrestling with Kirstie Allsopp, which, in retrospect, would have really rounded off a truly awful day.

Cleaning myself up, I finally managed to find my desk, and slumped into my chair, a defeated man. Slowly but surely, the gas hissed out of the seat's hydraulic system, leaving me six inches from the floor. Fantastic. Shouty Kev peered down at me over my terminal.

"D'you recommend anything in the canteen?" he shouted.

"Chicken," I replied, determined not to be the only one visiting Shit City that day, "Have the chicken."

Manky

It was first thing Sunday morning, not so long ago. More recent than I care to admit, in fact. I was already up and about, emptying the dishwasher and scratching my bollocks in front of News 24, the news channel for the discerning loafer. Mrs Duck was in the bathroom, and by the sound of things, she was washing her hair, a process that can, and usually does, take several hours.

This was bad news for me as although we are a two-bog household, the second toilet was still in a box in the garage, waiting for our useless, work-shy twat of a builder to finally get around to installing the plumbing. Worse, the previous evening had seen some particularly heavy red-hot curry action, and now it is time to pay the price with a ring-piece of fire. I was, in fact, busting for a crap, and it was only outstanding sphincter control that prevented me from redecorating the landing, and as I hammered on the bathroom door. This one was a code red.

"I'll only be a minute or two," I was told, and I wait as patiently as I could given the circumstances. Presently, the most urgent need subsided, and I was able to gingerly descend the stairs to the kitchen, knock out a cup of tea, scratch my bollocks a bit more and head outside to feed the dog.

It was at this point that I was overtaken by the most sudden, uncontrollable urge to empty my bowels, and judging from the pain, the previous poo had come back with a few friends. The turtle's head was touching cloth, and the bathroom was clearly occupied. Doom.

So here is my confession. You know what they say in the Round Table: Adopt, Adapt, Improve. Make the most of the situation you find yourself in, with the tools available to you. Situation: a biblical flood set to erupt from my anus. Location: Back garden, miles away from the nearest unoccupied lavatory. Tools available: one Asda carrier bag, a garden shed, a pet hamster. I know what you're thinking, and yes, small, fluffy Ryan Minogue survived.

Those of a nervous disposition may wish to look away now, for I have no shame in what I did. A man's shed is his castle, so they say - a small foul-smelling castle made of wood, notable for their lack of toilet facilities. But for this I cared not. Dashing headlong into my shed, garden tools and kids' scooters flying in all directions, I dropped my kecks and took the mother and father of all curry-powered craps into a plastic bag and wiped my arse on a handful of hamster bedding.

It was then that I realised that Adsa put little holes in their bags to stop idiots from suffocating themselves and preventing normal, sane people like myself from using them as squirty poo receptacles. And the dustbin was at the other end of the garden. Ideal for icing a brown birthday cake, perhaps; but not for early morning comedy dashes, spraying path, feet, dog with something nasty. Hot-bagging, it seems, is not all it's cracked up to be.

The bathroom window opened a few inches.

"Scary - why have you got the hose out at this time in the morning?"

The Hot Bag ended up in the dustbin, where it was pecked open on bin day by the seagulls, fuck my luck for living by the sea.

The Kate Winslet Story

Events seem to have run away with themselves, and I am forced to cave in to popular demands (not least from Mr Gaiman) to see The Kate Winslet Story published. Look, Kate, I'm really, really sorry, but you know how insistent people are…

Ah, Kate, how do we love you? It's a well-known fact that Berkshire-born actress Kate Winslet has got her baps out in every single film she has worked on, including the ones where the script stipulated that she remain fully clothed, the filthy mare. But that's what you get when you come from a part of Reading where nudity is virtually obligatory in her part of town. They've even built a block of flats in her honour down the Oxford Road, with a removable roof.

In fact, on the cusp of fame, she was a well-known face in the (ahem) lively west of Reading, where sane men know not to walk, and the knocking shop on the Oxford Road hasn't even bothered to disguise itself as a respectable establishment. It was clear that La Winslet was going to be a huge, huge star despite her habits of swearing like a trooper and smoking like a chimney.

Well, I didn't know, did I?

I had an absolutely valid 100 per cent cast-iron excuse for going down that end of Reading that Thursday evening.

I was buying pornography.

A young man's got needs, and the Oxford Road has a number of newsagents with impressive top shelves catering for just about every peccadillo and perversion known to humankind. All strictly legal, you understand. And this month's Big and Fruity, the magazine for greengrocer fetishists and lovers of root vegetables had just come out.

Me, I was after a copy of Fiesta and this week's Auto Trader. Honest.

I always went to the same shop, a) because of the astounding selection and b) it was right next to a side street which was good for a quick getaway should the worst come to the worst and people started looking at you in a funny way in the midst of your jazz purchase.

Scene set? Good. The trouser itch activated and wearing my best flasher mac, I headed for the Oxford Road to make a small purchase.

The coast clear, I dived into Mr Khan's emporium of fags, booze and smut and scanned the upper shelves (yes - plural) for suitable one-handed reading material. And Lordy, he knew how to hide the specialist stuff from view.

It would be several minutes before I could locate this month's edition of "Big and Fruity" and head for the counter. And I would have made it too, if it wasn't for the fact that the act of pulling this celebration of the juxtaposition of fruit and incredibly naked female flesh from the shelf and making for the till hadn't have brought me into direct collision with a Hollywood starlet, popping out to the corner shop for twenty Lambert and Butler.

In normal, comedic circumstances, you'd fully expect an explosion of pornography, the centre-spread fluttering to the floor between us. Happily, this didn't happen.

I merely prodded her in the left tit with a scud mag. A tit which, one day, would be painted by Leonardo di Caprio. The bastard.

"Ooh," she said. Unfortunately, this was not followed by the line "It's so hot in here", which, I gather, is obligatory in certain genres of filmed entertainment. "Ooh!"

"I'm terribly sorry, Miss Winslet" I said, "I appear to have assaulted you in a rather tender area with a partially-folded adult publication. I'm related to a doctor, perhaps you'd allow me to see to the wound." Which came out like this:

"Gneep."

I dropped my spoils back amongst the motor magazines and fled, heading up the side-street towards the handily parked Scary-mobile. Leaning against the door, I breathed a huge sigh of relief following my brush with disaster. She had a stare that could sink ships, and would one day do so.

And there she was, following me up the road, cancer stick between her lips, puffing away in the provocative manner that only an habitually naked star of stage and screen can manage.

Sid James stirred inside me.

As she passed your humble scribe toward Winslet Mansions, she gave me a pitiful smirk.

"Gneep."

I don't know about you, but I think I might still be in with a chance there.

Part V: The end bit

In which I offer special thanks to those who contributed to the stories in this volume, most notably my brother Nigel Coleman and Clive "Balders" Summerfield. Also, this book would be nothing without the various friends, neighbours, colleagues, relatives and unsuspecting passers-by who took part in my life of mirth and woe without realising they were, in fact, contributing to a work of literary genius. You know who you are, and I would appreciate you not suing me, thank you very much.

Finally, there are loads of people out there on the internet who have encouraged me in one way or another, and in no particular order, I'd like to offer my thanks:

Wil Wheaton. Actor, writer, excellent person who got me blogging in the first place: http://www.wilwheaton.net

Clive Summerfield, My arch-nemesis who has put up with me for decades: http://www.theuktoday.co.uk

Neil Gaiman. The greatest living English author, and unwitting influence of the Duck: http://www.neilgaiman.com

Paul Rose. Writer and genius: http://www.mrbiffo.com

Tim Ireland: http://www.bloggerheads.com

Fraser Lewry: http://www.blogjam.com

Joy Durham: http://joynews.blogspot.com/

Geraldine Curtis: http://www.madmusingsof.me.uk/weblog

Zoe McCarthy: http://www.myboyfriendisatwat.com

Rik Hughes. Exactly like me, only Welsh: http://rikaitch.blogspot.com

Maria Sparkes: http://www.agirlwitha.com/

Iain Purdie: http://www.moshblog.me.uk

Tina Hannan. http://www.misty69.com

Grant Wray: http://therandomthink.blogspot.com

D. Geezer: http://diamondgeezer.blogspot.com

Dawn Mason: http://wrathofdawn.blogspot.com

Arseblogger: http://www.arseblog.com

If I've forgotten you, I'm incredibly sorry – it's nothing personal. Perhaps you'd like to change your deodorant or something. And, grief, who cuts your hair? Tell me, and I'll go out and kick his guide dog for you. Allow yourself a few moments of inner warmth instead, safe in the knowledge that you'll be in Volume Two instead. There's lovely now.

Printed in the United Kingdom
by Lightning Source UK Ltd.
122044UK00001B/104/A